$ 34,95

2-2015

The LOOK of LOVE

Center Point
Large Print

Also by Sarah Jio and available from
Center Point Large Print:

The Last Camellia
Morning Glory

**This Large Print Book carries the
Seal of Approval of N.A.V.H.**

The LOOK of LOVE

Sarah Jio

CENTER POINT LARGE PRINT
THORNDIKE, MAINE

This Center Point Large Print edition
is published in the year 2015 by arrangement with
Plume, a member of Penguin Group (USA) LLC,
a Penguin Random House Company.

The text of this Large Print edition is unabridged.
In other aspects, this book may vary
from the original edition.
Printed in the United States of America
on permanent paper.
Set in 16-point Times New Roman type.

ISBN: 978-1-62899-438-4

Library of Congress Cataloging-in-Publication Data

Jio, Sarah.
  The look of love / Sarah Jio. — Center Point Large Print edition.
    pages ; cm
  Summary: "Born during a Christmas blizzard, Jane Williams receives a
rare gift: the ability to see true love. On her twenty-ninth birthday, Jane
receives a card from the midwife who delivered her specifying that Jane
must identify the six types of love before the full moon following her
thirtieth birthday or face grave consequences"—Provided by publisher.
  ISBN 978-1-62899-438-4 (library binding : alk. paper)
  1. Large type books. I. Title.
PS3610.I6L66 2015
813'.6—dc23

                                                                        2014041786

For the dear friends who
walked with me through my darkest hour
and never once let go of my hand, especially
Wendi Parriera, Natalie Quick, and Claire
Bidwell Smith. That is true love.

The LOOK of LOVE

Unless you love someone,
nothing else makes sense.

—E. E. Cummings

Prologue

In the fashionable fifth arrondissement along the river Seine, Elodie stands beside her flower cart watching couples stroll arm in arm. Love, she thinks, is not meant for her. Oh, yes, she could have a boy. An ice-cart driver, perhaps. A farmer in the countryside. A chimney sweep. One of those fellows outside the market who shine the shoes of wealthier men. But no. She takes a deep breath and plucks a ragged leaf from one of the peonies crowded in a basin of water. When she looks up, she sees the Count of Auvergne, Luc Dumond, his top hat towering above the crowd on the street. With his eyes fixed on hers, he crosses the cobblestone street, narrowly missing a horse and carriage.

The count frequents her cart to buy flowers for his wife, Marceline, whose severity, pinched face, and stormy eyes make for an odd pairing with his obvious gentle kindness. And so Elodie sometimes daydreams about what life might be like as a countess, his countess. She often gazes up into the windows of his elaborate city house, just across the street, and wonders what life is like inside its walls.

11

"Hello," Luc says to her, removing his hat.

"Hello," she says in return, a little flustered in his presence. "Your usual selection for the countess?"

As a tea maker might have a special blend, or a restaurateur has a dish that defines him, Elodie has a signature nosegay. Composed entirely of green blossoms—zinnias, chrysanthemums, and harder-to-find but entirely breathtaking roses in a shade of muted lime—this bouquet is made only once daily, and she keeps it in the back of the cart for Luc.

He doesn't respond immediately, for he is lost in her eyes. "They're green," he says suddenly.

Elodie shakes her head, puzzled.

"Your eyes."

She smiles. "Yes."

"They're beautiful."

"Thank you, sir."

"It's Luc." He pauses. "May I know your name, please?"

"Elodie."

"Elodie," he says, surveying the flowers before him, then pausing when he sees the engraving along the edge of the cart.

"What is the meaning of this?" he asks, pointing to the inscription, "Amour vit en avant."

Love lives on. These were her mother's parting words to her, on her deathbed. "Do not give up on love, my sweet Elodie," she had said through tears. "Do not become hardened like I did. Keep love in

12

your heart. Be open to it when it comes, even if the circumstances seem impossible. Trust it. And do not be afraid to fail. Because if you do, it will still live on." She placed her hand over her own frail heart. "It will live here. Love does not die. It lives."

"My mother's words are a comfort to me," Elodie says. "They guide me."

Luc smiles. "I would like to make a purchase."

She nods. "A small nosegay, perhaps? Something with—"

"I would like to buy all of the flowers in your cart."

She shakes her head. "Surely you aren't serious."

"I am."

"But what will you do with all of them?" she asks, grinning. There are hundreds of stems in today's cart. Hyacinths, roses, stock, the most fragrant peonies of the summer.

"I want to buy them for you," he says.

"For me?" she asks, stunned.

"For you," he replies. "So you don't have to work today; so you can meander as you please in the Paris sunshine." He tucks a stack of bills into her hand. "Walk with me?"

Genevieve, another flower cart girl and a friend of Elodie's, has witnessed their interaction from a distance. "Go," she says with a smile. "I will watch your cart."

"Shall we?" Luc asks, offering his hand.

Elodie knows no other choice: She takes it.

13

Chapter 1

2021 Pike Street, Apartment 602, Seattle
December 24, 2012

I steady my golden retriever, Sam, as I slide my key into my mailbox. Bernard, the apartment building doorman, looks away from the packages he's sorting and kneels down beside Sam to scratch his ears. "Morning, Jane," he says, looking up at me with a smile. "Did you hear? They say we're getting snow tonight. Four inches at least."

I sigh. We'll never get the flower deliveries out on time if the roads are icy. I collect the stack of mail and holiday cards inside the box, then cross the lobby to the front windows, which are lined with multicolored lights. Sam sniffs the Christmas tree in the corner as I peer outside. Pike Place is just waking up. Steam wafts from the awning of Meriwether Bakery, down the block. The fish-mongers are hosing down the cobblestones in front of their stalls. A flock of eager tourists carrying umbrellas (tourists *always* carry umbrellas) pause for a photo across the street, disturbing a seagull perched on a street sign overhead. He lets out an annoyed cry and flies off in a huff.

"Yep, those are snow clouds out there," Bernard says, nodding toward the window.

"How can you tell?"

"Come here," he says, standing and walking through the double doors. I follow him out to the street. "Let me give you a little lesson in clouds."

I feel the bitter cold on my face as I breathe in the frigid air, which smells of coffee grounds and seawater—aromatic and salty at the same time. Seattle. Sam wags his tail expectantly as a passerby reaches out her hand to greet him.

Bernard points up to the sky. "See those? They're cirrostratus clouds."

"Cirro-what?"

He grins. "They're the first cloud formations you'll see before a snowstorm. Look how they're thin and rippled, like fallen snow."

I study them with curiosity, as if they might contain a message written in meteorological hieroglyphs. A cloud language that I might be able to decode if I stare long enough.

"Now, look farther off over the sound," he says, pointing out to the distant clouds lurking over Elliott Bay. "Those are the snow clouds moving in. They're heavier, darker." He pauses and touches his hand to his ear. "And listen. Do you hear it?"

I shake my head. "What?"

"The way the air sounds muffled." He nods. "There's always an unexplained quiet before a snowstorm."

Sam sits at my feet on the sidewalk. "I think you might be right. There's something eerily quiet about this morning." I gaze up at the sky again, but this time I do a double-take. "Do you ever see things in clouds? Pictures? Faces?"

He grins. "Indeed I do. But what I see may be different than what you see. Clouds are illusive that way." He pauses for a long moment. "I think they show us what we *want* to see."

He's right. I do see something, and it startles me a little. I quickly shake my head. "Then I'm not telling you what I see, because you'll just laugh at me."

Bernard smiles to himself.

"What do *you* see?" I ask.

"A roast beef sandwich," he says with a grin, then reaches into his pocket. "Oh, I almost forgot. This came for you." He hands me a pink envelope. "The postman accidentally left it in Mrs. Klein's mailbox."

"Thanks," I say, quickly tucking the envelope into my bag with the other mail—mostly an assortment of unwanted Christmas cards. Perfect, happy, smiling families posing for the camera. Talk about illusions.

"Merry Christmas," Bernard says as Sam begins pulling on the leash.

"Merry Christmas to you," I reply. The words echo in my head. *Merry Christmas.* I don't feel merry. But I never do this time of year.

I round the corner and nod at Mel, the owner of the newsstand at Pike Place. He winks and points to the mistletoe hanging on the awning. "A kiss for old Mel?"

I play coy and smirk, and Mel frowns. "Not even on Christmas Eve, Janey?"

I lean in and give him a quick peck on the cheek. "There." I smile. "Are you happy now?"

He clutches his cheek and feigns paralysis. "Best day of my life," he says. Mel is at least seventy. He's operated the newsstand for forty years, maybe longer. A short, balding man with a potbelly, he flirts with every woman in the market, then goes home to a little apartment two blocks up the hill, where he lives alone.

"My Adele loved Christmas Eve," he says. "She loved mistletoe. She'd do it up big, with a roast and a tree and lights."

I place my hand on his arm. Although his wife passed away eight years ago, he speaks of her as if they'd just had breakfast this morning. "I know you miss her so much."

He looks up at the clouds, and I wonder what he sees. "Every damn day," he says. I see the grief in his eyes, but his expression changes when a woman, perhaps in her seventies, approaches the newsstand. She's tall and towers over Mel like the Columbia Center perched beside the much smaller Fourth and Pike Building. She has silver-gray hair and chiseled features. Elegant with a strand of pearls around her neck, she was no doubt very beautiful in her youth.

"Do you have the *Times*—the London *Times*?" she asks in a tone that telegraphs disappointment. Her voice is sharp, commanding, and I hear the telltale clip of a British accent.

I watch the two face each other, and my vision clouds a little, as it sometimes does. I rub my eyes as Mel grins jovially at his prim-and-proper customer. "The *Times*?" he exclaims. "Ma'am, with all due respect, this is Seattle, not merry old England."

The woman's eyes narrow. "Well, any proper newsstand would carry it. It's the only publication worth reading." She scans the racks of tabloids and newspapers. "So much rubbish these days."

Mel raises an eyebrow at me as the woman adjusts the collar of her trench coat and bristles past us.

He looks momentarily stunned before his face twists into a half smile. "Snobs!" he says. "Rich people think they own the world."

I glance over my shoulder and rub my eyes again, careful not to disturb my recently applied mascara, which is when I remember the appointment I have tomorrow with Dr. Heller, the neurologist I've been seeing for most of my life. The British woman has disappeared around the corner. "Maybe she's just unhappy," I say. "My grandmother used to say that most of the time, people don't mean to be rude; it's just their sadness showing through."

I'm hit with a sudden memory from childhood, when the first time I encountered deep sadness was the same day I first noticed a change in my vision. I was four years old, standing in the doorway of my mother's bedroom. Mom sat hunched on her bed, sobbing into her hands. The curtains were tightly drawn, and darkness stained the walls. My father hovered behind her, begging her forgiveness. He held a suitcase in his hand and was leaving that day for Los Angeles to follow a woman he'd met. He said he was going to marry her. Dad was in love, and Mom was heartbroken.

I don't remember my father's face, or the exact words they exchanged that rainy Seattle morning. I recall only my mother's deep sadness, and when my father placed his hand on her shoulder as if to say, "Please forgive me," I blinked hard. It was as if my eyes had completely fogged over, but not from tears, from something inside me. I remember taking a step back, rubbing my eyes, and stumbling in the hallway, where I waited until my father slipped through the doorway. If he had intended to say good-bye to me, he didn't get around to it. And so he left us—my brother, Flynn, oblivious, watching TV on the couch; me, confused and partially blind in the hallway; Mom, crying so loudly, I wondered if she might be dying.

I wanted only to cheer her up, so that morning, with a shaking hand, I offered her a cup of coffee. I'd watched her grind the beans and place them in the French press a hundred times, and I summoned the courage to try it myself. But my vision was still blurry, and I'd gotten it all wrong, and Mom was quick to tell me so.

"What is this?" she snapped.

"I made you coffee," I said in a squeak.

She looked down at the coffee cup and shook her head, then slowly walked to the kitchen sink and dumped it out.

I held my tears as I watched her walk back to her bedroom. Dad had failed Mom. And I'd failed her too. An hour later, Grandma came over and explained that sadness has a way of controlling our behavior. I never forgot those words, or the way Grandma summoned Mom, and the two of them rushed me to the hospital when I told them about my eyes, still mildly blurry an hour later. After an inconclusive CAT scan and a needle prick in my arm that made me cry, I went home with a sticker and a cherry Popsicle. We didn't talk about Dad anymore after that. And even now, as hard as I try, I can't picture his face. In my mind's eye, he remains a permanent blur.

Mel shrugs as he slices open a bundle of newspapers with a box cutter.

"Well," I continue, "I'm off to the shop. It'll be a busy day today. Last year Lo created this arrangement with poinsettias, holly, and rosehips, and I swear, every socialite in this city wants four for her holiday table." I sigh. "Which is not a bad thing, obviously. It just means that by the time this day is over"—I pause and hold up my hands—"these fingers are going to be arthritic."

"Don't work too hard, Janey. I worry about you."

"I love that you worry about me," I say with a slow smile. "But I can assure you, my life does not warrant any worrying. I get up and go to the flower shop, then go home. Simple, drama-free. No need for worrying."

"Sweetheart, that's *why* I worry about you," Mel continues. "I'd like to see you cut loose a little, find someone."

I smile and pat my golden retriever's head. "I already have someone," I say. "Sam."

Mel returns my smile as I wave good-bye. "I'm going to set you up with a fishmonger I met yesterday. His name is Roy. He could make you a nice fish dinner sometime."

"You do that, Mel," I say, rolling my eyes playfully as I lead Sam down the next block and open the door to Meriwether Bakery. Elaine waves at me from the counter. Her dark hair is pulled back into a neat ponytail. There's a dusting of flour on her cheek.

"Morning," I say. Sam jumps up and places his front paws on the counter, waiting for Elaine to toss a dog biscuit in his mouth. The bakery smells of burnt sugar and yeasty, fresh-baked bread. In other words, like heaven.

Elaine, a third-generation owner of the bakery, befriended me when I took over my grandmother's flower shop five years ago. We bonded over our shared love of chocolate croissants and white peonies, and we continue to trade them regularly. She wipes her brow. "We've taken forty-nine orders for pecan pie in the last hour. I may never make it home tonight." The bells on the door jingle, and I turn to see her husband, Matthew, walk in.

"Honey!" she chirps from behind the counter. Matthew, an architect with rugged good looks, walks toward us and leans across the counter to give her a kiss. They have the kind of life that makes everyone around them just a touch envious: two beautiful children, and a house on Hamlin Street overlooking the Montlake Cut with a Martha Stewart–approved flower garden and a backyard chicken coop that yields unlimited fresh organic eggs.

"Did you pick up the Lego set, the one Jack wanted?" Elaine asks, twisting her wedding ring around her finger.

"Got it," Matthew says, lifting a bag onto the counter. "Oh, and I got Ellie that American Girl doll she's been talking about."

Elaine exhales. "Good, because that would have

been a major Santa fail." She turns to me. "This man is my savior."

Matthew grins. "Hey, did you meet the new neighbor?"

Elaine shakes her head.

"I said hello to him this morning," Matthew continues. "His wife died last year. Just moved out from Chicago. I thought we might invite him over tomorrow for Christmas dinner."

"Sure," Elaine says. "If you think he'd want to come."

Matthew shrugs. "He just moved into town. I'm sure he knows no one. And besides, his daughter is about Ellie's age."

While Elaine is inclusive and welcoming, Matthew is that, amplified. At their Thanksgiving celebration, I sat across from a recently divorced colleague of Matthew's with a bulging mid-section and a perma-frown. Elaine took me aside in the kitchen and complained that if Matthew had his way, he'd invite every third person in Seattle to dinner.

"It's fine," Elaine says. "Tell him he's welcome."

Matthew nods, then turns to me. "Plans for Christmas? You know you're always welcome too, Jane. And who knows, maybe you'll hit it off with our new neighbor."

I meet his wink with an eye roll. "*You* are incorrigible, Matthew."

"Honey," Elaine says. "Leave Janey alone. She

doesn't need the matchmaking services of Matthew Coleman."

He grins.

"Besides," Elaine continues with a grin of her own, "you forget that Christmas is Jane's birthday."

I grimace. "Yes, I have the poor luck of being cursed with a Christmas birthday. At least I get both out of the way on the same day."

Elaine frowns. "You're such a grump."

I shrug. "I go into survival mode on December twenty-fifth. You know that. It's brutal."

"At least let me bring you survival rations, like a cake," Elaine says. "You refuse every year."

"Please don't," I say. "I'd honestly rather order takeout and have a *Scandal* marathon on Netflix."

"That sounds depressing," she says. "And what takeout place is open on Christmas Day?"

"Yummy Thai," I reply with a grin. "They're open every year. See? All covered."

Elaine sighs. "At least give yourself a vase of flowers."

I smile. "I can probably do that, yes."

"How's business going?" Matthew asks.

"Great," I reply. "Booming, actually."

If there is any constant in my life, it's flowers. My grandmother Rosemary founded the Flower Lady, Pike Place Market's original flower shop. It opened in 1945, shortly after the war, and when my grandmother's fingers became arthritic in the 1980s, my mom, Annie, took it over until she passed away when I was eighteen. Mom's assistant kept the place afloat until I finished college, and the baton was passed to me.

I grew up in the shop, where I'd sweep up leaves and petals and sit on the stool at the counter and eventually help Grandma arrange. "You're a born florist," she told me time and time again. "We have the special touch of knowing how to reach people, to make them feel."

And I suppose she was right. Mom had it too. We knew—we were born knowing, perhaps—how the right blend of roses and freesia can help a man tell a woman he loves her; how a tasteful combination of chrysanthemums and yellow tulips can express a heartfelt apology.

I ache for my mother then, as I always do this time of year. Mom used to love Christmas, and she'd make it beautiful in every way, decorating every spare surface of the apartment with ever-green boughs and cedar garland. She'd never settle for a small tree either. Despite the space limitations, we'd lug home the biggest noble fir at the tree lot.

Mom's cancer was sudden. A blessing, in some ways, as she didn't suffer long. And yet, only weeks passed between the diagnosis and her death. It didn't give me enough time to ask her the things I needed to ask her about life, and love. There I was, faced with losing the most important woman in my life, overwhelmed with the idea of cramming a lifetime's worth of wisdom into a few final days.

On the morning of her death, I intended to bring her flowers, as I had done every few days. But the doctor called me at six a.m. He said to come quick, that Mom may not have many hours left. So I came empty-handed, tormented by the thought of losing my mother, and regretful that she didn't have her beloved flowers beside her at the end.

But then I heard a faint knock on the door of Mom's hospital room. A moment later, a young woman with a volunteer badge appeared, smiling tentatively. "Excuse me," she whispered. "My boss said to deliver these flowers to your mother."

At the time, I hadn't stopped to consider how Mom knew this volunteer's boss. It seemed an insignificant detail. And besides, Mom made a habit of befriending people at every turn, even at the end of her life. "Thank you," I said, accepting the vase of flowers, with its gorgeous blend of blooms in stunning shades of pale green. "These are exquisite. Obviously your boss has excellent taste. Please, tell her thank you."

Mom smiled when she saw the vase. Her voice had grown hoarse, and in a whisper, she said to me, "The last time I saw an arrangement like that, I was here, in this hospital. I had just given birth to you, honey." Tears welled up in her eyes then. "But you know what? They didn't come with a card. I never knew who sent them."

I remember trying so hard to fight the tears as I watched Mom extend a shaking hand to touch one of the green roses in the vase, its petals as delicate as her pale skin.

When I think back to that cold morning in October when she took her last breath, I can still see her face: the look in her eye, her will to hold on, even a few minutes longer. And when the doctor entered the room and asked to have a word with me privately, I didn't want to leave her. Every moment was precious.

But Mom smiled and called me to her a final time. "Your eyes, my dear Janey, have always been the color of new growth," she said, placing her hand on my cheek. "Like the green shoots of spring on all the trees, like the flowers in this vase. You're special, my beautiful daughter. So special."

The tears came then. I couldn't fight them any longer. "Go talk to the doctor," she said, shooing me out the door. "And bring me back a coffee." She smiled to herself. "And not instant or drip. Espresso. I want to taste espresso a final time."

"I'll be right back," I said. "I'll only be a moment." I touched her cheek lightly. When I returned, with a double-shot Americano, Mom was gone.

My phone buzzes in my pocket as Matthew kisses Elaine good-bye and waves to me. "Merry Christmas," he says, heading to the door.

"Merry Christmas," I say with a smile as I reach for my phone. It's my older brother, Flynn.

"Hey," I say.

"Hey." He sounds down, which is typical of my big brother. He's melancholic, the way Mom described our father. While I have my flowers, Flynn has his art. A painter, with reasonable acclaim in the Northwest, he opened his own gallery a few years ago, as a way to surround himself with artists. The venture has paid off, both in being a successful stream of income and also in cementing him as a leader in the Seattle art community.

His good looks don't hurt either. And if you ask me, Flynn has always been much too handsome for his own good. All of my friends had crushes on him when we were growing up. And they still do. He's devilishly handsome, with his thick dark hair and light stubble on his chin. But at thirty-five, he still has no interest in settling down. Come to think of it, I'm not even sure if he's ever truly loved a woman. But, oh, have there been *a lot* of women in Flynn's life.

"What's going on?"

"Oh, I was calling to say happy birthday in case I forget to call tomorrow to say happy birthday."

I grin. "You are *such* a guy."

"I am. But at least I remembered, even if I'm a day early."

"Well, thank you, big brother."

"Are you going to come to my New Year's party?"

I sigh. Flynn hosts a raging party in his Belltown loft every year, and I make it my mission to do my absolute best to avoid it. Flynn's scene is one that, well, I tend to feel a bit obtuse in: anorexic-looking women in skintight dresses, men with fully tattooed arms, and loads of smokers crowded on the balcony.

"I don't know, Flynn."

"Oh, come on," he says. "You have to come. Maybe you'll meet someone."

"Meet someone? That's the last thing I need."

"Jane, have you ever considered the fact that a relationship could do you some good?" he says. "It's just you and Sam. Don't you get lonely sometimes?"

"My dear big brother," I reply, "we may be related, but I am not wired the way you are. I do not need another person to make me happy."

"You're bluffing," he says. "Everyone needs someone."

"And apparently some of us need a new person every night of the week."

"Please," he says.

"Well, who are we dating now? Did things work out with what's-her-name?"

"Lisa?"

I watch as Elaine fills the pastry case with lemon tarts, each with a sprig of lavender on top. "I thought her name was Rachel," I say.

"That was before Lisa."

"See?" I say with a laugh.

"Just come to my party, Janey, please?"

"I'll think about it," I reply.

"Good."

I blow a kiss to Elaine, and Sam and I walk out to the street and round the corner. The Flower Lady is in the distance. The sight of it still warms me, just as it always has, with its old grid-style windows and emerald-green awning. Loayza—Lo—my assistant, has rolled out the carts to the curb. Barrels of festive holiday bouquets beckon passersby, and I watch as a woman lifts an arrangement of red roses and boughs of fir to her nose. I smile to myself. Who needs love when you have rewarding work?

"Morning," I say to Lo, who looks up from the counter and pushes her dark-rimmed glasses higher on the bridge of her nose. We met in a college geology class and bonded over the fact that rocks made us drowsy. And so we took turns keeping each other awake on Tuesdays and Thursdays after lunch, at one o'clock, which is the very worst time to take a course that's focused entirely on limestone and tectonic plates. Miraculously, we both managed to finish the semester with a pair of B minuses.

"I hate poinsettias," she says with dramatic flair.

I hang my coat on the hook in the back room and reach for my apron. "So do I," I say, glancing at the orders on the computer screen behind the counter. "But look at this. This may be our highest-grossing holiday season yet." I roll up my sleeves. "Let's do this thing."

"Best-case scenario," Lo says, "we finish up by five so I can meet my date at six."

"A date on Christmas Eve? Lo!"

"Why not?" she says. "Who wants to be alone on Christmas Eve?"

To the average assessor, Lo could be (a) a hopeless romantic, (b) a dating genius, or (c) addicted to love. The number of men in her life is staggering, and she, not unlike Flynn, never seems to find any kind of lasting satisfaction with any of her conquests. Over time, I've begun to see that it's the game, the pursuit of love, that Lo enjoys. I have decided that she does not love *love,* but rather the idea of love.

"Oh, come on, Lo," I say. "There's nothing wrong with being alone on Christmas Eve. And besides, you could always come over to my house."

She grins coyly. "If all goes as I hope, I'll be spending the evening at Eric's house."

"You know," I say, shaking my head, "you're going to get coal in your stocking this year."

She smiles. "Oh, I'm tight with Santa."

I open the cash register and eye the till, then say with unabashed sarcasm, "Yeah, because he's an *ex-boyfriend.*"

Lo lets out a laugh. "He couldn't be. I don't date men older than forty-two, remember?"

"Oh, yeah," I say, smiling. "I forgot about your rules." I sort through a stack of checks from yesterday. "You like to write—you should write a book about dating."

"Like a memoir, you mean?"

"Yeah," I reply. "Or maybe you need a talk radio show. It could be called Lo on Love."

She nods. "I've thought about that. I mean, I do have a lot of material."

The bells on the shop door jingle. An older man walks in and pauses to look at the arrangements in the window. At first I don't recognize him, but when he turns around, Lo and I exchange glances. "It's Creepy Christmas Customer," she whispers to me. I nod.

And, to be fair, *creepy* might not be the best word. *Unusual,* maybe, for his presence is a bit of a mystery. He comes in every year on Christmas Eve and orders the most expensive arrangement in the shop, utters no more than five words, and tips heavily.

"He looks like the kind of person who killed his wife and keeps her body parts in his basement freezer," Lo had said once.

"No," I'd said. "He just looks lonely."

"I don't know," she had replied. "I don't like the way he looks at you."

And, I suppose, it's what gives me pause this

morning, and every Christmas Eve before this. This man pays attention only to me, not to Lo.

I take a deep breath and smile at him as he approaches the counter with a slight limp. He wears a pair of khaki pants and a rain slicker. "Hello again," I say cautiously. "Another Christmas Eve."

He nods.

"Will it be your usual arrangement?"

He nods again, and I immediately get to work on his flowers, snipping and blending until I have just the right mix.

"Will this do?" I ask, holding the vase out to him.

"It's perfect," he replies, eyes fixed on me.

"Good," I say, ringing him up.

"Merry Christmas." He hands me a wad of cash. He doesn't smile, just stares at me for a long moment, and for a tiny second, I can see a flicker of feeling in his eyes. Sadness? Regret? Flowers have a way of stirring up emotion in people. Memories of love found and lost, Christmases past, new beginnings and finish lines—all can be conjured up by petals and greenery. Perhaps that's why he comes every year. To remember.

"Merry Christmas," I reply as he walks out the door, bells jingling as it closes behind him.

Lo leans over my shoulder as I count out the one-hundred-dollar bills on the counter. "One thousand dollars?" she says, annoyed. "The dude is weird."

I shrug. "He's definitely odd—but hey, I'm not complaining." I tuck the cash in the till. "This will pay for those two windowpanes that need fixing up front."

Our mysterious customer is forgotten the moment a man in his midforties enters the shop. He's tall, with slightly graying hair and a strong-looking face, a bit weathered, as if he's spent too many summers at the beach, but the look suits him somehow.

"Can I help you?" Lo asks, walking toward him. He pauses, the way most men pause when in Lo's presence. She's beautiful in an old-fashioned way: porcelain skin; dark, perfectly straight hair (a unique combination passed down from her relatives in the Basque region of Spain); an ample chest and tiny waist.

The man rubs his forehead. "Yes," he says quickly. "I'm stopping in to pick up an arrangement of flowers for . . . Christmas. My . . . we . . . we have a lot of family in town. I thought we could use something for the table."

Lo smiles and points to a display of decorative urns filled with red roses, white tulips, and greenery. "Definitely consider one of these," she says. "It's a statement, but won't overpower the table."

The man casts a quick glance at the arrangement, before his eyes fix back on Lo's. "You're perfect—I mean . . ." he stammers, "you definitely know flowers. It's perfect."

She grins as she carries the arrangement to the cash register, where she rings him up.

"Merry Christmas," he says slowly, before turning to the door.

"Merry Christmas," Lo says with a grin.

Once he's left, I place my hands on my hips. "Lo, he's way too old for you."

She pretends to busy herself with an arrangement.

"And I know you're going to hate me for confronting reality, but there's the tiny, inconvenient fact that the man is *married*. Don't tell me you didn't see the gold band."

She shrugs. "Oh, I didn't notice."

"You're impossible," I say, half-amused, half-annoyed.

"Oh, Jane, stop being such a prude. You know I'd never go out with a married man." She looks thoughtful for a moment. "But it could make an interesting chapter in the book."

I scowl at her.

"Kidding," she says.

"Good."

Bing Crosby's voice croons over the speakers as we turn back to our work. Earlier, Elaine suggested that I make myself a flower arrangement, and in spite of the orders I have to get to, I find myself reaching for the green roses in the bucket behind the counter, which I intersperse with winter greens. For me, for Mom.

• • •

I send Lo home at a quarter to five so she can get ready for her date, and after Juan, our delivery driver, picks up the last batch of arrangements at six thirty, I decide to call it a day myself. I zip up my coat, attach Sam's leash, and step out to the curb, where, on a whim, I decide to toss one of the last fir wreaths on my arm. I reach for the flower arrangement I made earlier, then lock up the shop.

The market is quiet, but it's not the usual dinnertime calm. It's a lonely quiet. It's the sound of people who are elsewhere—drinking warm drinks beside roaring fires, seated next to loved ones, where they belong. It's the sound of people belonging.

I sigh and walk ahead. It doesn't matter. I don't need to be with anyone on Christmas Eve. I am not like Lo. I am not like Flynn. I am not like, well, anyone. I am content with Sam and a good book, a glass of wine, and then bedtime. Holidays are overrated, especially this holiday.

I pass the newsstand and wonder what Mel's doing tonight. The lights are dim in Meriwether Bakery, and I wonder if Elaine finished the pie orders for the day. I imagine her on Hamlin Street holding a platter with a turkey or a roast, or whatever people eat on Christmas Eve, presiding over the family table, beaming with love. I walk through the empty lobby to the elevator. Bernard has gone home for the night, and I think of him

36

too. I think of him settling in with a hot toddy beside his wife, Sharon, thinking about the snow clouds.

The elevator doors open, and I press the button for the fourth floor. A moment later, I unlock the door to my apartment and walk into the dark entryway. Sam laps up water from his bowl, and I set down my keys. I lift the wreath from my arm and hang it on the nail inside the door, then set the vase of flowers on the mantel, where Mom would have placed them.

"Merry Christmas, Sammers," I say. He's the only one who can hear the weakness in my voice, the tiny tremor. I reach into my pocket to locate my cell phone, which is when I find the pink envelope I tucked away this morning.

I turn on the light in the kitchen and eye the unfamiliar handwriting. There is no return address, but the envelope is postmarked Seattle. Curious, I tear open the flap and lean against the counter as I survey the birthday card, then begin to read the message written inside:

Dear Jane,

   You don't know me, but I met you on the day of your birth. On that day, you were given a gift, a rare and special gift, passed down to a select few through the ages, one that affords you the ability to see love in all of its forms in a way that

37

others cannot. But with this gift comes great responsibility and a task that must be completed before your next birthday, before sunset on the day you turn thirty. The rest I must tell you about in person. Will you please meet me at my apartment in Pioneer Square the day after Christmas? We'll have tea at two. I'm in the Waldron Building on Main Street. Apartment 17. I'll be expecting you.

Yours,
Colette Dubois

I set the card down on the counter as if it could quite possibly be contaminated with anthrax.

I shake my head, then slip off my shoes and walk to the window seat in the living room that overlooks Elliott Bay. It's been a long day, and I'm exhausted. I hear Bernard's voice in my head then. "Four inches of snow tonight . . . See those, snow clouds . . . They show us what we need to see."

The sky is dark, but in the glow of the street-lights below, I see a flurry of snowflakes in the air. A layer of white is just beginning to stick to the street below.

I think of the birthday card on the counter and the cryptic words inside: ". . . you were given a gift . . . one that affords you the ability to see love in all of its forms in a way that others cannot." I think about how foggy love has been for me, so unclear. And how, even though I deal in a business of love and help people express theirs through flowers, I know nothing of it myself. Nothing at all. I think of my college boyfriend who broke up with me for my roommate; the chef who criticized my cooking, then called it off after tasting my apple tart (which I secretly bought from Meriwether); the medical student I dated last year for two weeks, who turned out to be also dating every third woman in Seattle.

Me? A person who can identify love? Some joke. I consider calling Flynn right now and telling him off. This is absolutely something he'd do. And if I do go to that apartment in Pioneer Square, it will surely be a setup. I'll knock on the door and one of his single guy friends will be there ready to take me on a charity date. I cringe.

Sam nuzzles my leg, and I scratch his neck. "You're all I need, Sammers," I say, then press my nose against the window and watch the snow fall from the sky like flour, coming from a great sifter in the sky. That's when I remember the image I saw in the clouds this morning. I didn't tell Bernard, of course; nor will I tell anyone else. But it was there, as big as life: a heart. A perfectly formed heart, dangling from the sky like a Mylar balloon.

Chapter 2

2201 Hamlin Street
Christmas Day

Jack and Ellie wake up their parents the way most young children do on Christmas morning, with unmeasured exuberance. Elaine is jarred from a deep sleep by a child jumping on her bed. There's a knee on her chest and a pair of small hands tapping her cheeks. She opens her eyes and tries her best not to groan. The sun has not yet shown its face, and she was up until two a.m. wrapping presents after a long day at the bakery. But it's Christmas morning; everyone knows that children make the rules on Christmas morning. And somewhere in the kitchen there is an espresso machine that will produce a double-shot Americano with her name on it. She yawns and turns to her husband. "Here we go," she whispers with a smile.

The two of them follow their children downstairs and Elaine is struck, as she sometimes is in quiet moments of family togetherness—at the breakfast table on Saturday mornings, for instance, or on the random Tuesday night before bed when the kids are brushing their teeth together—at how perfect her life looks. They could pose for a picture on a postcard of the beautiful American family, the type you see in a magazine, in which the husband wears a polo shirt and tucks his arm around his wife, who looks effortless in a wrap dress and heels, while their two towheaded children smile with angelic expressions. And in that moment, as she watches her husband and their two children bound down the stairs, she is overcome with the feeling of being on the outside looking in. She is suddenly a stranger, standing in the three inches of fresh snow outside, wiping the foggy window with her mitten, and peering into the life of a perfect family, in a perfect house, in a perfect world. But Elaine does not feel perfect, and she has not for a very long time.

"You coming, Laney?" Matthew says.

Elaine, standing motionless at the base of the stairs, snaps out of her frozen state and nods. "Yeah," she says quickly. "Let them get started on their stockings. I'm going to go make some coffee."

Christmas morning comes and goes like a tornado. An hour later, Elaine and Matthew are surrounded by crumpled wrapping paper, and the children have run off to play in other rooms with whatever toy has captivated them most. Quiet descends on the house.

Elaine looks at her watch. "I should call Jane; it's her birthday. Do you think I should insist that she come over for dinner tonight? You already mentioned it to her yesterday, but I know she's cautious about intruding, and I want her to feel welcome. I—"

Matthew places his fingers against her lips. "Jane will be fine," he says, eyes sparkling. "Remember our wedding day?"

Elaine and Matthew were married on Christmas Eve twelve years ago, during a candlelight service at a Presbyterian church on Fifth Avenue. The pews had been decorated with holly and boughs of cedar, and they'd had their guests join them in singing "O Holy Night" before the close of the ceremony.

"Yes," she says, reminiscing. There was snow on the ground, and her white ballet slippers got soaked when she walked up the steps to the church. As a result, she walked down the aisle barefoot.

"I'm sorry," she says suddenly. "I forgot your anniversary present this year."

Matthew smiles. "I didn't forget yours."

He never does, this husband of hers. He remembers every holiday. Every occasion. And marks them with a card, a vase of flowers, or a gift. Without fail.

"There's one last present under the tree," he says.

Elaine frowns. "You're a better human being than I am."

"Perhaps," he says cheekily. He reaches beneath the festive branches, then hands his wife a small white box tied with a red ribbon.

She pulls the ribbon free from the box and lets it fall to the floor. Could it be? Did he remember? They've talked about it over the years, casually, but she mentioned it to him just a few months ago. The charm bracelet she had as a girl, the one she lost at the top of a carnival Ferris wheel when she was twelve. She'd decorated it with charms representative of the moments of her life—a tiny wedding cake from her grandmother, a garden spade from her father, and that little half of a broken heart from her best friend, Angela, that every girl in the 1980s had in some fashion or another—and in a moment of horror, it had slipped off her wrist. When she went to look for it, it was as if the earth had swallowed it up, and with it, all of her childhood memories. For her whole life, she's hoped to find a replacement for it. Has Matthew finally found one? Did he remember?

Her eyes sting with tears as she lifts the lid of the box and pulls back the double layer of tissue paper. And in an instant . . . her heart sinks.

"Pretty, aren't they?" he says, smiling confidently, pointing to the old bureau ahead, the one with the glass knobs that the kids shattered accidentally, years ago, when they attempted to "fix" the house with a hammer they'd found in the garage.

"They're . . . yes," Elaine says breathlessly. Tears well up in her eyes, and she forces them back as she lifts one of the antique knobs out of the box. "Perfect."

Matthew kisses her lips lightly, then stands up to stretch. "Time for some coffee," he says, making his way to the kitchen.

Elaine hates the way she feels. Ungrateful. Idealistic. Childish, even. But something has stirred inside her. Inside her perfect life, inside her perfect home, and her perfect marriage, there is a disconnect that she cannot ignore. She feels it in small moments and big. And as she looks at the glass knobs in the little box in her hands, she feels it once again.

The doorbell rings at four, and in the whirlwind of Christmas Day and cooking, Elaine has almost forgotten that they are entertaining guests for dinner. She looks up from the sweet potatoes she's mashing when Ella bursts into the kitchen grinning from ear to ear. "Mom, look who came! The new neighbors!"

Elaine licks a splattering of sweet potato puree from her index finger and glances at the doorway, where a man and a young girl about Ella's age stand.

He is in his mid-to-late forties, balding slightly, and not especially tall. His eyes meet Elaine's, and she drops the spatula in her hand.

"Let me get that," the man says, rushing to her side.

When they both kneel down at the same time, their eyes meet again.

"Sorry," he says, handing her the spatula. "I'm Charles."

"Oh," Elaine says. "Yes, the new neighbor. Welcome. Do you go by Chuck or Charlie or . . . ?"

"Just Charles."

She grins. "Hello, Just Charles."

He shakes his head, a bit stunned. "That's funny."

"What?" she asks.

"It's just that . . ." His voice trails off for a moment. "It's just that, well, my late wife said the very same thing the day I met her." His voice is nostalgic, a little sad.

"Oh, I'm so sorry," Elaine says. "I hope I didn't—"

"We were married twelve years, before she passed away last year," he continues.

She doesn't know what to say, so she doesn't speak, and instead places her hand on his arm.

"It's OK," he says. "I'm doing OK."

"I've been married twelve years too," she says.

Charles nods. "The last anniversary was hard. We'd always do something unexpected. One year I took her up in a hot air balloon. The year before she died, I hired a string quartet to serenade her at her office."

"How beautiful," Elaine says. "The way you

describe it, I can see the clouds and hear the notes." She feels a pang of envy when she thinks of the way Matthew has typically handled special occasions over the years, most often with a box of chocolates and a Hallmark card.

Charles grins, glancing at the bowl in front of Elaine. "My grandma used to make sweet potatoes," he says. "Every Christmas."

"With marshmallows?" she asks.

"It's criminal not to have marshmallows," he says, smiling.

Matthew appears in the kitchen. "Good, the two of you are acquainted. Now we can open the wine. Laney, I told Charlie that he's going to love this street. We're all a bunch of highly productive winos."

Elaine and Charles open their mouths and say at the same time, "It's just Charles."

Matthew pats Charles on the back. "Charles it is, then." He grins at Elaine. "Has she been evangelizing about sweet potatoes again?"

"Well, I—"

Matthew grins. "I'm more of a mashed potato man," he says. "But you know what they say— happy wife, happy life." He pats Charles's back again. "So what brings you to Seattle from Houston?"

Charles grins. "Microsoft," he says. "Like most other émigrés in Seattle, right?"

"Ah, yes," Matthew says. "Then you picked a

great street. Your commute over the bridge will be a breeze from here."

He nods. "I was lucky to find this house. My real estate agent tells me there was quite a bidding war involved."

"We were lucky enough to be grandfathered in," Matthew says proudly, tucking his arm around his wife's waist. "Elaine's grandparents owned this house."

Charles smiles. "It must be nice to live in a home with so many memories."

"Yes, I suppose," Elaine says a little wistfully. "And Matthew's right. You can't beat this street." She hands a spatula covered in sweet potato puree to Ella for a taste. "But I guess I have a bit of real estate wanderlust. I've always wondered what it would be like to live on a houseboat." She thinks of her friend Lo's charming floating home on Lake Union.

Charles's eyes brighten. "You know, that has always been my dream too. People say you can't make it work with kids, but I disagree."

"Life jackets," they both say at the same moment.

A momentary uncomfortable silence falls on the kitchen, before Matthew speaks again.

"Charles," he says. "Let me show you the work we had done to the fireplace last fall. I think our homes are built in the same way. You could easily make some similar improvements."

The two men disappear to the living room, and Ella stands beside her mother in the kitchen and helps herself to a stray marshmallow on the counter. "I let Chloe play with my new American Girl doll," she says.

"That was sweet of you, honey," Elaine replies.

"They're nice," Ella continues. "I'm glad they moved here."

Elaine looks toward the doorway and takes a deep breath. "Me, too."

Chapter 3

I open my eyes and am at once assaulted by the brightness streaming through my window. I'm on the couch, where I must have dozed off the night before, and Sam is sitting beside me, panting. I notice the half-empty wine bottle sitting on the coffee table beside me as I stretch, then walk to the window, where Seattle is awash in white. I smile when I notice three children happily building a snowman on the street corner below. A white Christmas.

I walk to the kitchen and put a Nespresso capsule in the machine and watch as the shot pours into the little white espresso cup. As I take my first sip, I notice the pink envelope I received yesterday, with the strange message inside. I reach for my phone and pull up my brother's number. It rings three times, and then I hear his cranky, tired, and likely hungover voice.

"Hello?"

"Flynn, that wasn't funny."

"What are you talking about?" he asks. "And what time is it?"

"Merry Christmas to you too," I say, annoyed.

"Oh right, and happy birthday."

"Is there a lady in your bed?" I ask.

"No, of course there isn't." But I hear a woman's voice in the background.

"I can tell when you're lying," I say. "Anyway, I'm talking about the card you sent. Not funny. Did you really think I would go through with it? Did you think I'd go to that apartment so you could set me up with one of your friends?"

"Janey," Flynn says, yawning. "I have no clue what you're talking about."

I glance at the card again. "Really? You didn't send it?"

"No," he says. "In all of my years as your brother, have I ever sent you a birthday card?"

"No, you haven't."

"OK, we're settled on this, then." He yawns again. "Want to come over later?"

"Nah, I'm supposed to make an appearance at Elaine's."

"Well, then if you're going to deny your family on Christmas, and your birthday, at least come to my New Year's party," he says. "Promise?"

"I said I'll think about it," I remind him with a grin.

"OK," he says. "Then tell me what this birthday card thing is all about."

I stare at the Main Street address. "I'm sure it's nothing," I say, but the truth is, the card stirred something in me, from the very moment I laid eyes on it.

• • •

I stop at the flower shop and pick up one of the last peony-and-poinsettia arrangements before driving to Hamlin Street. The house, just off the Montlake Cut near the University of Washington, was owned by Elaine's grandparents. When they passed, she bought it with Matthew, and together they remodeled it and made it their own. The home overlooks the gray water of Lake Washington, which is choppy and stormy today.

I park, then gather my purse, the bottle of wine on the seat, the grocery bag with presents for Jack and Ellie, and the flower arrangement, then look out the window at the house. The old white Dutch colonial is dusted with a generous layer of snow. A snowman stands in the front lawn, and I imagine Matthew helping the children build it earlier, and I think of how lucky Elaine is to have such a life—idyllic, like an old Currier & Ives print.

She greets me at the door with a hug that almost knocks me over. "You came! I'm so happy. I thought you were going to blow us off."

I grin, handing her the wine and flowers. "I have presents for Ellie and Jack too."

"Oh, honey, you didn't have to, but they'll love having gifts from you!"

"Aunt Janey," Ellie says with a squeal. She hugs my legs, and I am instantly glad I came. "We have new neighbors," she says. "Come meet them!"

I follow Elaine and Ellie through the house to the kitchen, where a man in a gray sweater stands at the stove stirring a pot of gravy. Elaine smiles. "Charles, this is one of my dearest friends, Jane."

Matthew smiles. "And she's single."

Elaine elbows him. "Charles, you'll have to forgive my husband. He's always trying to set up our single friends."

I give Charles a knowing smile, which he immediately returns. "Pleased to meet you, Jane," he says.

Beside him is a little girl, and before he can introduce her, Ellie does. "And this is my new friend Chloe. She just moved to our street and we're going to be friends."

"That's wonderful," I say, turning back to Charles. I watch as Elaine hovers over the pot he's stirring, then dips a spoon into the mixture. "Needs more salt," she says, and Charles is quick to offer the saltshaker he sees on the counter.

My vision clouds then, and I rub my eyes. I scold myself for the extra glass of wine I had last night. Still, when Elaine uncorks the bottle I brought and pours me a glass, I take a long sip.

"You OK, honey?" she asks.

"Yeah," I say quickly. "My eyes are just bugging me; that's all."

"It's Jane's birthday today," Matthew says to Charles.

"Happy birthday," he says. "One of my best friends was born on Christmas. Special people, you are." He's speaking, but he's not looking at me. His gaze is fixed on Elaine, and I see her eyes light up in a way I haven't seen in years. She's leaning against the counter and tugging at her white apron, which is splattered with a patina of culinary ingredients from countless dinners cooked over the years.

Matthew tucks his arm around his wife's waist and points to the brown paper bag on the island. "I had to go to three stores, but I finally got the flour you like."

"King Arthur," Elaine says, lugging the flour out of the bag. "Matthew knows I won't bake with anything else."

I think about the details of marriage. The thousands of tiny facts that make up a life with someone. The way two people can spend a lifetime becoming connoisseurs of the details. The brand of flour, or toothpaste, or large kitchen trash bags (drawstring or no?). Radio station preferences in cars. The precise spot on the sofa that makes one or the other happy. The minutiae, the fine print, of love. By all appearances, Elaine and Matthew have mastered it.

Elaine looks at the kitchen wall clock. "If I can just get this cake batter made and in the oven, we should be able to eat at five."

I take a seat on a barstool beside Matthew. As

Ellie and her new friend Chloe walk out to the living room, he watches his wife proudly. "Elaine's making her grandmother's famous olive oil cake," he says to Charles and me.

"I have to admit, it's an acquired taste," she says. "And I won't be offended if no one wants to eat it. Grandma made it every year on Christmas, long before it became hip to bake with olive oil. She had it every year as a girl on Christmas morning. You know what the secret ingredient is?"

I shake my head.

"Citrus," she says. "Of course, you can use whatever you have, but Grandma preferred blood oranges."

"I love blood oranges," I say. "The color is so gorgeous."

Matthew smiles in Charles's direction. "And what is your opinion on blood oranges, sir?" It's painfully obvious that he's trying to nudge us along in conversation. But if he's aware of this, Charles doesn't seem to let on. He looks up suddenly, at Elaine. "Was she from Sicily?"

"Yes," she replies, a little surprised.

"My grandmother was too," he says. "I've never met anyone, apart from my mother, who keeps that tradition."

Elaine is momentarily speechless, but I watch as she collects herself. "Well, good, then," she says. "You can help me juice the oranges."

• • •

After dinner is served and the desserts are devoured, we say good night to Charles and Chloe, and Matthew and the children head to the basement to watch a movie. Elaine and I refill our wineglasses, and in the quiet of the living room, in front of the tree, we sink into the couch beside the fire.

"Do you think it was a nice Christmas?" Elaine asks, watching the flames dance before us in the fireplace.

"It was a beautiful Christmas," I say. "You make it beautiful."

She shifts positions and takes another sip of wine before turning to me. "You're lucky, you know."

"Me?" I let out a little laugh. "I'd hardly say that. You, on the other hand, are lucky."

Elaine shakes her head. "Jane, you have your whole life ahead of you, and you can make it anything you like."

I scrunch my nose. "Well, so do you. You're only a year older than me, darling."

"No," she says. "I'm not talking about age. I'm talking about the difference of being settled and set versus being open to new possibilities."

I nod and turn back to the fire. How strange to hear Elaine speak this way, when for so long I've looked at her life as the pinnacle of perfection, the destination on the road to happiness. The house. The husband. The kids. The life. She has it all.

I place my hand on her arm. "What is it, honey?" I ask. "Tell me."

She's quiet for a long moment, then wipes the hint of a tear from her eye and picks up a little white box from the coffee table and hands it to me. I lift the lid to find two shiny glass knobs, the old-fashioned kind that you'd find on an antique dresser. "Matthew gave me these for our anniversary," she says.

"Well," I say, "they're pretty."

"Knobs, Jane. Knobs."

I wonder if I am missing an important detail. "Is there something wrong with . . . knobs?"

She shakes her head. "There's nothing and everything wrong with them."

I nod with understanding. She doesn't have to explain any more.

Elaine wipes another tear from her eye. "Look at me getting all weepy," she says, turning to me with a summoned smile. "I hate that I get this way on Christmas Day."

"Try having it be your birthday on top of it all," I say, squeezing her arm again.

"I'd be a wreck."

"But you're not," I reply.

She nods vacantly and turns again to the fireplace. We sit together in silence, watching the logs crackle and hiss.

• • •

Lo is standing behind the counter when I arrive at the flower shop the next morning. "Morning," she says cheerfully. "I see you survived another birthday."

"I did," I say, hanging my coat on the hook in the back room. I set my purse down under the counter. "How was your night?"

"Oh, good," Lo says. "Dom Pérignon with Lorne."

I raise my eyebrows. "Lorne, huh? A new one?"

"Yes, he's an investment banker by day and a closet poet by night," she says dreamily. "I think I like him."

I smirk playfully as I turn on the computer to review the orders that have come in online overnight. "You always like men on the first date."

"Of course I do," she says. "They expire after the third date. I get bored after that."

"You're like a man, you know?"

She shrugs. "So what if I am? Women would do well to behave more like men."

Sometimes I admire Lo's bold take on love. But I worry about her too, and I wonder if she's too caught up in the game to ever be happy. I sigh and reach into the pocket of my jeans for a rubber band to pull my hair back into a ponytail, which is when I find the strange birthday card I received in the mail. I tucked it in my pocket this morning, intending to show it to Lo.

"Hey," I say, turning to her. "Will you do me a favor and read this? I have no idea who it's from or whether it's some kind of practical joke."

Lo takes the card and reads it over. "That's like no other birthday card I've ever seen," she says.

"I know, right?"

She nods. "And the handwriting looks familiar, for some reason." She looks thoughtful. "It reminds me of a guy I dated last year. Tristan, yes. He had the most beautiful handwriting."

I roll my eyes. "So you're saying this is from Tristan."

"No," she says. "And besides, I'd never let you date him. He was a narcissist. You know how I knew?"

I smile at her. "How?"

"His grocery shopping lists," she says assuredly.

"Shopping lists, huh?"

"Yep," she says. "You can spot a narcissist a mile away by the amount of money they spend on paper products."

"Paper products?"

"Yes—you know, paper towels, disposable napkins, boxes of tissues."

"Lo, you can't be serious," I say with a laugh. "That makes no sense."

"Believe me, it's a *thing*. They've documented it in research studies. Seriously, the dude went through a roll of paper towels every single day." She shakes her head at the memory. "And he'd write out those shopping lists in that gorgeous handwriting of his. Too bad he didn't have a gorgeous heart to match. They never do." She looks at the card again. "But, I don't know, this might be worth checking out. I mean, maybe . . ."

"Maybe what?"

Lo shrugs. "Maybe you have some crazy ability." Her eyes brighten. "Like, what if you could time-travel?"

I let out a little laugh.

"Just think. You could take me with you back to 2004, back to that asshole who broke my heart. Except this time, I wouldn't let him break my heart. I'd break his."

Jed Harrison. Yes. The man who is, quite possibly, the reason Lo is the way she is today. She loved him—even wanted to marry him. And it turned out he was already engaged to the beautiful daughter of a Seattle real estate tycoon. In the end, his love was a business decision. And Lo was laid off.

"Well," I say, "I admit I'm a bit curious to know what this woman has to say."

"Then check it out," she says. "And if you want, I'll go with you, just to make sure it's not some kind of sex slave operation where they kidnap you and ship you off in a crate to some foreign country where you end up as part of some harem of women for a sheik."

I grin. "A sheik, huh?"

She nods. "Hey, ever heard of a sapiosexual?"

"A sapio-what?"

"Sapiosexual," she repeats. "It's a person who's attracted to intelligence, to the human mind." She smiles to herself. "Evan said he's a sapiosexual. And at first I was a little annoyed. I mean, does it mean he isn't attracted to me physically? But no, the more I thought about it, the more I realize that it actually was quite a compliment. If I ever write a dating book, I think I'll include that as a section."

"You *will* write a dating book," I say, printing off the thirty-three new orders.

Lo grins as she looks up at the clock. "Hey, let's get our work done and then rendezvous with this mystery card writer of yours. What do you say?"

"Maybe," I say, glancing at the pink envelope on the counter. Its presence is hard to shake, and I know, somehow, what I must do.

The old brick building doesn't look like much from the street. I stare at the card again to make sure I've gotten the address right. Waldron Building, Apartment No. 17. "I don't know, Lo," I say hesitantly. "I think we should turn around."

"No way," she says, as a panhandler passes by and mumbles in our direction. Lo shoos him away with a flick of her manicured hand. "Now you've got me curious. I want to see what this is all about."

I look around Main Street. Pioneer Square has a grittier vibe than Pike Place, but if you're looking for a taste of old Seattle, it's here, where old lampposts preside over the streets and visitors line up for tours of the city's once–fully operational underground city.

"What if it's a hoax?"

Lo rolls her eyes. "Then we'll get the hell out of here."

"All right," I say tentatively, stepping ahead to the building's double doors with elaborate brass hardware that looks like an ornate relic from the 1920s. I imagine all of the flappers and prohibitionists who might have walked through the entryway as I push open the heavy door. Inside, the lobby smells musty and perfumed. I scan the placard on the wall and see the name Colette Dubois beside apartment number 17.

When the elevator bell dings and the doors open, we step inside.

"This is crazy, you know," I say as we move upward. My palms feel sweaty.

"Don't be scared," Lo says, smiling. "We'll go in briefly, check it out, and leave if it feels sketchy. In and out, OK?"

"OK," I say with a sigh, except I don't feel OK. I feel scared and anxious. I'm possibly about to be told something about myself that I have no **knowledge of—or, worse, find out that I'm on the** receiving end of a very cruel practical joke.

On the eighth floor, we walk down a long corridor until we come to a door where the brass numbers one and seven hang crookedly against the elaborate woodwork. I knock quietly at first, but when there's no answer, I try again, this time louder. I hear footsteps beyond the door, and my heart rate quickens.

The knob begins to turn and the hinges on the door creak. A cloud of incense-fueled air drifts out as a thin woman with silver hair spooled into a bun looks us over. When her gaze meets mine, her stern expression melts into a smile. "Ah, Jane," she says in a thick accent that I immediately identify as French. "I'm so glad you're here. Please come in."

Lo follows me inside the apartment, which looks like an illustration of 1890s Paris. Thick blue velvet drapes block out the light from the large bay window. Antique armoires hold trinkets that range from porcelain ballerinas to intricately painted vases. The floor-to-ceiling bookcases completely consume the right wall, where a ladder attached to a wheeled track provides access to even the highest shelf.

"Please sit down," Colette says, pointing to a couch upholstered in indigo velvet. The cushions are threadbare. "I'll make us some tea."

Lo and I sit in silence, until she elbows me. "I feel like we're in a movie right now."

"I know," I say. "I'm getting the same vibe."

Colette returns holding a tray with a steaming teapot and three cups. She sets it down on the coffee table and sits in the chair opposite us, folding her hands in her lap. "It's good to see you, Jane," she says, before turning to Lo. "And who have you brought along?"

"This is my friend Lo," I answer, while pouring a cup of tea for Lo and then myself. "I—"

"I'm glad she could come," Colette says, but her smile fades. She looks at Lo, then at me again. "You'll need someone to keep you accountable."

"Accountable?"

Colette nods. "But I must ask, do you trust her?"

"Of course I trust her," I say a little defensively. "Lo is one of my oldest friends."

"All right," the older woman says with a satisfied nod. "Then she must vow to never repeat what we discuss here today."

I look at Lo and swallow hard. Before I can open my mouth, she does. "Cross my heart and hope to die," she says with a wink.

Colette purses her lips. "Good, then," she says. "Jane, I'm sure you are deeply curious about my birthday greeting and why I've invited you here today."

I smile tentatively. "I admit, I'm a little confused."

"And probably skeptical," she adds.

"Honestly, yes."

"I understand," she says. "I was too, at your

age. But, Jane, you must listen to what I'm about to tell you, and you must accept it."

I look at Lo, who is captivated, then back at Colette. "And if I agree to your conditions?" I ask.

Colette stands up and walks to the bookcase on the far wall. She wheels the ladder to the center and climbs to a high shelf, where she pulls out a single book, then returns to her chair.

I eye the aged book in her hand. It's bound in leather, weathered by the sun. Its spine is tattered, and I spot a water stain on the edge.

"I will tell you a story," Colette says. "It begins in Paris, in 1893." Colette pauses to open the book to the first page. "There was an impoverished but beautiful girl named Elodie who sold flowers on one of Paris's most prosperous streets. She kept her cart outside a great home owned by Luc and Marceline Dumond, the Count and Countess of Auvergne. Marceline was deeply jealous of Elodie, for her husband, Luc, had become besotted with the young flower girl. He showered her with gifts—furs and elaborate jewelry—all within plain view of his wife. When she realized that Elodie returned her husband's love, Marceline's anger knew no end, but not because she loved Luc. No; in fact, there was little love in Marceline's heart. Her marriage was a business arrangement between two wealthy Parisian families. And yet, she was deeply embarrassed and jealous. On the night of a masquerade ball, which Elodie would attend at the invitation of Luc, Marceline enacted her revenge. In her employ was a Gypsy man, known in dark circles as a caster of spells powerful enough to render his target paralyzed, or syphilitic, or blind or dumb. He arrived at the party in costume, having been richly compensated to wreak havoc on Elodie. But when he reached for her hand on the dance floor, he felt, in her presence, a strange and unknown force. He felt a palpable aura of love so intense, he could hear the songs of a thousand children, the whispers of lovers across the city. With Elodie, he was in the presence of love. Great love."

I inch closer to the edge of my seat. "So did he place the spell on her?"

Colette shakes her head. "No, he did not. He couldn't bring himself to do it. Elodie was like a perfect rose, and he could not trample her. So he did the opposite."

I furrow my brow. "The opposite?"

"He did not curse her that night. He gave her a gift."

I look at Lo, then back at Colette.

"He gave her the gift of being able to see love. From that moment forward, Elodie could walk into a room, a crowded café, a parlor on the edge of town, and she could see love in all of its truth and beauty." Colette looks at me for a long moment, and I feel goose bumps erupt down my arms and back. "I have this gift too, dear. As do you. The gift was passed down to me, and I gave it to you on the day you were born at Swedish Hospital."

I startle. "You brought the green bouquet. My mother remembered you until the day she died."

"Yes," she replies. "That hue is Elodie's legacy. Her story is yours, and it is mine."

I shake my head. "I know nothing of love."

Her eyes lock on mine. "But you do. It's been inside of you all your life. And you must fulfill certain conditions of your gift before your thirtieth birthday or . . ." Her voice trails off.

"Or what? I turn into a pumpkin?"

Colette lays her hand on the ancient book. "Here, in these pages, are centuries of recordings. When the Gypsy gave Elodie her gift, it came with a very important challenge. In order to secure love in her own life and access the vision to see it, she had to identify the six types of love."

"Six types of love?"

Colette nods. "You may already know of them. A woman with our gift in the nineteen sixties foolishly made a copy of one of the pages of this book, and it was discovered by a noted psychologist in the nineteen seventies, who wrote a best-selling book on the topic."

Lo clears her throat. "I've heard of that book," she says. "It's called *The Colors of Love*, right?"

"Indeed," says Colette, turning the page in the book. "But what people don't know is that the concept of that book originated from the wisdom in *these* pages, the six types of love." She pauses for a moment. "Have you recognized true love in your own life?"

"That's a personal question," I say, "and I'm not sure how to answer it."

She sets her teacup on the coffee table. "I mean to ask, have you seen love in your own life, in the people you're close to? If you have, it's impossible to ignore the signs."

My heart beats faster as her words wash over me. I've never been in love, not really. But have I seen love in others? I pause to remember the way my grandmother spoke of my grandfather, the one who died when I was barely three. She used to look up to the sky longingly and say, "I miss my guy." And then I think of my late mother, and the father who left when I was so young that his face will always be a blur in my mind. Their love had been intense and deep. He'd serenaded her with a mandolin outside her apartment on a warm Seattle night. She told the story over and over again, mostly after a second glass of wine. The memory of their love never ceased to send shock waves through her veins. It simply never let go. And she didn't either.

I turn to Colette and search her face. "How can I be sure I've seen love when the experience is so different for everyone?"

"Ah, you are right, my dear," she replies. "There

is not one form of love. There are six, and in fact, many shades in between."

"Fifty Shades of Love," Lo says with a snicker.

I give her an annoyed look.

"Wait," I say. "So this . . . gift . . . that you say we have. You say there are others who also have it, or have had it?"

"Yes," Colette says. "Fourteen, in fact."

"How did they . . . ? What did—"

"How did their stories end, you mean?" She nods to herself. There's regret in her eyes. "Some fulfilled their legacy and, in turn, led fulfilling lives. Others, well, did not. And that's not what I want for you, Jane. I want you to be able to also experience the love you see in the lives of others. I want you to have that for yourself."

I shake my head. "But that's just it," I say. "I can't *see* love."

"Ah, but you can, dear," Colette replies. "Your vision, it's been a little off all your life, has it not?"

"Well, yes," I say. "But I have a tumor on my optic nerve. I've been seeing a neurologist since I was tiny, and my medical team thinks they're getting close to understanding the exact cause of my episodes."

"It's your gift," she says matter-of-factly, "not a neurological condition."

I swallow hard. "I hate to disappoint you, but my vision is clouded by a medical abnormality, not some romantic condition."

"Describe your vision problems to me," Colette says. "What happens, and when?"

I look at Lo, then back at Colette. "Well, it's been going on all my life. For a long time, I just assumed that everyone's eyes clouded up at one point or another. It worried Mom, and she took me from one specialist to another. For a long time, they thought it was anxiety or something psychological, because it seemed to come on when I was in social situations, never when I was alone. My blue-eyed mom used to try to cheer me up by saying that it was a result of my being the only member of our family with green eyes. 'Your eyes are as vibrant as the green gladiolus,' she would tell me. 'The secret name of that flower is "sword lily," the bloom that signifies the power to pierce the heart.' " I look at Colette then. "You have green eyes too," I say, a little stunned.

"I do." She smiles before continuing. "All the women with our gift share that trait."

I shake my head in disbelief.

"Tell me more about when your vision changes," she says.

"For me, the timing has always been random," I reply. "I can be walking down a street, or talking to friends, or gazing into a crowd, and there's a halo effect in my sight. For so many years, doctors told me I was having ocular migraines. Sometimes I get headaches associated with it;

but mostly just this foggy, cloudy aura, and often really intense pressure. It's hard to explain."

Colette nods. "And when's the last time it happened?"

I stop to think for a moment. "Yesterday, at my friend Elaine and her husband Matthew's house."

"Ah," Colette says knowingly. "And this happened in their presence, when the two of them were together?"

"No, actually," I say. I pause for a moment, remembering Elaine standing in her kitchen yesterday, making Christmas dinner. "It happened when she was mashing sweet potatoes, talking to a new neighbor. His name was . . . Charles." In an instant, I recall the glance they shared.

Colette clasps her hands together in her lap. "You can see why our gift comes with great responsibility."

I shake my head. "You can't possibly be implying that Elaine is *in love* with her neighbor? Because you couldn't be more wrong. She only met him yesterday. And she and Matthew are so happily married that it makes most people nauseated."

"Our vision doesn't lie," she says insistently. Her green eyes flash. They're a deeper, darker shade than mine, almost emerald in hue. "What you saw yesterday was true, no matter how hard it is to believe."

I close my eyes tightly, then open them again.

"Hard to believe?" I say. "More like impossible to believe."

"Love itself, dear, doesn't make much sense," she continues. "Its very nature is confounding. Why, for instance, would a count fall in love with a flower cart girl? Or a seemingly happily married woman find herself inexplicably drawn to a stranger in her kitchen on Christmas Day? Love is not always logical, but when you see it, you know it. And, Jane, *we* can see it."

At once, my mind is flooded with memories, of cloudy vision and smiling faces, of the banging sound of MRIs and needle pricks, of glasses with thick lenses and medication. I hear Dr. Heller's voice in my head. "You're special, Jane. Yours is a condition rarer than any I've seen."

I take a deep breath.

"It will take time to sink in," Colette says. "You're feeling the same shock I did when I first learned of my gift. But I implore you to heed my words today, for your very future depends on it." She turns to the book again and flips to an interior page. "It's all explained here. Before sunset on your thirtieth birthday, you must identify the six types of love. You must have seen them and recorded the names of two people, as well as their story, for each category. Or . . ."

Her voice trails off, and in that moment of silence, I feel a tug at my heart. Truth? Understanding? I'm not sure. "Jane, you see, if you fail at this, you lose the ability to experience love for yourself. And a life without love is . . ." She pauses as she extends the book to me. Her eyes pierce mine. "Well, it is perhaps the worst fate of all, Jane. No matter what you feel about our meeting, no matter what you believe at this moment, promise me you'll at least consider what we've talked about today. Eros, Ludus, Storge, Pragma, Mania, and Agape. You must identify them, and you must not fail. Promise me you won't."

Because I am momentarily frozen, Lo takes the book from Colette and nods. "Don't worry," she says. "I'll make sure she doesn't."

"Thank you," Colette replies, standing up. We follow her to the door and find our coats hanging on the rack. I notice an old flower cart by the door, the type you might have seen in nineteenth-century Paris packed with nosegays of lilies of the valley and big white peonies.

I reach for the book in Lo's hands. "After I, er, after I do my part, and write the names in the book, what do I do with the book?"

"You will be its caretaker," she says. "Until you notify the next woman of her gift."

"The next woman? But how will I know?"

Colette smiles to herself. "There will be a child, and you will be drawn to her, on the day of her birth. You won't have to wonder. You will simply *know*." She nods. "Before sunset on your next birthday. The circle must be completed by then."

I reach for the doorknob but then turn around to face Colette once more. "Wait," I say. "I'm a stranger to you. Why do you even care if I succeed or fail at this so-called gift? What does it matter to you?"

She smiles to herself. "We are a sisterhood, dear. In a world where all are blind, we see." She places her hand on my arm. "You mustn't fail."

Chapter 4

Hr ow can we help you?" Lo says to an attractive man as he walks through the door of the flower shop. Lo handles our male customers with such skill that by the time they're ready to make a purchase they are either head over heels and asking for her phone number or charmed into submission and eager to buy any item she recommends.

"I have a problem," the man says. He's wearing a fedora and a well-tailored pinstripe suit.

Lo grins. "Nothing that a flower arrangement can't fix."

"That's what I'm hoping," he says, cocking his head to the right, somewhat playfully, at Lo. "Here's the thing. I messed up. I broke a woman's heart, and I, well, I want to mend it."

"Mend her heart, eh?" I hear the sarcasm in her voice. She doesn't like this man. Not one bit. "And, may I ask, how bad was the, er, heart-break?"

"Bad," he says. "Listen, I'm not proud of it, but I cheated on her."

At my place behind the counter, I bite my lip. It never ceases to amaze me how men regard florists as therapists. One whiff of a rose and they spill their guts.

"I see," Lo says, taking guarded steps toward our front-end case, where we keep the type of arrangements a certain subset of the population likes: vanilla combinations of roses and baby's breath, with the occasional carnation thrown in for good measure. No matter how inventive, creative, and imaginative you can get with floral design, some people just want boring. "And you're looking for flowers that say, 'I love you. I'm sorry. Take me back.'"

"Yes," the man says, looking at Lo as if she has psychic abilities. "Exactly."

"Right, then," she says, opening one of the refrigerator doors. "Then I'm going to suggest pink roses, with a generous helping of baby's breath." I cringe as I watch her reach for the vase.

"This is perfect," the man says.

"Good," Lo replies with a sly smile.

As she swipes his credit card, another customer enters, the man in his forties from the other day. "Want me to help?" I say to Lo, who looks up and catches his eye.

"No," she says, looking ahead intently. "You have all that paperwork to do, and you have a hair appointment this morning, right?"

I nod.

"I'll take him," she says as Mr. Cheater walks out the door.

I can see the way her hips sway as she approaches him. Lo is a pro at the game of love, and I love to watch her do her thing, even if I sometimes disapprove of her tactics.

"Well, hello again," she says, smiling and tucking a lock of her hair behind her ear.

He scratches his head, accentuating his gold wedding band. *No, Lo, no.*

"I need something simple," he says. "Peonies, maybe. With freesia?"

Men aren't typically familiar with peonies, so I know Lo is impressed. "Oh, what's the occasion?" she asks, obviously prying.

He rubs his forehead. "It's, well, it's for some-one special."

"A lady in your life?" she says, walking to the back counter.

"Yes," he replies.

"Your wife?"

He hesitates, then shakes his head. "We're going through a rough patch. But no, these are for my mother. Tomorrow would have been her wedding anniversary, but my father passed away last year."

"I'm sorry," Lo says, "and about your wife too." But on the latter point there is no true concern in her voice, only curiosity. "Are you separated?"

"Well, we're headed that way," he says, shaking his head. "I mean, can I be honest with you?"

She nods with rapt attention.

"I'm trying to go through the motions of someone trying to save their marriage, but"—he rubs his forehead—"I just don't know that my

76

heart's in it." He sighs. "That probably sounds awful."

Lo places her hand on his forearm. "Or honest."

He grins. "Well, thanks. I guess that's all we have, our truth, right?"

She nods. "That's what *I* always say. You've got to own it."

He grins.

"And so you find yourself in a flower shop," she continues.

He looks around. "Yes, here I am. Again." He smiles. "I'm Grant."

"I'm Lo," she says, extending her hand.

My vision clouds just then, and I rub my eyes as I always do, but this time, I feel a thousand goose bumps on my arms, because I *know*.

Lo creates a classy arrangement—peonies, hyacinths, and greenery in a square vase—then she sets it on the counter. They admire it together. "You know," she says boldly, "life's too short not to be happy."

"I know," he says. "I know this all too well right now."

She smirks. "Then what are you going to do?"

I shoot her a look. Lo can be unfiltered, but I don't always love it when she's so direct with our customers.

"You're right," he says, staring at the enormous arrangement on the table at the center of the shop. The ceramic vase, as large in diameter as a decent-size cherry tree, is peppered with white and pink roses, sprigs of stock, and freesia, calla lilies, and shoots of bells of Ireland for dramatic flair. Following in my grandmother's floral tradition, we create something new, and enormous, every few days. Sometimes someone buys it, sometimes not. But it made Grandma happy to walk into the shop and see such grandeur, and it makes me happy.

Grant's eyes light up momentarily. "Is that for sale, by chance?" he asks, pointing to the large arrangement.

"It is," Lo says, confused. "If you'd rather buy that one for—"

"I'll take it," he says, walking to the center table and lifting up the vase, which partially obscures his face. "Both of them."

"You have excellent taste," she says, grinning as she takes his credit card.

"Have dinner with me," he says suddenly. "Monday night."

She looks at me, then back at Grant. "Yes," she says decidedly. "Yes, I'll have dinner with you."

"Good," he says, grinning. "I'll swing by here at six and get you?"

"Come and get me, yes," she says flirtatiously.

He walks to the door, then turns back with a smile. "See you soon, then."

Lo eyes the enormous arrangement on the counter, which he seems to have forgotten. "Wait," she says. "You forgot this one."

He turns to face her a final time, grinning. "Those are for you."

Once the door is closed, I turn to Lo. "*What* just happened?"

Her smile is infectious, and the corners of my mouth lift as I watch her staring at the flowers in front of her. "An amazing man asked me out, is what happened," she says, looking up at me.

"Honey, he's married. Don't go there."

"But you heard him," she continues. "He's separated, or almost separated. But, anyway, he's done."

"But you don't really know that, Lo. And he's too old for you. Remember, you said you'd never date men in their midforties."

She looks lost in thought for a moment. Then her eyes flash. "Did you see it?"

"What are you talking about?" I say, though I know exactly what she's talking about. I know what I saw.

"Did you see any signs of *love?* Did your vision change? Jane, tell me."

"No," I lie. I feel a guilty pang, and yet, I'm overcome with doubt. *What if Colette was wrong?*

"Oh," Lo says. I can hear the disappointment in her voice. Does she feel a spark with this man, something that sets him apart from the others? Does she want me to confirm it? "Well," she says, quick to recover, "who's to say that love can't grow?" She sighs and tugs at her sweater dress. "I'm going to have dinner with him. And what will be, will be."

Mary owns a hair salon two blocks from the market. Initially, it was a hole-in-the-wall space, just large enough for a few chairs, a sink, and a small reception desk. She fell in love with its rustic hardwood floors and one exposed brick wall when she found it ten years ago, and as a result, she stayed. She was able to open a wall and take over the neighboring space two years ago, which provided room for two other stylists, but the salon retained its cozy feel.

When I walk in, Mary is at the reception desk speaking to one of the stylists. Mary is a year younger than I am, and gorgeous, with auburn hair and olive skin. She's married to Eli, a musician. And it's a certifiable fact that they are one of the most beautiful couples in Seattle.

She waves and points to the empty chair, the one I've sat in year after year and laughed, or cried on days when I miss my mom. I sink into the familiar seat and sigh.

Men may spill their guts to florists, but stylists have that effect on me. For a decade, Mary has been listening to my secrets as she cuts my hair, but I hesitate to share what Colette has told me. I think about how I can ask her advice without worrying her with the details of the burden I now carry.

"Hi, honey," she says, running her fingers through my long blond hair, which is in dire need of a foil, and, well, perhaps a whole new style.

"Hi," I say in an exhausted tone.

"Oh," Mary says. "You don't sound so good." A true friend can understand your complete emotional state from a single word.

"I was feeling sentimental and decided to look through my mom's keepsakes," I say. "You know what a hopeless romantic she was, in spite of the way my father broke her heart. There was an old book with a holiday fable, the story of a woman with a rare gift: the ability to see whether people were in love or not."

"Oh, what a perfect tale for this time of year," Mary says.

"So her dilemma got me thinking, what if someone like you or me had to make the decisions she did? If a person has revelations about the love in the lives of people she cares about, should she tell them? Or is that, well, meddlesome, somehow?"

Mary nods. "As in, if she sees that a husband loves his wife, but the wife loves someone else, or vice versa?"

"Exactly," I say. "It's delicate, isn't it?"

"Very," she replies. "If someone told me that Eli wasn't in love with me, well, I don't think I'd want to know. It would ruin me."

"Here's the strange part," I tell her as she guides

my head back into the bowl and begins shampooing my hair. "The end of the book is blank, almost as if I'm meant to fill it in, even though I've never been in love myself."

"Well," Mary continues, reaching for the conditioner, "I imagine she could help people come to their own conclusions, make educated decisions without telling them outright, you know?"

My eyes narrow as she rinses my hair. "Sort of nudge them in the right direction? Like a gentle matchmaker?"

"Yeah, that," she says, "and also, well, just help them along their path. Play cupid a little."

"I can't stop thinking about this story," I say. "She has no sense of love in her own life. In that way, she's blind."

Mary raises her eyebrows as she blots my hair with a towel before running a comb through the ends. "Blind? I get that, I guess. I've felt a little lost lately, with Eli on the road so much. Anyway, I'm doing what a lost one does: remodeling the kitchen." She shrugs. "Eli surprised me at Christmas with the plans. We'll finally get rid of those circa-1982 cabinets."

I sit down in a chair in front of the mirror, and she reaches for her scissors. "That's great," I say, remembering an observation about home remodeling being a way to mask, or dull, the inevitability of a broken relationship. As if custom cabinets and fresh paint can fill the gaps of love gone wrong. But I don't say that to Mary. I just smile. "I bet it'll look beautiful."

She nods a bit vacantly. "He's been gone so much this past year," she says. "Honestly, I'd rather have him home than have a new kitchen."

"I'm sure," I say. "But he's on a tear with his music, isn't he? You must be so proud of him." When they married, Eli was an unemployed songwriter, but five years ago, he got a big break when one of his songs was picked up by a Hollywood producer and put into a movie that ended up winning an Academy Award. It injected life into his career, and last year, he signed with a major record label.

"I am," she replies, then bites the edge of her lip. "I mean, I sound like a jealous wife or something. It's not that I'm not happy for him; it's just that, well, it's really hard to be married to a musician. Especially a touring musician. A touring, incredibly hot musician."

Eli is hot, yes. In Lo terms, he's "sizzling." The type of guy who can walk into a bar and attract the eyes of every woman in the room, even the married ones. Eli is highly aware that he possesses this ability, and for Mary's sake, that has always given me pause.

"I can only imagine," I say. "But you wouldn't have it any other way, would you?"

She sighs. "No, I wouldn't. He's the love of my

life." She reaches for the hair dryer and round brush. "But I'd be lying if I didn't admit to wondering about his life on the road, wondering about all the amazing women he meets. They throw themselves at him, Jane. I've actually witnessed it."

"*You* are an amazing woman, honey," I say, locking eyes with her in the mirror in front of me. "He's married to the very best one. You have nothing to worry about."

She shrugs. "We've been talking about starting a family."

"Oh, that's wonderful," I say. "You'd be a great mom, Mary."

"We'll see," she says. "We've been trying for about six months now. No luck yet. I mean, his infrequent trips home don't really help matters."

"Well, if it's meant to happen, it will happen."

Mary nods. "Yes, you're right. Eli gets home soon." She finishes blow-drying my hair, then turns me around to face the mirror. "There."

"Thanks," I say. "Perfect, as usual."

"Big plans for New Year's Eve?"

I shake my head. "My brother's throwing one of his usual parties, and he's hell-bent on getting me to go."

"Oh, how is Flynn doing?"

A long time ago Flynn had a crush on Mary, but knowing his track record with women, I did not encourage it. "He's all right," I say. "Roaming from one woman to the next, you know." I grin. "Nothing new."

Mary spritzes my hair with hair spray that smells like citrus. "Well, I think you should go to his party. You never know who you might meet."

I roll my eyes. "No, I know exactly the type of guy I'll meet, and he'll be an artist, probably have a sleeve of tattoos and wear skinny pants, and possibly suspenders."

Mary grins. "You're too picky, Jane. Those guys can be great too."

Just then, the salon door opens and an older woman walks in. I immediately recognize her as the British woman who recently passed Mel's newsstand at the market. She is so polished and proud, and yet her presence has a lonely tenor to it. When her eyes meet mine, I smile, but she quickly looks away.

"What's her story?" I ask Mary in a whisper.

"Oh, Vivian," she says in a hushed tone that matches mine. "She comes in every Thursday for a wash and blowout. She doesn't say much. For a long time, I thought she was an ice queen, but . . ." Mary stops and shakes her head. "Do you know what happened to her husband?"

"Her *husband?*"

"Yeah, she was married. I had to use some serious detective skills to connect the dots. One day she paid with a check, and I noted her last name. A quick Google search turned up quite a story. Jane, she's the widow of Alastair Sinclair."

I shake my head. "The name doesn't ring a bell."

"It didn't for me at first either, but I did some more searching. He was a big deal. Knighted by the Queen for his humanitarian work in Africa. From what I can tell, she was fairly involved too." Mary shakes her head. "He died in a helicopter accident ten years ago in Africa. With his mistress beside him."

I gasp. "Oh, no." I look over at Vivian sitting at the far end of the salon, staring down at her manicured hands, face pinched into a frown. "No wonder she's bitter."

Mary nods. "I suppose she has the right to be. To lose the love of her life and find out that his heart belonged to another in the same moment."

I think of Mel, the antithesis of Vivian's larger-than-life late husband. Could he thaw the ice around her heart?

After lunch, I drive downtown for my monthly appointment with my neurologist, Dr. Amy Heller. She's been following my condition since childhood, and after Mom died, she became my mentor and mother figure, although she couldn't be any more different from Mom. Where Mom was a romantic who'd sometimes put on her favorite Billy Joel song, "And So It Goes," and listen to it over and over as she cried, practical

Dr. Heller regards life with fact, not feeling. Nothing stands in her way, and as successful as she is, I've often wondered if she's happy.

"Hello, Jane," Dr. Heller says, taking her usual seat beside me in her exam room, with its beige walls and windows that look out over Seattle's Capitol Hill neighborhood. "And how are we doing this week?"

Dr. Heller speaks in "we's" not "you's." When her patients have cancer, *she* has cancer. When they have migraines, she rubs her aching forehead too. No, Dr. Heller may not be an emotional woman, but she does have the gift of empathy.

"We're . . . OK," I say.

"Just OK?"

I swallow hard as I begin to relate the details of my visit with Colette.

Dr. Heller sets my chart down, then nods. "So let me get this straight. A woman you've never met told you that the changes in your vision can be explained as your ability to see"—she pauses to clear her throat—"love?"

"Yes, in short."

"And do you believe this woman?"

I shrug. "I don't want to, but she spoke about my condition in a way that, for the first time in my life, made sense."

"What?"

"Well, she said that I have until sunset on my thirtieth birthday to identify the six types of love

87

as they appear in my life, or I risk losing the ability to ever find meaningful love myself."

She takes off her glasses, rubs the lenses with the sleeve of her white coat, then replaces them.

"You think this is all nuts, don't you?" I say.

"No," she says. "I do not. Jane, do you know the old parable about the maiden and the fox?"

I shake my head.

"It goes like this: There once was a beautiful maiden in a kingdom far away. She watched as her four younger sisters were married off to eligible suitors, but the maiden, despite her great beauty, remained unmarried. A wise old woman in the neighboring village told her that for her to ever find love and marry, she'd have to identify a red fox in the forest under moonlight. Well, red foxes are exceedingly rare. But the maiden accepted the challenge. And night after night, year after year, she consumed herself with finding this elusive red fox. And then, one night, she found her fox, standing on a mossy rock in the moonlight. Moments later, it was shot with an arrow, by a prince on horseback, who immediately noticed the maiden's great beauty. They married, and she became the princess of the land. So I ask, was it the fox or was it the maiden's persistence to be thanked for her collision with love?" She nods to herself. "Jane, I believe in science, not magic. I believe there's a logical explanation for most everything. And while this journey may not cure you of your condition, it may give you some sort of understanding into yourself. And in that, you have my full support."

"Thanks," I say, just as the door opens and Kelly, one of Dr. Heller's longtime nurses, pokes her head in. "Dr. Heller, Dr. Wyatt needs to have a word with you."

"Tell him to come in," she says.

Kelly and Dr. Wyatt enter the room.

"Sorry for the intrusion," he says to me.

"It's no problem," I say. I watch as Dr. Wyatt, a handsome, slightly younger doctor, hands a chart to Dr. Heller. Kelly looks on as they exchange a few words about another patient, which is when my vision begins to cloud.

"Sorry about that," she says a moment later, after Kelly and Dr. Wyatt exit. "Male physicians," she says with a sigh. "They come in so cocky, and when it turns out they're wrong about something, well, don't even get me started. I just had to . . ." Her voice trails off when she sees me rubbing my eyes.

"It's happening, isn't it? You're having an episode."

I nod.

"We need to track this. We need to see this on imaging. I'll fast-track an MRI. If we're lucky, we'll pick up the tail end of this. Hurry, Jane."

Kelly, the nurse, returns with a wheelchair and pushes me hurriedly down the hall.

"You OK, sweetie?" she asks in the elevator.

I rub my eyes again. The fog is lifting now. "Yeah," I say. "But you have to tell me. How long has she loved him?"

"Honey, whatever do you mean?"

"Dr. Heller," I say. "How long has she loved Dr. Wyatt?"

Kelly laughs nervously. "You'll have to ask her about that," she says, wheeling me down the long hallway to the imaging department.

Chapter 5

1301 4th Avenue

Flynn opens his eyes and turns to his right, where a nude woman sleeps beside him. Her blond hair is spread out on the pillow, and her mascara is smudged beneath her eyes. He sits up and notices the empty wine bottle on the nightstand beside him as the events of last night, still foggy, slowly come into focus. He was at his art gallery in Pioneer Square for his friend Ryan's new body of work. His paintings weren't memorable, or even very good, but Ryan was a friend, and Flynn couldn't say no to hosting a friend's exhibition. Thankfully, Ryan's wealthy family dutifully bought every single canvas.

Flynn climbs out of bed quietly. He doesn't want to wake what's-her-name. Jenna? Cara? Julie? Is she a cocktail waitress or a dental hygienist? An esthetician or a flight attendant? He can hear his sister's voice in his ear then: "You only date one kind of woman: bimbos." But what does Jane know about love? At least Flynn *has* a love life.

He steps quietly onto the cold hardwood floors beneath his feet, careful to avoid the floorboard that creaks three paces from the bed. One creak and what's-her-name would call him back to bed.

Not that that would be a tragedy. But Flynn has a code of conduct. And morning sex, though quite enjoyable, is not something one does after a one-night stand. Morning sex is for relationships. Morning sex is for love. And Flynn has never been in love.

He thinks about this as he stands naked in his kitchen, gazing out at the city beyond the floor-to-ceiling windows of his eleventh-floor loft apartment. He scoops the pre-ground espresso into the machine and pulls a shot. As he listens to the familiar hum of his espresso machine, a gift from a girlfriend whose face six years post-breakup is now fuzzy in his mind, he thinks about his life. Thirty-five. Never married. Never in a serious relationship. And maybe he'll always be this way.

He takes a sip of his espresso and looks out the window at the apartment building directly across the street, where he stares into the first bank of windows on the eleventh floor. Flynn wonders if she's awake yet, the woman he sometimes sees cooking in her underwear, or nothing at all; crying late at night, or early in the morning; working in the spare bedroom that she uses as a pottery studio, spinning her wheel with such concen-tration, such intensity, he cannot look away. And then she emerges from her bedroom. She wears a white tank top and a pair of red panties. Her long brown hair is pulled back into a messy ponytail and it swings from side to side as she wends her way into the kitchen, where she pours a cup of coffee into an oversize white mug before walking to the window. She looks out across Fourth Avenue to Flynn's apartment. For a moment, time stands still as their eyes meet. Flynn lifts his hand to wave just as he feels a pair of thin arms around his waist.

"Whatcha lookin' at?"

He turns around to face the woman from last night. She's wearing one of his T-shirts, her long tan legs exposed beneath. And he remembers the way he lifted them this way and that only hours before.

"Oh, nothing," he says quickly, pulling the blinds down.

"Come back to bed," she says seductively.

"I shouldn't," Flynn says with a grin. "I've got a packed schedule today."

"Oh," the woman says, a little injured. "Tonight, then?"

He shakes his head. "I'm busy tonight too, sorry."

"Call me, then?" she asks, with puppy dog eyes.

"Of course . . ."

"It's Julia," she says.

"Right, exactly. Julia."

"I gave you my phone number last night. So you have it. I mean, if you wanted to call. We could go out sometime. Do this again."

"Right," he says, making a mental note to delete her number from his phone. It's not her fault. She's twenty-five, beautiful, and just so . . . typical. Flynn knows women like Julia well. They were psychology majors in college, but now work in advertising or marketing. They order fruity drinks at bars and spend all their money on expensive shoes and handbags. They laugh about vapid things and bat their eyelashes at him. And so he dates these women. He buys them their fruity drinks and takes them to restaurants and tells them things they want to hear, while he waits for *it* to come along, even if he doesn't quite know what *it* is.

Julia manages to find her clothing, strewn across his bedroom from last night. She dresses, and he gives her the obligatory good-bye kiss. After the door clicks closed, he pulls on a sweatshirt and laces up his running shoes, then opens the blinds and looks out the window again, across Fourth Avenue. She sits at her pottery wheel. He loves watching her work. And he's thought, dozens of times, that he should walk over and introduce himself. He could invite her to display her pottery at his gallery. It would be a perfectly natural thing to do. A business opportunity. And yet, when he thinks about doing it, his stomach quivers, though Flynn never gets nervous. Point to any beautiful woman at a bar and he'll walk up to her.

But this woman? She looks up from her wheel then and adjusts her dark-rimmed glasses with the edge of her hand, and Flynn feels weak. She sees him again. And this time, she lifts her hand up to wave to him. He smiles, but she looks away quickly. He watches as she suddenly leaps up from her chair and runs to the door. She peers through the peephole and then pauses with trepidation.

After a long moment, she unlatches the lock and opens the door, slowly. She takes a few steps back, as a man walks through the door. He's carrying flowers, an enormous vase of pink roses. She takes them in her hands, but Flynn can't tell if she's smiling. He can't see her face. He can only see the man, tall and businesslike in a well-tailored pinstriped suit. He takes off his hat, a fedora (who wears fedoras?), and his silver hair is the only indication that he's older than she is. Flynn hates to admit that this man is handsome, perhaps better-looking than he is.

The man points to the couch, and the woman nods slowly, as if she's hesitating. Flynn knows he should look away, but he can't. He is trans-fixed by every detail of this living room scene, every detail of her life. Who is he? Clearly he's in love with her. But is she in love with him?

The woman walks to the window, and Flynn's neck erupts in goose bumps once again when she catches his gaze. But this time, her eyes are sad, distant. She reaches her arm higher, and in one movement of the wrist, the blinds are lowered and, once again, the iron curtain is drawn.

Chapter 6

New Year's Eve

Lo is hovering over an arrangement of gerbera daisies when I walk into the shop. "When will people lose their love for these flowers?" she says with a sigh. "They're so cliché."

"But they pay the bills," I say with a smile.

Lo smirks. "I wouldn't trust a man who gave me gerbera daisies."

"What if what's-his-name gave you them?"

She pauses for a moment as if I've just hit her in the Achilles', then shakes her head. "He wouldn't. He gets it."

I set my purse down on the counter and fiddle with the stereo system, then pop in Lo's Sarah McLachlan CD. "So you're still going out with him."

"Grant, yes," she says. "You disapprove, I know."

I shrug. "I do, but I'm starting to sound like an overprotective mother." I fix my eyes on hers. "Just be careful, OK?"

"Deal," Lo says with a smile. "Are you going to Flynn's party?"

I nod. "Reluctantly."

"Oh, Jane, you'll have fun. Drink some champagne. Talk to a boy. Enjoy yourself a little."

"Easier said than done. Especially among the kind of guys in Flynn's circle."

"What are you going to wear?" she asks.

"I have no idea."

She nods and walks to the back room, where a bunch of freshly dry-cleaned dresses hang on the door. "I just picked these up from the cleaners. We're the same size. Take your pick."

I shake my head. "I can't pull those sorts of dresses off like you, Lo."

"Of course you can," she says, pulling the plastic wrapping off of them and selecting a black dress that's cut low on top and daringly short. "This would look perfect on you."

I hold it up, then shake my head. "I'm not so sure."

Lo nods. "I'm sure." Then she reaches in her bag. "And take my Louboutins," she adds, handing me a pair of black patent leather heels. "You'll wow in these."

"I don't know," I say, kicking off my UGGs and slipping one on.

"They fit," she says. "Perfect."

My phone rings, and I reach for it on the counter. I don't recognize the number. "Hello?"

"Jane, this is Dr. Heller."

"Oh, hi," I say.

"Have I caught you at a bad time?" Her voice sounds a bit more serious than normal, and I feel a surge of adrenaline.

"No, no, this is fine. Is everything OK?" I think of the recent MRI. Did she have bad results?

"Yes," she says. "At least, I think. But it's about your MRI. Jane, the results were quite puzzling. In fact, we've never seen anything like it. The temporal lobe was lit up in a way I've never witnessed on imaging."

"What does that mean, exactly?"

"We're not entirely sure," she says. "At least not at this moment. I'm sending your scans to some of the country's top experts to see if they can offer some alternate explanations. But the reason why this concerns me, at least for now, is that the type of activity revealed in your scans is most often seen in people who have had significant seizures, even strokes. But we know your health history, and I don't believe that you've had either. It has to be something else. There has to be some other explanation."

I nod to myself. "Dr. Heller, a long time ago you told me about the various parts of the brain. I was twelve, I think. You showed me a diagram of the different sections and I recall thinking that it was really gross. Remember?"

"Yes," she says. "I do."

"So what is the temporal lobe responsible for?"

Dr. Heller is silent for a moment. "It's part of the limbic system. It regulates our emotions and is the place in the brain that researchers have been able to measure . . ."

"Love?"

"Well, Jane, no one can scientifically measure love, but yes, feelings, emotions, affection."

"Love," I say again.

I arrive at Flynn's party at eight. I feel awkward in Lo's dress and shoes, and as I peek my head through the door, I tug at the hemline nervously. For 2.5 seconds, I consider turning around, running back to my apartment, and changing into my typical uniform—a pair of black leggings and a sweater—but Flynn sees me instantly and gestures grandly from the bar in the kitchen. I'm trapped.

"Jane!" he calls out. "You made it!"

I smile and walk to the bar, where I kiss my brother on the cheek.

He hands me a glass of champagne. "Look at you," he says. "You look *stunning.*"

"I'm glad you think so," I say. "I feel like an idiot in this dress, honestly. Lo made me wear it."

"How is Lo?" he asks.

"Good," I say with an eye roll. "Up to her usual antics. Tonight's she's out with a married—well, ambiguously separated—man."

Flynn raises an eyebrow. "Oh?"

"And who is your woman of the hour?" I ask facetiously.

He hesitates for a moment and looks out the window of his loft apartment, where the city lights sparkle all around, then snaps his head back to a group of young women standing across the room.

"Good luck with that," I say with a grin.

"Hey, there's someone I want to introduce you to," he says.

"No, please," I say. "Not another guy in a band. Or an artist."

Flynn shakes his head. "He's a writer, actually. Just relocated from New York."

"A writer, huh?" I take another sip of my champagne and yawn. Sam woke me up at five a.m. needing to pee, and I wasn't able to get back to sleep.

Flynn takes my hand and leads me across the room to the door that opens onto the balcony, where a group of people are packed together smoking or locked in deep conversation.

"Cam," Flynn says to a man in the far corner. His back is turned to us, and all I can make out of this stranger is his gray tweed suit jacket and dark hair.

He turns around to face us, and I take a step forward, then realize the heel of one of my shoes has gotten lodged in the metal grate of the balcony. "I think I'm stuck," I say.

"Here, let me help you," my brother's friend says, laughing.

I grip Flynn's arm for balance as my cheeks burn with embarrassment. I slip off my right shoe, painfully aware of the chipped pink nail polish on my toes, as Cameron kneels down to free the heel from the grate. I slip the other heel off before it succumbs to a similar fate.

Flynn grins. "Now that we have this problem solved, Cameron, I'd like you to meet my sister, Jane. Jane, this is Cameron Collins."

He extends his hand. "Nice to meet you, Jane. Please, call me Cam."

He's about my age, and definitely fits the scene at Flynn's, with his plaid shirt, slim-fitting pants, and a hint of stubble on his chin. But there's something different about him too. Preppier? Smarter? I'm not sure, and I can't quite pinpoint if I like it or despise it.

"Cam just moved here from New York. He's a correspondent for *Time*. He writes about medicine."

"Oh," I say. "What sorts of topics do you cover?"

"Neuroscience, mostly," he says. "Between the research that's coming out of the University of Washington and what's happening in the bio-technology space on South Lake Union, Seattle is a medical writer's paradise."

Flynn looks at me, then at Cam. "My sister's been seeing a neurologist her whole life. You two have something in common."

Cam raises his eyebrows curiously as I shoot Flynn an annoyed look, then turn back to Cam. "It's not that interesting," I say.

"I'm sure I'd find it interesting," he replies.

A woman who looks vaguely like Kim Kardashian approaches Flynn and they head back inside.

"So you're his little sister, huh?" Cam asks, grinning.

I nod. "How did you say you knew him?"

"We went to college together," he says. "I attended the University of Washington for one year before transferring to NYU for journalism. I lived with Flynn for one crazy semester."

I grin. "Yeah, I'm sure it was."

Cam's gaze is intense, and I find myself looking away every few moments to avoid eye contact. "You're not much like him, are you?" he asks.

"Well, I don't know about that," I say, feeling my cheeks burn again. "What do you mean, exactly?"

His expression softens. "You just seem different; that's all. Good different."

I smile. "I mean, I love my brother to pieces, but a serial-dating hipster, I am not."

He reaches for an open bottle of champagne on the table outside and refills my glass. I take a long sip. "What do you do for work?" he asks.

"I'm a florist."

"A florist." He grins. "I don't think I've ever known a florist."

"My mother owned the shop before she died," I say. "And my grandma, before her. It's called the Flower Lady. It's a Pike Place institution."

"The Flower Lady," he says, genuinely impressed. "I passed your shop the other day, I think, when I was down getting a Dungeness crab melt at Beecher's. Ever had one?"

"Yeah," I say. "It's lunch's equivalent to crack cocaine."

Cam chuckles. "I bet you have great cocktail party fodder about the emotional moments you see in your line of work. Like men who get all nervous before big dates or proposals. A lot of cheesy love stuff."

I raise one eyebrow. "Cheesy love stuff," I repeat. "Obviously you're not a romantic at heart."

He shrugs. "I guess I take more of a logical, scientific understanding."

I furrow my brow. "I'm sorry, but love is hardly *scientific*."

"Oh, but it is," Cam replies. "I don't mean to come off as rigid, but I think we as a culture overthink love. The concept is highly logical, actually. You choose to be with someone, or you don't."

"You make it all sound so simple."

"Well, it is, when you break it down." He smiles. "How about you? Ever been in love?"

I cock my head to the right. "Coming from someone I've just met, that's an awfully personal question."

"Sorry, you don't have to tell me," Cam says,

sensing my hesitation. "Having covered neuro-science in depth, here's my takeaway: Whether we believe we're in love or not, I think we're responding to a chemical reaction in the brain. Neurons talking to other neurons. The collision, the spark. Bam—love, or what we think is love. And then it dissipates as it always does. There's a whole science to it. And whether you define it as love or not, it never lasts. It can't. The brain isn't made to sustain that feeling of intoxication you get from a new romance. Even the greatest love stories turn into pots and pans."

I grin. "Pots and pans, huh?"

"Exactly," he says. "Eventually routine takes over."

"If there is truth in your words, there is also sadness."

He nods. "Because we want the kind of love that sells movie tickets. Everyone does. But it just doesn't happen, and if it does, it doesn't last."

I feel a shiver come over me, and before I know it, Cam has peeled off his jacket and draped it over my shoulders.

"You didn't have to do that," I say.

"But I did," he says. "You were shivering."

"Right," I say with a grin. "Logical."

I finish my third glass of champagne and pour myself another. I feel light and uninhibited now.

"Let's go in and grab some food before the teenagers eat it all," he says with a wink.

I follow him inside. Flynn catches my eye from across the room and motions for me to come over.

"Go," Cam says with a smile. "I'll catch you later."

I hand him his jacket, then walk over to my brother.

"Oh, I didn't mean to interrupt," he says. "It looks like you two are hitting it off."

I grin. "I'm not so sure I'd say that." I glance across the room at Cam, who's now chatting with an Asian woman who's wearing a "Happy New Year" headband. "But he *is* interesting. And how about you? Which girl gets the privilege of kissing you at midnight?"

Flynn looks serious for a moment, then leads me over to the window. He points at the apartment across the street. "See the window with red curtains, with the lamp on the coffee table?"

I nod.

"A woman lives there," he says, rubbing his forehead. Then he lowers his voice to a whisper. "Jane, she absolutely possesses me."

"Have you met?"

He shakes his head. "No, I just see her every day. She makes pottery, and I sometimes watch her work. God, it's beautiful. Her intensity, her determination, the way she moves her hands."

"Why didn't you invite her to your party?"

"I don't know," he says. "I guess I'm—"

"Feeling scared to talk to a girl for the first time in your life?"

"Yeah," he says. "And here's the thing. I think she's sad. Deeply sad. Sometimes I'll get up at three a.m. to get a glass of water in the kitchen, and I'll see her doubled over on the couch, crying. A man came to visit her the other day, older than she is. He brought her flowers. But I could tell by the way she looked at him that he'd hurt her somehow."

Just then, the woman appears at the window. It's too dark for me to make out her face, but I watch as she lifts her hand as if to wave at Flynn, and he does the same. In that moment, my vision begins to fog, and the familiar aura covers my sight like a thick bank of clouds. I look away and rub my eyes.

"You OK, Jane?"

"Yes," I say quickly. "I must have gotten something in my eye. I'll just run to the bathroom."

"Use the one in my master," he says. "There's a line for the powder room."

I nod and walk through Flynn's bedroom, where a couple in their early twenties is making out on the bed. They sit up like two teenagers who've just been caught by their parents.

I close the bathroom door and lean against the countertop so I can get a good look at my eyes. I open and close them several times, then take a deep breath. *Should I tell Flynn what I see? Would he believe me? Or would it ruin it for him? Would it send him running scared the way he's done in the past when he's gotten too close to a woman, too close to love?*

I think of Colette next. *If I do accept her challenge, to identify the six different types of love, how will I know I've seen them for what they are? What if I get it wrong?*

I walk back to the party and help myself to another glass of champagne. More people filter into Flynn's apartment, couples and singles and women in sparkly, sequined tops. I find myself chatting with two men in their midtwenties. One's a drummer in a rock band; the other is an artist. By eleven, the lights dim. Flynn turns up the speakers, and dance music fills the air. A girl who looks like she's long since had too much to drink begins gyrating, and a group of her friends join her. My little drummer boy takes my hand suddenly and leads me into the center of Flynn's living room. Before I know it, his arms are around my waist and he's pulling me close.

"I'm not really much of a dancer," I say, attempting to step back, but he pulls me closer.

"I'll teach you, then," he says.

"But I—"

I feel a hand on my shoulder. I turn around and see Cam. "There you are," he says, smiling at me before turning to the drummer. "Sorry, I'm afraid I'm going to have to retrieve my girlfriend. She

107

tends to embarrass herself on the dance floor." Cam shoots me a playful glance. "And we can't have that, can we?"

"Oh," the drummer says, immediately removing his hands from my waist. "Sorry, dude."

"No harm done," Cam says, confidently weaving his fingers through mine and leading me back across the room.

"Why did you do that?" I ask with a curious smile.

He winks. "Because I think you're the type who's much too nice to say no."

"That's not true," I say indignantly.

"Then why didn't you tell him no?"

"I was going to," I say. "Just as soon as—"

"Exactly," he says self-confidently. "Besides, it's almost midnight. And there's the matter of who I will kiss."

"This, coming from a man who doesn't believe in love?"

"Yes," he says. "But that doesn't mean I don't want to kiss you."

"You're bold, you know?"

"I know," he says with a self-assured look that I'm not sure if I love or loathe. "But I'm right."

I think of Flynn again and the woman in the apartment across the street. I think of Elaine. I'm starting to add it up in a way that I can't deny. "What if I told you something that would disprove your bah-humbug theory on love?"

"Ah," he says. "I'd be intrigued, but I have to admit, I'm a difficult one to convince."

He's right, and when I look into his eyes then, I know my confession is like a runaway freight train. For a reason I cannot explain, I must tell him. "What I said earlier about my neurological condition being uninteresting—well, that wasn't entirely true. You see, I was born with a special . . . ability," I say.

"What, like the ability to roll your tongue into crazy shapes?"

I laugh. "No, it's . . . much bigger than that."

"Then what is it?"

"Well," I say with a sigh. "So, I can see . . . love."

Cam stares at me for a long moment, then bursts into laughter. "You're *funny*."

"No," I say, "I'm serious."

"So let me guess, do little hearts fly out of people's heads when they're in love? Do you hear birds chirping in your ears? No, wait, is Cupid in on this? Do you see him puncturing hearts with bow and arrows?"

"You're mocking me," I say. "I shouldn't have told you."

His smile fades away. "You're actually serious?"

"I am," I say. "I've had vision issues my whole life. I've seen a neurologist since I was a kid, and the latest thinking is that I have a tiny tumor on my optic nerve. And, and . . . I don't even know why I'm telling you this." I pause to rub my eyes. I've had too much champagne. I regret the last glass. But I'm in this deep, so I decide to finish. "Last week, on my birthday, I got a card from a strange woman who was present on the day I was born. She knew all about my gift. And, anyway, she told me things, big things."

"Well," Cam says. "I don't quite know what to say."

All around us people are chanting. *Ten, nine, eight, seven, six.* The countdown to a new year. My head spins when I feel Cam's lips on mine, and when he presses his body against mine, I don't pull back. In fact, I seem to melt into him. And for a moment, I don't know where he ends and I begin.

"Happy New Year," he says.

"Happy New Year," I reply.

"So, did you or did you not?"

I look up at him, confused. "What are you talking about?"

"Love," he says. "Did you see love when we kissed?"

"It doesn't work like that," I say. "Nothing in my own life is clear."

"Ah," Cam says with a wink. "That's convenient."

I look up at him and shake my head. "You think this is all a bunch of bullshit, don't you? You think I'm lying to you." I take a step backward. "This was a mistake. This all was a mistake."

I tear off the "Happy New Year" hat I seem to have acquired and toss it on the couch as I wend my way through the living room. I find my shoes by the front door and grab my bag from Flynn's closet. I take one final look behind me. I don't see my brother, so I push through the door and head to the elevator. I want nothing more than to be home, out of this horrible dress, and in my bed with Sam lying on the floor beside me.

Chapter 7

4572 Sunnyside Avenue

Mary hears the chime of the doorbell and lets out a long exhale. She almost wishes that she would have canceled the appointment with the contractor today. She has so much to do before Eli's return. Somehow, details of the kitchen remodel seem almost meaningless when her husband's homecoming is imminent. She wants the house to be just right—the bed made with new flannel sheets; his favorite dessert, apple crisp, ready to be baked, with vanilla ice cream in the freezer. They'll open that bottle of 2002 Dom Pérignon she received as a gift from a client two years ago. Surely, he'll see the love in her eyes, the love she knew he missed. He'll give up his intense touring schedule and focus on recording. They'll build a home studio for him in the backyard. Mary smiles to herself and imagines them clinking glasses together, Eli looking at her the way he used to, with eyes of love. She'll have to find something new to wear, of course, something stunning. A red dress, maybe. Eli loves red.

The doorbell rings again, and she walks to the front entryway.

"Hello," she says to the man standing on the stoop. "You must be from Ridgeway Construction."

"Yes," he replies. His accent is thick, and Mary immediately places it as Italian. In a moment, she's transported back to her year abroad in Rome, where she danced the night away with men named Dino and Giovanni. "My name is Luca," he says.

"Come in," Mary says, smiling. He's handsome, in a quiet way. Tall, with strong features, but soft, kind brown eyes. "You must be from Italy."

"Yes, I am," he says, tucking a lock of hair behind his right ear. It's wavy and unruly, and just as he's tucked it away, it falls back over his eye. "I live here for two years only."

Mary smiles at his sentence construction. "Well, I hope you've enjoyed Seattle, then."

"I like it very much," he says. "In Italy, I make cabinets. And here I make cabinets. I do what I love."

"Me, too," Mary says. "We're in the lucky minority." She points to the kitchen. "So I explained to Ridgeway that I would show you around today, and the demolition should start next week. You see, my husband is coming home tomorrow, and I'd like us to have some time together before everything's torn up. I imagine there'll be a lot of dust."

"Of course," Luca says quickly. "I understand."

Mary leads him to the kitchen, and together they stand near the fireplace. When they purchased the house, Eli didn't like the idea of a fireplace in the kitchen. "It's such a waste of space," he said. But Mary had always loved the thought of having a log flickering away in the fireplace while she cooked dinner. "My mother had a fireplace in her kitchen in Italy," Luca says. "It makes memories for me."

"My grandmother had a fireplace in her kitchen," Mary says, reminiscing, "in an old farmhouse in Skagit Valley. All through the cold winters and rainy springs she'd keep a fire burning. My sister and I used to love to sit by it and warm ourselves while she cooked."

Luca sets his bag down on the kitchen table and pulls out the architectural renderings for the new space. "There must be a mistake," he says. "This plan show no fireplace."

Mary nods. "My husband wants it out." She finds herself speaking in a very convincing manner, as if perhaps she's trying to convince herself. "We'll need the space on that wall for the Sub-Zero," she says. "There just isn't room for the old fireplace, sadly."

Luca nods as Mary's cell phone rings in her pocket. She glances at the screen. "Sorry," she says. "It's my husband calling from New York. I have to take it."

"It's OK," Luca says, turning back to the plans.

Mary walks out to the living room. "Eli, hi!"

"Hello, beautiful," he says. She loves his terms of endearment.

"I miss you so much," she says. "I can't wait to see you tomorrow."

There's a long pause, and at first Mary wonders if the call was dropped. "About that," Eli finally says. "I'm going to have to stay out here for a few more weeks. All of my shows at the venue have been sold out, so my manager wants me to stay awhile longer, possibly follow up with another leg of the East Coast tour."

"But I . . . I thought you were coming home tomorrow," Mary says, her voice faltering. "I miss you so much. This distance is killing me."

"I know, beautiful, I know. And I'll be home right after this next round of shows. We could use the money, with the kitchen remodel and all." Mary thinks of Luca in the kitchen, poring over the drawings, which she'd just as well toss in the kitchen fireplace and incinerate.

"Right," she says, almost robotically.

"Thanks for understanding," he says. "Call you later?"

"Sure," she says.

Mary stands stunned in the living room for a long moment. A single tear streams down her face as she glances at the mantel, where a framed photo of her and Eli on their wedding day sits. She turns around when she hears footsteps behind her. Luca stands across the room. She almost forgot he was there.

"I'm sorry, I interrupt?"

With the edge of her wrist, she quickly wipes away the tear on her cheek.

"Are you OK?" Luca asks, walking toward her. His eyes are big and filled with concern. She notices, for the first time, a scar beneath his right eye.

"Yes," she says quickly. "I'm fine."

"Sit down," he says.

She nods.

"Why you cry?"

Another tear falls onto her cheek, and this time Mary doesn't try to conceal it. "My husband isn't coming home."

Luca nods as if he understands, but he doesn't. This world is too impossible for him to make sense of. Here is a woman, a beautiful woman, and her husband has let go of her hand, just as his fiancée let go of his four years ago. She walked into the café in that pale blue dress, told him about the other man, and broke his heart so badly, it still aches.

He doesn't say anything. There are no words that will mend her, and besides, even if there were, he knows he could not string them together into a sentence that would be well understood, much less meaningful to her. So he sits beside her on the couch as the clock on the wall ticks, and he offers her his only gift: his presence. They will go over kitchen construction plans another time.

"I'm sorry," Mary says, standing up quickly. "You must think I'm a lunatic."

"A lunatic?" he says.

She smiles. "It means . . . a crazy person."

Luca grins. "You are not crazy, no."

"Well," she says, reaching for a tissue from the box on the side table. "Maybe you can come back tomorrow. I'll have my act together then."

"Of course," he says. "Tomorrow."

The word echoes in Mary's ears long after Luca has left. Tomorrow. Tomorrow. *Tomorrow.* The problem is, she heard the tone in Eli's voice on the phone—the doubt, the hesitation. And while Mary's tomorrows once looked bright, she now has to squint through the darkness to see.

Chapter 8

February 12, 2013

Dark, wet clouds hover low over Pike Place Market, and I feel mist on my face as I walk to the flower shop. I stop in to see Elaine and grab a chocolate croissant on the way.

"Hi, honey," she says from behind the counter. Her eyes look more tired than usual. Dark shadows lie beneath. And she's lost weight, at least five pounds. I wonder if she's been sick.

"Eat something," I say with a grin. "Nobody likes a skinny baker."

Elaine forces a smile and readjusts her ponytail. "I haven't had much of an appetite these days," she says, pausing for a long moment before looking at me again. Then she shakes her head. "Actually, there's something I'd like to talk about." She indicates a corner table. "Can you sit down for a sec?"

"Of course," I say. She grabs two chocolate croissants, and I follow her past pink and red heart decorations. I remember Valentine's Day is in two days.

We sit down, and Elaine lets out a sigh. "I think I've been hibernating for a really long time."

"What do you mean, hibernating?" I ask.

"I mean . . . ," she says, pausing. "Sometimes we can just go through the motions in life. We pick up the dry cleaning and go to our kids' soccer games and put a new box of tissue on the bedside table. We do it all again and again." A tear falls from her eye. "Jane, I've been doing this for so long. I've been so numb for so long. Living a seemingly happy life, but not being truly present in it. Not *feeling* any of it. Hibernating. And then"—she pauses to wipe a tear away—"something woke me up. And, Jane, I'm scared."

I reach for her hand under the table and squeeze it tightly. "Elaine, you can talk to me about this. Just let it out."

She nods, just as Matthew walks in. "Hey, you two," he chirps. "Jane, I'm about to come over to see you." He wraps his arms around Elaine's shoulders and gives her a squeeze. "Got to order this beautiful wife of mine her yearly two dozen roses."

Elaine forces a smile. I can tell that whatever she was about to tell me hasn't hit Matthew's radar.

"Here's the thing, Jane," he says, giving Elaine a quick shoulder rub. "When you've been married as long as we have, there's not much point in the element of surprise."

I smile, but I can see fresh tears in Elaine's eyes.

"I should get back," she says, composing herself. "We're slammed with Valentine's Day prep."

We both look up when the door to the bakery opens and a familiar face appears. "Mary," I say, waving.

"Oh, hi," she says, grinning.

"You remember my friend Elaine and her husband, Matthew, right?"

"Of course," Mary says. "And, Elaine, I have to tell you, I've developed quite a craving for your black-bottom cupcakes."

Elaine smiles. "It's funny you should say that. I was just talking to a woman this morning who is thirty-nine weeks pregnant, and she says she's eaten one every day for the entirety of her third trimester. And she's as thin as a rail; go figure."

Mary looks at me, then back at Elaine, and smiles knowingly.

"Wait," I say. "Mary, you're not . . ."

"Pregnant?" She is radiant, and yet there's a flicker of sadness in her eyes too. "No. Impossible. But Eli's coming for a quick visit next month, so it's possible."

Elaine walks behind the counter and returns with a small box of cupcakes. "For good luck," she says. "Come back anytime. We'll keep that future baby adequately fed on butter and sugar."

Mary grins as she stands to leave. "Thank you."

"Jane," Elaine says, retying her apron strings. "Let's catch up later."

"Sure," I say, catching her eye. I remember the connection I saw between her and Charles, the new neighbor who came over on Christmas Day.

Matthew watches as his wife slips back behind the counter, then turns to me. "Mind if I follow you back to the shop and get those flowers ordered for Elaine?"

"Of course," I say, and we walk together to the door. The air outside is crisp, and the market is bustling. I confide in Matthew about my fears about Eli, how he hasn't been home in months.

He frowns. "I just don't get how a person can be that selfish, how someone could throw away such a beautiful life in search of greener pastures."

In that moment I think of Charles. I think of Elaine's hesitation this morning. Matthew is like a man standing on a hill on a calm, sunny day, unaware of the dark storm cloud creeping up behind him. I feel a pang of sadness for him. The atmosphere is changing, and he isn't prepared for a new environment.

Back at the flower shop, I help him with his usual order of roses. "Do you think she's happy?" he asks. His face is still, thoughtful. There's concern in his eyes.

"Elaine, you mean?"

He nods and scratches his head a little nervously. "She's just seemed a little off lately," he says. "I don't know, distant." He sighs. "You know what my biggest fear is, Jane?"

I shake my head. "What?"

"It's been my fear since we met, that crazy night

in Belltown a thousand years ago. I saw her from across the room, and, I swear, the earth shifted on its axis. The atmospheric pressure changed. I had no idea why she even walked up to me. I have no idea why she chose me. I've never known. But she did, and it has been the greatest gift of my life. This beautiful, amazing woman chose me. And I'll always be living in fear that one day she'll wise up and realize that she made a huge mistake."

"Oh, Matthew," I say, placing my hand on his shoulder. "That's not true." But when I say the words, I feel a quiver deep inside, because what I'm about to say may not be true. "Elaine loves you. Very much."

He nods and forces a smile. "Thanks," he says. "Well, listen to me going on and on. Must be something about florists."

I grin. "Yes, we do have a way of getting people to share." I point to the cards beside the register. "Don't forget the card."

He selects one from the rack and scrawls out a few words, then signs his name. He nods to himself and tucks the card into the envelope. "I don't deserve her. I've always known it. I married way out of my league."

Not many would agree with Matthew's self-deprecating assessment. After all, he's handsome, successful, and kind—all desirable qualities in a husband. And yet, he's always taken a second seat to Elaine. Her personality is bigger, her wit sharper, her confidence bolder.

"That's not at all true," I say, trying to reassure him.

He runs his finger along the edge of the envelope, looking lost in thought for a long moment. "Well, every day I get to wake up with my dream girl. It's the greatest joy of my life."

I smile. "That's beautiful. Did you write that in the card?"

He shakes his head. "No, I just wrote 'Happy Valentine's Day.'"

We both look up as Lo walks into the shop carrying two buckets of fresh greenery. Matthew says good-bye, and once the door's closed, Lo asks, "Isn't he your friend Elaine's husband?"

"Yeah," I say, watching him disappear into the market beyond the windows. "Something's not quite right about those two right now, but I don't know what's going on."

"Keep an eye on them," she says. "It could be something for that ancient book of yours. Speaking of, have you thought much more about what that French woman, Colette, told you?"

"I have," I say. "In fact, her words play on continuous loop in my mind."

Lo nods approvingly.

"But," I continue, "I did something really stupid on New Year's Eve."

She grins. "Oh did you, now?"

I roll my eyes. "No, *that's* not what I mean. There was this man, this writer. I was really tipsy, and we got to talking about love. He had this compelling quality that made me want to tell the truth, and I just let it spill right out, about my gift."

Lo looks thoughtful. "And what was his reaction?"

"He thought I was joking, of course. Or making it up." I shrug. "I was stupid to tell him."

"Maybe you told him because you liked him."

I shake my head. "No, he's really not my type."

"Jane," Lo says. "You don't have a type."

"Well, if I did, he wouldn't be it. Besides, he's a friend of Flynn's. He knows how to reach me, and he hasn't called. I mean, not that I expected him to or anything, but—"

"Wait," she says, holding her hand to her forehead. "I can't believe I forgot to tell you. There *was* a man who stopped in briefly last week looking for you. I'm so sorry, Jane; I completely spaced." She bites the edge of her lip. "What did you say his name was? The writer guy?"

"Cam."

"Yes, that was him, I think. Kind of tall, stubble on his chin. Dark glasses. A bit hipster."

"Yep," I say, perking up. "So he stopped by? What did he say?"

"It was busy," Lo says. "There was a line of people at the counter, so I didn't have time to talk to him. But he asked if you were in and said to tell you he stopped by. I'm so sorry I didn't think about it until now. I should have." She fumbles around in the drawer and pulls out a notebook. "He left his phone number."

I tear the edge of the page and stare at his phone number and name. His handwriting is messy, like most men's, but I like the way the *C* in his name is big and bold.

"So are you going to call him?" Lo asks with a grin.

"I might," I say. "Or I might not." I tuck the piece of paper in my pocket.

Lo grins nostalgically. "I had dinner with Grant again last night. He's been texting me all day." She sets a pair of shears down and turns to me. "He took me to Vashon Island." She beams. "Can you believe I've lived in Seattle my whole life and I'd never been? Jane, it was so dreamy. And when we got to the restaurant, this little place along the beach, it was completely empty. There was just one table set up, with a single candle on it. He rented out the entire place so we could be alone."

I remember the way my vision clouded when I saw them together, even in that first exchange they shared. It was real; I saw it. And yet, this man gives me pause. While his grand gesture at the restaurant could be interpreted as an incredibly romantic one, it's also proof of his desire to keep Lo in the shadows.

"It was so . . . natural," she says. "We love the same movies, the same music. His favorite place in the world is Key West."

Lo loves Key West, and she once broke up with a boyfriend who had no interest in renting a convertible and accompanying her on her annual trip to the Keys.

"I've never felt this kind of connection before," she continues. "And this is going to sound totally stupid and cliché, but it's like I've found the other half of me. I swear, we can finish each other's sentences."

I smile at my friend, so beautiful and fierce. She could have any man she wants, and yet she chooses Grant, married and possibly unavailable. "I'm happy for you," I say. "I really am. But take it slow with this one. You both have a lot to lose. You have the potential of experiencing great heartbreak. And he has children, a family, Lo. Don't forget that I was once a little girl whose father left. I know how it feels."

She sighs. "I know, and I hate it. I hate it so much that the love we're forging could cause pain to others." She closes her eyes. "But at the same time, I can't deny these feelings. What if he's the man I'm supposed to be with? What if he's my one?" She lowers her voice to a near-whisper. "He told me that he believes he's living the wrong life."

"Do you think he's being sincere?"

"I do," Lo says. "He's miserable with his

wife. They couldn't be any more different. He's a dreamer, spontaneous. She's measured, logical. They're practically separated anyway. They don't even sleep in the same bed. He's always in the guest bedroom."

"Be careful with your heart," I say. "I don't want you to get hurt."

"I never get hurt," she says playfully.

It's true—in love, Lo always knows how to keep the upper hand. But this time? I have a feeling that if a rogue wave hits, she might go down with the ship.

That afternoon, I pass Mel's newsstand. He looks up from a box of magazines, beaming, in a shirt and red bow tie, a change from his usual jeans and sweaters with patched elbows.

"You're looking awfully fancy today," I say, smiling.

His eyes dart right, then left. "Have you seen her yet today?"

I don't catch the reference. "Her?"

"Vivian."

"Vivian?"

He takes a step closer. "The Queen of England."

"*Oh,*" I say, recalling the British woman who gave Mel a talking-to about not carrying the *Times*, and whom I saw at Mary's salon. "I do remember her."

"Thinks she's better than everyone," Mel says,

adjusting his bow tie. "I'm going to show her that we have plenty of class here in Seattle."

I smile to myself. "I saw her getting her hair done. She's an elegant one. You have a crush on her, don't you?"

He frowns. "A crush? On her?" He shakes his head. "Not me. For starters, she's—"

"You have a crush on her," I say, grinning, as I reach for a copy of the *Seattle Times*, before waving to him and heading down the sidewalk toward my apartment. Just as I reach for my keys, I hear my name.

"*Jane?* Is that *you?*"

I turn around to find Katie, a friend from high school, who went on to attend law school and became a successful immigration attorney. She's just as beautiful as ever, with her shiny brunette hair and big brown eyes. She stands beside a man who is equally attractive. Tall, with the kind of chiseled, handsome face that you'd find in a fashion ad for Eddie Bauer or maybe Abercrombie & Fitch. "Josh, this is my old friend Jane," Katie says, "the one I was telling you about, who I met when my parents moved to Seattle. Jane took pity on my eating lunch alone every day and invited me to share her table. She owns the flower shop in the market."

Josh takes my hand. "Pleased to meet you," he says with a smile, before wrapping his arm around Katie.

"Josh and I are engaged," she says. "We're getting married this summer."

I immediately hug her. "Katie, that's wonderful news!"

Josh caresses her cheek lightly, and she leans in closer to him. Their connection is electric, and my vision immediately clouds, but not in the typical hazy way. This time it's a full-fledged fog, which startles me. I remember the bench on the sidewalk behind me, and I take a few steps back and collapse onto it.

"Uh-oh, you're not feeling well?" Katie asks.

"I'm fine," I say. "I'm just a little fatigued. We've been busy at the shop today, and I forgot to eat lunch."

Josh points to the record store across the street. "You two have girl talk for a bit," he says. "I'm going to run over and see if they have that Dylan album I've been looking for."

Katie smiles to herself as he walks across the street. She watches his every step, then turns back to me proudly. "Is he the hottest thing you've seen in your life or what?"

I smile, grateful that my vision is returning to normal. "Yeah, I'd have to agree with you. He's very handsome."

"Oh, Jane," she says, "and our chemistry is . . . well, let me just say that we can't keep our hands off each other."

"The last time we talked was last fall, and you

were going through that awful breakup with Chris," I say. "I'm glad to see you so happy."

"Thanks, Jane," she says. "I can't even explain it. I've never been with anyone I've clicked with like this, which makes me think that I've never really known love until now. Does that make any sense?"

I nod. "It does."

Katie looks ahead to the record store. "A lot of people believe they're in love when they're not. I certainly did. Remember how much I wanted to marry Chris? I thought he was *it*. But looking back, I never had the type of connection I have with Josh. Nothing will ever compare to the way he makes me feel. And I didn't even know I could feel this way; then, bam—I meet him in a coffee shop in Ballard one Sunday morning, and my world is changed forever. That's how love goes, I think. It just hits you upside the head like Popeye with a baseball bat."

I grin. "Like Popeye with a baseball bat, huh?"

"Well, that's how it felt for me," she says. "It was intense." She pauses for a moment. "Jane, I want you to be in our wedding. I was going to call you this week, but running into you is even better. Would you? It would be such an honor to me if you'd say yes."

"Of course I'll say yes, Katie." I don't tell her about my gift. I don't tell her that the love I saw between her and Josh is so powerful, being in its very presence weakened me. I am only happy for my friend.

After taking Sam on a quick walk, I call Dr. Heller. "Something happened today," I say.

"Another episode?"

"Yes, but it was stronger than anything I've experienced." I tell her about Katie and Josh. I describe the fogginess of my vision, the way my eyes clouded over almost completely.

"Interesting," Dr. Heller says. "And it sounds like you still believe that these symptoms have something to do with love."

"I know you think I'm nuts, but I do. At least I think I do."

"Well," Dr. Heller says, "I'd like you to come in, and soon. I want you to have another MRI. There's a clinical trial that I've been watching closely with you in mind. It may give us some entirely new information about what's going on in your temporal lobe. Jane, I'm worried that these episodes are doing more damage to your brain than we think, and if there's an opportunity for intervention, I think we should take it. There may be treatment options we haven't considered before."

I can't help but think of the way my vision changed in Dr. Heller's office shortly after her interaction with Dr. Wyatt.

"Dr. Heller, there's something else, something I didn't tell you about the last time I was in the office."

"Oh?"

"I didn't want to say anything because it was about . . . you."

"I don't understand," she says.

"That day, my vision clouded while I watched you speaking to Dr. Wyatt. Do you follow?" I pause for a moment. "You love him, don't you, Dr. Heller?"

There's a silence, and for a moment, I worry that she's hung up the phone.

"Please," I finally say. "I hope I haven't offended you. I just thought you should—"

Dr. Heller clears her throat. "Jane," she finally says. Her voice falters a little. "All you have to know is that I could never, ever love Dr. Wyatt. And there is nothing more for us to discuss on the matter."

"Of course," I say. "I got it wrong; I see that now." But I know that I haven't. Love knows no bounds. Whatever restrictions Dr. Heller has placed on her love, it was still there, as clear as day. I saw it.

"All right, I'll see you at an appointment soon, Jane," she says in a distant, distracted voice. The mere mention of Dr. Wyatt makes her emotional, and Dr. Heller is never emotional.

I say good-bye and set the phone on my coffee

table, then pull out the scrap of paper with Cam's number on it. I stare at it until the digits appear to dance.

"This is Jane," I greet him after he picks up on the third ring. "Jane from New Year's Eve. I own the flower shop." My voice is jumpy and sporadic, and my palms feel suddenly sweaty.

"Right, Jane. Hi. I thought you blew me off."

"No, sorry," I say. "My assistant forgot to give me the message until today. I . . . I wanted to get back to you."

"I'm glad you did," he says confidently, with a touch of amusement, which instantly annoys me. "I wanted to see if you'd have dinner with me one night."

"Dinner?"

"Yeah, you know, the meal that people eat every day around six or seven, or, more fashionably, at eight or eight thirty?"

"You're funny," I say sarcastically. "And what makes you think I'll say yes to having dinner with you?"

"Because I'm arrogant," he says. "And I know you like me."

"You *are* arrogant," I reply.

"I have to work out of the New York City office for the next three weeks, but I'll be back the first full week of March. Let's meet that Wednesday night. We'll start with drinks. Lowell's in the market? Five thirty?" He pauses, then continues,

"I'll take your silence as a yes. See you then."

I set the phone down and shake my head while simultaneously grinning. On the coffee table is today's copy of the *Seattle Times* that I picked up from Mel's newsstand earlier. I flip open the newspaper and my eyes scour the front page, then flip beneath the fold to a headline that reads: WOMAN REACHES PEOPLE WITH FLOWERS. The photo is grainy and black and white, but I recognize the woman immediately: Colette.

I scan the first few paragraphs of the story:

> A native of Paris, Colette Dubois was raised in a flower shop on the Left Bank. When she came to Seattle in 1972, she brought her love of flowers with her and began working in the flower shop at Swedish Hospital. That position soon turned into a unique position at the hospital, "special supervisor of floral affairs."
>
> "Basically what I do," she says, "is make sure that the hundreds of flower arrangements that arrive at the hospital each day get to the people they're supposed to."
>
> And then there are the patients who aren't sent flowers. Dubois finds a way to brighten their day. "We have a team of donors and volunteers who source flowers from weddings and special events and

134

repurpose them for people in the hospital who need cheering. There are a lot of things I don't understand about life, but over the years I've learned one thing: Never underestimate the power of flowers to reach someone's soul."

When asked what her favorite flower is, Dubois offers a quick response. "Gloxinia," she says. "It's the flower that represents love at first sight."

Chapter 9

220 Boat Street #2

L o takes a long look at herself in the mirror. Thirty is approaching, not that age matters much to her. She'll still be sexy at forty, fifty, sixty-five. She knows that. It's her good genes. Her mother, after all, has a boyfriend twenty years her junior.

Men. Lo knows them well: what makes them tick, what makes them quiver. She's had a lot of them, after all. Young ones. Old ones (before her self-imposed rule of forty-two, that is). Rich ones. Poor ones. She lets them in her bed but never into her heart.

And then there's Grant. He walked into the flower shop like an arrow, or a perfect sword lily, and she felt it pierce her. She felt *him*.

Lo sighs, circles her eyes with a black eye pencil, then smudges the edges before applying mascara in swift strokes.

Rain pelts the roof of her Lake Union houseboat. It would be a nice night to stay in, with a glass of wine and a good book. Normal people do that. But Lo is not a normal person. Lo has the need to fling herself into the world. To be on the arm of a man. To be adored. Jane asked her once why she filled her schedule with so many dates. She asked her, point-blank, if she was uncomfortable being alone, if she peppered her life with men and noise to quiet her own voice, to numb some sort of pain. But Lo shrugged off her friend's words. She changed the subject. And then she went home and put on a tight Helmut Lang dress and went dancing with a man named David.

She slips on her heels when she hears a knock at the door. It's Grant, here to take her out to dinner at a secluded restaurant in West Seattle, where no one is likely to recognize them. After all, he is still married. This is a fact that nags her like a swollen mosquito bite on the farthest corner of her back that she can't quite reach.

"You look stunning," he says, standing in the doorway. He's wearing a long-sleeved dress shirt with the top button open, dark jeans, and a pair of Italian leather shoes. His smile makes her melt in a way no other man's has.

"You don't look too bad yourself," Lo quips.

"Ready?"

She nods, locks her door, then takes his hand. Her heels clack along the dock. She likes the way his hand feels in hers. She likes the way she feels standing beside him.

At the restaurant, they slip into a dark booth in the far corner. Instead of sitting across from each other, they nestle in on the same side, and Grant reaches for Lo's hand under the table, knitting their fingers together. They eat, they drink, but mostly they're lost in this secret moment, this delicious, connected place. They've barely touched their wine, and yet both of them are drunk, on love and desire.

"What are we doing?" Lo asks. "*This* . . . What is it?"

Grant doesn't hesitate. He kisses her hand. "It's love," he says. "I know it." He closes his eyes tightly, then opens them again. "I know it, I know it, I know it."

She smiles. "I do too," she says. The words fly out of her mouth, and in a surprising way, she hardly recognizes her own voice. In fact, she hardly recognizes her own *feelings*. And it frightens her. She looks away from him and refolds the napkin in her lap.

"Is it already ten?" Grant says then.

It could be ten or eleven or three in the morning. Lo doesn't know; nor does she care. Time is frozen, somehow. She glances at her cell phone. "Yeah."

He rubs his forehead. "I have to get home. My alibi was that work dinner I had earlier. If I stay out any later, I—"

"I know," Lo says quickly. "I get it."

He runs his hand along her thigh and pulls her closer to him. "Don't be sad, baby," he whispers. "We'll figure this out."

She nods and looks away. She knows his

situation is complicated, to say the least. He's going to leave his wife just as soon as his attorney helps him formulate an exit plan, one that won't leave him hemorrhaging money or cut him out of shared custody of his two daughters.

"You know what this feels like?" Lo says, as Grant pulls out his wallet and sets cash on the table.

"What?" he asks, taking her hand in his again.

"It feels like we've been climbing a mountain," she explains. "Everest. We started out at the same base camp and began our climb together. But I climbed faster. I always do. I made it to the top, and I can see you down there on a ledge below. I keep wanting to throw you a rope to help you up. I keep wanting to yell down for you to keep climbing."

"I'm climbing," he whispers in her ear.

"But what if you run out of oxygen? Or what if your gear fails you? Or what if—"

"What if I'm attacked by angry mountain ants?"

"Yeah, angry mountain ants," she says with a smile.

Grant returns her smile, then presses his nose against hers. Their eyes lock. "I will never, ever stop climbing to you," he whispers.

They are perfect words. And it should be enough, this promise of his. But Lo finds herself wanting more. She can't help it. She wants all of him. Every lazy Sunday morning. Every glimpse of the moon from the bedroom window. Every good-morning and good-night.

His cell phone buzzes, and he pulls away, their moment shattered. "It's home calling," he says. Lo knows that "home" means his wife, and she hates it. She hates the secrecy. She hates his unavailability. She hates all of it.

"Right," she says, turning away. She won't let him see her tears. She thinks of her favorite Billy Joel song, "And So It Goes," the one Jane's mother introduced her to. The lyric, "In every heart, there is a room, a sanctuary safe and strong." Yes. This is where she will tuck away her love, her fear that it will not be actualized. No man has entered this room in her heart.

But then Grant whispers three words in her ear that make her want to hand him the key: "I love you."

"I love you," she whispers back.

The words are simple and sure. And they change everything.

Chapter 10

March

Dr. Heller shines a light into my eyes. "And how has your vision been lately?"

I shrug. "Just a few flare-ups; nothing major after that incident with my friend Katie at the market." I remind her of the intensity of the feeling and how I struggled for balance.

"You know," I continue, "it's all starting to make so much sense. I was a shy kid. I hated making eye contact with people. I kind of went through life with tunnel vision. I kept my head down. I didn't know it then, but when I became curious about people, it activated my gift. It caused me to see things I didn't want to see."

Dr. Heller nods, but she doesn't look entirely convinced, and I know she's still jarred by what I told her about her and Dr. Wyatt.

I pause to remember my first episode, on the morning my father left our family. I was too young to understand it then, of course, but I saw love, real love, though the lens of heartbreak. I recount it to Dr. Heller.

"It's an interesting coincidence," she says, reaching for my chart. "But I believe there is a medical, scientific explanation here that we haven't explored before, especially in light of your most recent brain scans. You see, the tumor on your optic nerve seems to be growing. I don't want to alarm you, but I've recently consulted with the physician at Johns Hopkins who's finishing up the clinical trial I mentioned at your last visit. He and I have looked at your scans together, and we believe you may be suffering from a very rare and serious condition called Crane's syndrome, which eats away at the temporal lobe slowly at first, but then, like a cancer, increases in speed." She lets out a sigh that tells me she's concerned, perhaps very. "Jane, our biggest worry for you at this juncture is that, not unlike seizure activity, these episodes may be damaging your brain function. My hope is that with intervention, we can stop them from happening, stop the progressive damage to your brain."

I clasp my hands tightly in my lap. "And if we don't . . . intervene?"

"I believe it's our only hope," Dr. Heller says honestly.

There's a knock at the door. "Come in," Dr. Heller says. A moment later Dr. Wyatt and the nurse, Kelly, walk in.

"Kelly, take her vitals, please," Dr. Heller says before turning to Dr. Wyatt. He's jarringly hand-some, with salt-and-pepper hair and the type of sculpted face and brown eyes that would make him a good candidate to play a handsome doctor on TV. "Did you hear from your colleague?"

Dr. Wyatt nods, then turns to me. "Jane, we've consulted with a top neurologist at Hopkins, an old mentor of mine. He thinks you're in true danger of cognitive decline if we don't"—he pauses to look at Dr. Heller—"if we don't operate."

I shake my head. "Operate?"

Kelly straps the blood pressure cuff to my arm as Dr. Heller exchanges a knowing look with Dr. Wyatt. "Jane," she says. "It's a lot to take in, I know. But there is a procedure that we believe will stop these episodes from continuing. It involves cutting off blood flow to the tumor residing on your optic nerve. We think you're a great candidate for it."

My heart beats faster as Kelly takes my blood pressure. I look at her, then at the two doctors beside me. My vision begins to cloud. I rub my eyes.

"Jane, are you all right?" Dr. Heller says, her face awash with concern.

"It's happening again," I say. "I told you that I saw—"

"Lie down," she says quickly. "Kelly, get her some water."

Kelly nods and runs out the door. Dr. Wyatt takes a step back. "I'll leave you two now," he says. "Let me know if you need me. I'll be down the hall."

Dr. Heller gives him a grateful smile, then turns back to me. "I'm worried, Jane, that if we don't put this operation on a fast track, your health is only going to decline."

"How much time do I have to decide?"

"I don't know," she says. "But the longer you wait, the greater the risk."

My mind is swirling with the consequences of the medical ultimatum I've been given, and there is only one person who can help me make the decision. According to the *Seattle Times*, Colette must be here in the hospital, working wonders with flowers.

"I'm looking for a staff member," I say at the reception desk to a dark-haired woman with a prominent nose and gold hoop earrings. "Her name is Colette. She runs the flower program for the hospital, I think."

"Oh, yes, Colette," the receptionist says warmly, looking up from her computer and pointing. "Her office is just down the hall, across from the gift shop."

"Thank you," I say, walking ahead to a single open door. I peer in without knocking. Inside, there are plentiful flower arrangements and some balloons. I notice one that reads, "You Are a Champion."

Colette stands in the corner. She's wrangling an unfortunate arrangement of carnations onto a cart. I grimace at the overuse of baby's breath. "Oh, hello, Jane," she says, smiling, when she looks up and sees me.

"Hi," I say, taking a step forward. I feel timid in her presence. "I didn't know that you worked here until I saw the article in the *Times*. I . . . there's something about flowers, isn't there? And green eyes. We're a certain type of woman, aren't we?"

Colette tucks a strand of her gray hair behind her ear and walks to the door. Once it's closed, she indicates a chair beside her desk, brightened with a potted gloxinia in bloom. "Sit for a moment, won't you?"

I collapse into the chair, and my eyes well up with tears. "They want me to have brain surgery."

She nods and takes a step toward me.

"Is it true what my doctor said?" I ask. "That these episodes, this temporary vision loss, are wrecking my brain?"

"The truth is hard to come by," she says. "No one will understand our gift the way we do." Her eyes narrow. "But let me ask you this: Do *you* feel that your brain is being . . . what did you say, *wrecked?*"

I shake my head. "No, I wouldn't say that. At least I don't think so. But Dr. Heller has so much urgency about the idea of surgery. And I've trusted her my whole life."

Colette clasps her hands together. "As much as

people may try to draw conclusions, there is no scientific explanation for what we experience. There was a woman in the late nineteen fifties who faced a similar medical dilemma. Her name was Felicia Harcourt. It's not clear whether she possessed insufficient strength to handle her gift, or if there was some other factor at play. But she ultimately consented to a lobotomy. She spent the rest of her life in an institution. Look in the book. Her pages are blank. She didn't complete her journey."

"What should I do?" I ask in a trembling voice.

"There is only one thing you must do: Identify the six types of love," Colette says. "And, Jane, you must succeed. You must. Promise me you will."

I wipe away a tear. "I'll try."

"Good," she says.

I reach out and touch one of the gloxinia's purple rosettes. "Why do you devote your life to flowers?"

She's quiet for a long moment, then takes a deep breath. "Because it's my way to experience love."

I think about her words as I walk out of the hospital and drive back to the parking garage at Pike Place, as I take Sam on a walk, and as the March sunshine warms my face.

"You look hot," Lo says to me later. It's a little after five, and at five thirty I'm supposed to meet Cam for drinks at Lowell's.

I tug at my skirt. "Do you think I overdid it a bit? I'm thinking about going home and changing into jeans."

"No way," she says. "You look great. And I know you're not really accustomed to dating, but this, my friend, is what people wear on dates. They step it up a notch, and you have done that beautifully."

I sigh. "I don't know. I don't even know if I really even like this guy. He's kind of . . ."

"Kind of what?"

"Outspoken, for one. Overconfident. Cocky."

"Cocky is a good trait in a man," Lo says with a laugh. "Well, confidence. It's a turn-on. You'll see."

"I'm not so sure," I say. "And also I'm a little worried, because I told him about my . . . thing."

"The love thing, yes," she replies, pulling the cash out of the till.

"I wish I hadn't told him."

"Well, you did," she says matter-of-factly. "And you probably did because you felt, at a gut level, that you could trust him."

"Well, I'm still nervous."

"Dating is brutal," Lo says as she bundles the cash and checks into a stack and tucks them into an envelope that she'll deposit at the bank later. "You know what I've been thinking about a lot lately?"

"What?"

"Something my mom used to say," she continues. "She said twenty-nine is the most dangerous year of a woman's life."

I crack a smile. "We're both twenty-nine. What do you think she meant by that?"

Lo looks thoughtful for a moment, then nods. "She said that at this age, we're on the verge of our futures in a way we never have been and never will be again." She pauses for a moment as if trying to extract the memory of her mother's voice from the depths of her mind. Like me, Lo lost her mother as a teenager. It's one of the many reasons we bonded in college. "It's a pivotal time. And she warned me that some women get lost in it, this big year. They get lost in the fog or end up in a place they didn't ever want to be. Others make poor choices, terrible ones. And then there are those who live boldly and loudly and take life on. I think my mom said, 'Take life by the balls.' I like that." She sighs. "Anyway, it's a dangerous year. So we have to be wise."

I think about Lo's words as I walk to the market. Lowell's is just a few steps ahead, and somewhere inside, Cam will be waiting at a table. I think about Colette, too, and how she insisted that I complete my journey before my thirtieth birthday—well, before sunset on my thirtieth birthday. Twenty-nine. I wonder if she also believes it's a dangerous year.

148

My phone rings a block away from the restaurant. I see Flynn's name on the screen and answer.

"Hey," I say.

"Hey yourself," he replies. "Doing anything for dinner?"

"Yeah, I'm meeting that writer, Cam."

"A date!"

"Yes," I say. "I guess you could call it that."

"So you like him, I take it?"

"I think so."

"Well, he's a good guy, Jane," Flynn continues. "A really good guy. Did he tell you about Joanna?"

"Who?"

"His girlfriend who died."

"Died?"

"Yeah, it was horrible, and I don't know the whole story, just bits and pieces from his friend Adam who lived with him after all of that in New York, but anyway, it was awful. They were engaged, I think, at the time. He was driving the car, up to someone's weekend house upstate, and I'm not really sure what happened, but there was an accident, a bad one. Cam came out unscathed, but Joanna wasn't so lucky. She was in a coma for a long time, and never recovered. Amnesia, a traumatic brain injury, stuff like that. Cam actually took a leave of absence from his job for a year and cared for her. Adam went to visit him in the thick of it, and he said it was the most amazing thing he's ever seen a man do for a woman. He bathed her, he spoon-fed her. He taught her to walk again. Talk about love."

"That's so sad, and inspiring," I say. "What ended up happening?"

"She ended up having a stroke," Flynn says. "It was a complication from her brain injuries."

"How . . . tragic," I say. "I'm shocked."

"Yeah," he says. "It changed him, I think, as any hardship changes a person. Man, can you even imagine loving someone and then having all of that taken away from you in the blink of an eye?"

"It makes sense now," I say. "That's why he's so jaded about love. He had it, then lost it."

"Yeah," he says again. "But I don't know if I'd call him jaded, Jane. He's just more serious now, I guess. He knows nothing in life is certain."

I think about Flynn's words as I walk inside the restaurant and see Cam already seated at a table. He sees me immediately and waves.

I bypass the hostess and walk to his table. "Hi," I say, feeling a flutter in my stomach as I sit down.

"You look great," he says.

I take off my coat and drape it across my chair. "Thanks." I feel his eyes on me, but instead of returning his gaze, I glance around the room.

"Ever been here before?" I ask, willing my eyes back to his, which are still fixed on me.

"No," he says. "It wasn't a place Flynn and I would have frequented our first year at school, and I haven't been back in Seattle for long." He pauses for a moment. "Wait, wasn't a scene in *Sleepless in Seattle* filmed here?"

"Yeah," I reply, "that scene with Tom Hanks and his friend when they talk about—"

"Tiramisu," we both say at the same time.

I smile and look away.

"I can't believe we haven't seen each other since New Year's," he says.

"Yeah," I say. "It's funny how life just speeds along." I bite my lip and scold myself for making such a sterile, benign comment.

"Well," Cam adds, "I'm glad we finally reunited. I've been thinking about you."

My eyes meet his. "You have?"

"I have."

He's confident—bold, even. Lo would approve. But I still don't know how I feel about his bravado.

"Have you thought about me?" he continues.

"Well, I guess," I say, feeling the color grow in my cheeks.

"You know what I can't get out of my mind?"

I shake my head. "What?"

"What you told me about yourself that night," he replies. "About your gift. Your ability to"—he pauses to hush his voice—"to see love."

"Oh," I say. "I had hoped we wouldn't go there."

"Why?"

"Because it's . . . complicated."

"Do you trust me?"

"Trust you?" I say with a grin. "I hardly know you."

"But you trusted me the night we met," he counters. "Why not continue to trust me?"

I nod. "You have a point."

The waiter delivers two martinis that Cam ordered before I sat down, and we clink glasses before each taking a sip.

"Here's what I'd like to know," Cam says. "When you're out places where couples gather, what's it like for you?"

"Well," I say a little cautiously, "it can be interesting."

"How so?"

I tell him about a typical episode, and he shakes his head in amazement or disbelief, or both. "I'm fascinated. So you're saying that if you look around the room, you'll probably see something that will trip off your . . . gift?"

I nod. "Love is all around, in many forms. And if it's real love, I'll see it."

"Does it hurt?" Cam asks, sinking his chin into the palm of his hand.

I shake my head. "No, not really. It mostly feels

like pressure in my head. And then my eyes feel like they're clouded over. I've lost my vision entirely at times. It's disorienting, a little unpleasant, but not painful, per se."

He looks thoughtful, then nods. "There must be a scientific explanation for this. There has to be."

"You sound like my neurologist, Dr. Heller," I say with a grin.

He nods. "I mean, no offense, but I just don't think I can buy into all the voodoo."

"Who said anything about voodoo?" I spar back.

"I'm sorry," Cam says. "I didn't mean it like that. I'm just trying to wrap my head around all of it."

"My head might not belong to me much longer," I continue. "My doctor wants me to have surgery."

"Surgery?"

I recount the dismal prognosis I was given today.

"What are you going to do?"

I shrug. "I don't know. Honestly, sometimes I think I'd be better off with a lobotomy."

He grins. "Well, I know a fair amount about those."

"And how is that?"

"Oh," he says, "nothing that interesting. I've poked around on the subject for articles in the past." He pops an olive into his mouth from his martini glass. "Anyway, it was years ago, and nothing I want to bore you with."

I think about my conversation with Flynn about Cam's late girlfriend. Is he drawn to topics of the brain because of Joanna's injuries?

"How did you come to be a medical writer?" I ask.

He looks momentarily thoughtful, as if considering whether to peel back a layer and reveal a truth about himself, but the look in his eyes quickly changes. "It pays a hell of a lot more than writing about sports," he jokes.

I smile, and when the waiter asks if I'd like another martini, I say yes.

"See those two over there?" Cam says, changing the subject. He indicates a young couple engrossed in conversation, with an open bottle of red wine on the table in front of them. I look away from them quickly.

"They're young," he continues. "They're good-looking. They're obviously into each other. Do you think they're in love?"

I roll my eyes. "Do we have to do this?"

"Yes," he says with a devilish smile.

I sigh and look back across the room. I let my eyes search the couple in question. I watch them sip their wine and exchange witty banter. The woman, dressed in a low-cut blue tank top, reaches across the table and places her hand on the man's wrist, just briefly, and he smiles. I squint, then brace myself for what I expect to come, the fog bank that will inevitably roll in.

I wait, but nothing happens.

"What is it?" Cam asks. "What do you see?"

"Nothing."

"Nothing?"

"Nada."

He shakes his head. "You mean, they're *not* in love?"

"Not that I can see."

He takes a sip of his martini. "But they look so . . . happy."

"Happy doesn't always mean love," I say. "You'd be surprised how many people you think are in love are really not."

"So they're faking it?"

I shrug. "*Pretending* is the word I like to use. I think people want to be in love. They want to have perfect lives and project that to the people around them."

"But you can see through all that," Cam says.

"Yeah, I guess," I say.

"But mostly you don't want to see it?"

I sigh. "It feels like I'm interfering."

"How so?"

"Well, what if you knew that your best friend's wife didn't love him? Would you tell him? Or what if your brother was madly in love with a woman who didn't return his affection? Would you say something?"

Cam nods. "Interesting, yes." He smiles and takes another sip of his martini.

"You still don't believe me, do you?"

"It's not that I don't believe you," he says. "It's just that it still doesn't add up, logically, for me."

"Love isn't logical," I say.

"And we're at an impasse again," he continues. He looks around the restaurant again, then indicates a couple by the front window. "How about those two? What do you see?"

I sigh again. "You really want to know?"

He nods. "But let me guess," he says. "No love connection between them. I don't mean to come off as rude, but they're completely mismatched. She's way too beautiful for him. Look at the guy. He's bald and, what, five foot seven on a good day?" He shakes his head. "I vote no."

I turn to see the couple Cam is so interested in, and I can immediately see why he's made such a stark analysis. The woman *is* beautiful. Model beautiful. And the man, yes, he is not handsome. Not in the slightest. I nod at Cam, just as my vision begins, unexpectedly, to cloud. I rub my eyes.

"What is it?" he asks, leaning forward.

I nod and close my eyes tightly. "Yep, it's love. Big love."

"Big love?"

I nod, eyes still closed. "You should feel the pressure in my head right now."

156

"Are you OK?"

I blink hard. "I will be," I say. "I need to head to the restroom." I hold on to the edge of the table to steady myself, but I've misjudged the strength of my legs, and they buckle underneath me.

When I open my eyes, I feel stunned, and my head hurts. Cam is hovering over me, and so is the man from the window table. He's dabbing my forehead with a napkin. I see a bloodstain on the edge of it. *My* blood?

"Jane," Cam says. His eyes are big and filled with concern. "Jane, can you hear me?"

"Yes," I mutter. "What happened?"

"You fell and hit your head," he explains.

"Knocked yourself out cold," the man with the supermodel girlfriend (wife?) says. "Left you with quite a goose egg and gash on your forehead. But no major damage done. I see no signs of a concussion."

Cam looks at the man, then back at me. "Still, if you feel nauseated later, or suddenly sleepy, it wouldn't be a bad idea to head to urgent care. Concussions can be sneaky. I know from my research."

The man nods. "Yes, if there's nausea, make sure she's seen right away."

Cam grins. "Pretty lucky to fall at a table across from a neurosurgeon."

"I'm Andy Westfield," the man says. "I work at Harborview Medical Center. And this is my wife,

Anna. It's our tenth wedding anniversary. We met here twelve years ago." He exchanges a sweet glance with his wife. "I still don't know what she sees in me. Well, we'll let you get back to your dinner. You're going to be fine."

I smile. "Happy anniversary. And thank you."

Cam offers me his hand, and I feel a fluttering in my stomach as I take it and let him help me to my feet.

"I'm so embarrassed," I say as I take my seat again.

"Don't be," Cam says. He carefully considers his next words. "You know, I'm beginning to believe you."

My eyes meet his then, and in this moment, I feel that he sees me. Not just my exterior, but me. He sees *me*.

"I'm glad," I say with a grin. "I'm so glad."

Chapter 11

1112 Broadway E. #202

Josh takes his fiancée's hand to help her out of the car. Katie is blindfolded, and has been for the past ten minutes. Josh has a surprise for her. A big one.

"Can I take this thing off now?" she pleads. "I'm dying!"

"Just a moment longer," he says, closing the car door, then leading her up the walkway to the three-story Capitol Hill brownstone he purchased for the two of them. The Realtor just delivered the key this week, and he stared at the shiny brass for a long time. Katie deserves a mansion, of course, a castle, but he dropped every last penny of his savings into the brick townhouse standing before them now, and it's pretty spectacular in its own right. Newly renovated, its three floors include a chef-quality kitchen with a six-burner Wolf range, an upper-floor home office, where Katie can work, and a master bathroom with a shower stall built for two. Josh's heart rate quickens when he thinks of their co-shower this morning.

It's a terrific street, too, with great neighbors; just yesterday he met one of them, a neurologist by the name of Dr. Heller. She mentioned that the local public elementary school is walkable, and that their music program won a national award recently, which made Josh think about the life he'd live with Katie here. The children's voices in the yard. Their future.

"Josh, I have no idea what's going on," Katie says impatiently. "It's not even my birthday. What in the world do you have up your sleeve?" She wraps her arms around his neck and runs her fingers through his hair.

He loves it when she does that. No other woman has touched him the way she does. Then again, there has never been another woman like Katie. She is a force—in life, and in bed. He smiles to himself as they reach the front door of their new home. "OK," he says, slipping the key into the lock, then pushing the door open before pulling off her blindfold. "Welcome home, beautiful."

Katie covers her mouth with her hand. "Josh, are you kidding me?"

"That would be a pretty cruel joke if I were," he says.

"Josh!" she screams. "This is the house. *The* house. The one I saw online. The one I showed you. I thought you were completely spaced out."

"Not true," he says with a grin. "I went to have a look at it the next day."

She shakes her head in amazement. "But I

thought you said it was too expensive, too urban?" She looks at her fiancé with astonishment and then falls into his arms. "You are the most wonderful man on this planet, do you know that?"

He winks at her, then reaches for her hips and pulls her closer to him. "Come here. I'm going to carry you over the threshold."

She loves the way his strong arms lift her up, the way he holds her like a prize, a treasure, as he walks through the doorway. He sets her down in the entryway, and she runs her hand along the railing.

"Do you like it?" Josh asks. "I mean, it won't be forever. But I think it's a pretty great place to start our life together."

"It's perfect," Katie replies.

"Come on," he says, taking her hand. "Let me take you on a tour."

She follows him through the house until they end up in the master bedroom. "Our bed will be great here," he says, pointing to the far wall. "That way, we can wake up and see the sunrise." He points ahead. "See, there's even a little view of the lake. See that?"

She nods. But she's not looking at the lake. She's looking at Josh. She's overcome with desire for him then, this man she loves with every ounce of her being. It's intense, palpable. Their eyes meet, and they kiss, deeply, passionately.

"We have it so good, you know?" she says. "I

don't think there ever was a woman who loved a man as much as I love you."

"We do have it good," he says. "We have the very best kind of love."

She nods. "You know what they say about stars?"

"What do you mean?"

"That some of them burn hot, then fizzle out," Katie continues. "They're short-lived. And others burn low and slow. They're less bright, but they go on for thousands and thousands of years." She shakes her head. "We're some mutant combo of both. We burn hot, and we burn long."

Josh pulls her to him so her body presses tightly against his. He lifts her sweater over her head and lets it drop to the hardwood floor. She unbuttons his shirt next, then unfastens his belt. Moments later, there is skin on skin, mouths entangled, bodies fused together. And then, cries of pleasure echo against the bare walls.

They are home.

Chapter 12

May

Pike Place Market is laden with the bounty of late spring, and the flower shop is bustling with customers who want to take home a token of the season. On this Tuesday afternoon, Lo and I have bridesmaid dress fittings for Katie's upcoming wedding, and though I hate to close the shop early on such a peak business day, I don't hesitate to honor the request of a friend.

My phone rings just as we're about to lock up the shop. It's Mary. And she's in tears.

"Honey, what's wrong?" I ask.

"I'm pregnant," Mary says.

"Oh, that's wonderful, you must be—"

"He's not coming home, Jane."

"What do you mean?"

"He met someone," she says. "Her name is Lizzie. She works in the marketing department of his new record label."

"Did you tell him about the pregnancy? Did that change things?"

"I might as well be adopting a dog, for all he cares. He's not coming home."

"Oh, honey," I say. "There are no words."

"There aren't," Mary continues, laughing and

crying at the same time. "Happy-sad. That's what I am."

"Ready?" Lo asks after I tuck the phone in my purse.

I tell her about Mary, and we both agree that Eli is the most selfish man in the history of men.

"Let's walk," I say with a sigh. "The bridal shop's up on Westlake, but it's such a nice day."

Fresh produce brims from vendors' stalls, and everywhere there is the sense of possibility. People are in better moods after the long winter and drizzly April. Even the seagulls seem happier. But not Lo.

"Sure," she says.

She seemed off when she arrived at work this morning, but I didn't pry. "Are you going to tell me what's bothering you, or am I going to have to guess?" I ask.

She shrugs despondently.

"Oh, no," I say. "So things aren't working out with Grant."

"That's the paradox," she says. "It's working out. Beautifully. I've never felt more into a man in my entire life. And for the first time, I really am thinking about a future with someone. With him. And that uncharted territory seems so . . . murky."

"Why?"

"Well, for starters, there's his wife."

"Oh," I say. "So he hasn't left her."

"It's complicated," Lo says quickly. "He has two kids with her, and they're fairly wealthy, so there'd be a lot of money to divide. It's a lot to consider."

"But how do you know he's worth waiting for?"

"Connection," she replies.

"What do you mean?"

She smiles. "It's hard to put into words. It's as much a feeling as it is the way your stomach flutters when you think of him. It's the feeling of being reached and reaching someone. It's the feeling of being seen by someone for who you really are and being adored for it. That, for me, is connection."

"And yet?" I ask, sensing the weight of her words.

"I feel that he's hesitating." She wraps her shiny brown hair into a ponytail with the rubber band on her wrist. "I sometimes wonder if he likes this arrangement, being to and fro, being secretive."

"As in, he wants to have his cake and eat it too?"

"I guess you could say that," Lo replies. "I think he likes the rush he gets from seeing me, and then he goes home and has the comforts of married life."

"You said he sleeps in the guest room."

She nods. "But he once let on that his wife is an amazing cook. And she buys his clothes, takes them to the cleaners. That sort of thing."

"So what he really wants is a lover and a housewife."

Lo smiles. "Men. Why do we even bother with them?"

"This one is getting to you more than the others," I say, raising an eyebrow. "Why?"

"I've grown accustomed to maintaining an edge, Jane," she says. "And I've lost it, even in my subconscious." She clears her throat. "I've been having a recurring dream."

"That sounds intense."

"It's a cold, windy night, and I'm standing alone on a deserted gravel road through the forest. I kick at the gravel, waiting for Grant to drive up to me, open the car door, and say, 'Get in.'"

"Kicking the gravel," I repeat.

She nods. "The action must signify waiting, impatiently, in that middle place." She frowns. "I *hate* the middle place."

"The imagery is so passive," I say. "You're letting someone else be in the driver's seat, call the shots."

"What else can I do, Jane? I love Grant. All I want is for him to take my hand and live a life with me."

"I'm sorry, Lo."

This morning, she blended white tulips with white hyacinths, and the effect was stunning. Her flower arranging skills are perfection, perhaps better than mine. "Do you know what my grandma told me about tulips?" I ask.

"She knew the secrets of every flower," Lo says.

"Tulips are the only flowers that continue to grow, up to an inch or more, after they're cut. Have you ever watched them? They reach toward the sun, seeking it, reveling in it. They are strong, even as they fade. Their petals take on a wrinkled grace and fall like brave teardrops." I nod. "You're a tulip, Lo." I reach for her hand and squeeze it. "You are graceful through pain. And you never stop pushing forward."

"Thanks, Jane," she says. "I needed to hear that today."

When we arrive at the bridal shop a few minutes later, Katie waves us inside.

"Hi!" she exclaims, throwing her arms around us. "Can you believe I'm getting married next month?"

"Care for some champagne?" the saleswoman, pretty, in her early thirties, asks. Her eyes are downcast, as if she might have been crying earlier and is trying to hide the signs.

I look at Lo, then at Katie, and shrug. "Why not?"

She hands us each a flute, and as I watch the bubbles float and dance in my glass, I think about the woman standing beside me. A person would have to truly believe in love, or perhaps be very jaded, to work in a bridal shop. I glance at her ring finger and see that she is unmarried. When Katie and Lo wander off to gawk at a Vera Wang dress, she pulls a tissue from her pocket and dabs her eye with it.

"I'm sorry," she says. "I'm having a very hard day."

"That seems to be going around," I say.

Tears well up in her eyes, but she smiles through them, as if trying to be braver than her grief, smarter than it. "Nothing is all right in my life right now," she says. "This time last year, I was a bride. I walked down the aisle with the very best intentions and hoped for a future with someone I loved, or thought I loved."

"What happened?"

"It turned out that everything I thought I knew about him was a lie, an illusion," she says. "His job. His past. His promises. All lies." She dabs her eyes with the tissue again, and I think about my gift and how I could have saved her from this heartache. But could I have told her?

We sit down on the bench, and I watch as groups of women ooh and aah over their respective brides-to-be. "Do you like working here?"

"To be perfectly honest, no," she says. "I only work here part-time, to make ends meet. This job pays my rent. When I'm not here, I'm working on my art."

"Oh, what sort of art?"

"Pottery," she replies.

I think of Flynn. He'd like this woman. He'd like her beauty, of course, but he'd also like the cracks in her porcelain. She isn't like the other women he's dated, vapid and airbrushed. "My brother owns a gallery in Pioneer Square. I should introduce you two."

"Oh, thank you," she says. "But I'm really shy about my art. I haven't been able to share it—well, besides with my cat. Cezanne's a kind critic."

I smile. "It must be hard to be surrounded by so much happiness when you're feeling sad."

She shakes her head. "This is not what I'd call a happy place."

"What do you mean?"

"Bridal shops are filled with artificial happiness," she explains. "Of course, you see the happy brides come in now and then. But they're usually the ones who couldn't care less about their dresses, or the bridesmaids' dresses. They are simply happy to be marrying the one they love." She shakes her head. "But those types are rare. Most people don't marry for love. They marry for the idea of love."

"Did you?"

"Looking back, yes. I knew on my wedding day I should have heeded the hesitation I felt in my gut. I wish someone would have taken me aside and said, 'Don't marry him.'"

"Would you have listened?"

"I might have."

Katie and Lo return with an armful of bridesmaid dresses. "Any favorites?" I ask Katie.

She smiles and shrugs. "To be honest, you girls pick. I'm not that hung up on bridesmaids' dresses."

I exchange a knowing look with the saleswoman.

"Katie seems so happy," Lo says on our walk back to the market.

"Yeah," I say. "I see it, you know. Love. When they're together. It's intense, Lo." I pause to remember the way my vision clouded in their presence. I should be happy for them, and I am. But I'm also destroyed by the mere idea of never seeing that same kind of love in my own life, of being blind to it.

"You're having drinks with Cam later, right?"

I look at my watch and smile. "Six o'clock at Il Bistro."

"He's pinged your heart," Lo says.

I let out a nervous laugh. "I don't know if I'd say *that*."

"Well," she says, "I don't have your gift, but I can tell you a thing or two about what I see. And I think you're smitten with this man."

"Smitten?" I say. "I'm not so sure. Intrigued, yes; but I'm also a little cautious. There's so much I don't know about Cam. He's a bit of a mystery, actually."

"First of all," Lo says, "you're way too cautious for your own good. And second, mystery is an ideal quality in a man."

I nod. "There's a side of Cam that he keeps hidden. For example, he rarely talks about his career or his writing. I had to stalk him online and read his stories to get a sense of what he cares about, what inspires him."

"And what is that?"

I hesitate. "People, well . . . like me."

"What do you mean?"

"His coverage area is neuroscience. Just Google his name and you'll find a ton of articles on all manner of brain science." I shake my head. "I don't know."

"So he writes about the brain and is dating a head case," Lo says with a grin. "Photographers marry the models they shoot. Chefs go home with hostesses. So you are aligned in that way. I don't see the big deal."

I grin. "A head case, huh?"

"Better than a basket case," she says with a sarcastic smile.

Before I change into a skirt and a flowy top, I take Sam on a quick walk through the market, blowing a kiss at Bernard, who's on the phone, as I pass through the lobby of my building. I pass Meriwether but don't see Elaine at the counter, so I continue on.

"Hello, beautiful," Mel says. "Need anything? A copy of *Vogue*? A newspaper?"

"Thanks, but no," I reply. "I've got to get Sam

back." I lower my voice to a stage whisper. "I'm going on a date tonight."

Mel beams. "With the *writer?*"

"Yes."

He nods. "Good-looking chap."

"Wait, you've met?"

"Yeah," he says. "He was down here yesterday. Said he worked for *Time*. He asked me if I knew the owner of the Flower Lady, and of course I said I did. He seems like a curious fellow. But that's the journalist in him, eh? He said the two of you were friends."

I smile, but something seems off. "That's funny," I say. "If he was in the market, I wonder why he didn't stop in to say hi."

"He asked a lot of questions, but he didn't give up much information," Mel replies quickly. "For all I know, he was in a hurry to get to an interview or whatever those journalists do."

"Yeah," I say. "What did you think of him?"

"He seemed like a smart enough fellow." His eyes fill with the type of concern I imagine my father might have felt had he stuck around. "Just use your noggin, sweetheart."

I smile. "I will. I always do. Perhaps too much. I'm trying to think with my heart a little more."

"Good," he says. "But as much as you think with your heart, be sure to let your brain call the shots. You've got a good head on your shoulders, Jane."

Just then, the British woman, Vivian, strolls by. Her heels clack on the cobblestone, and her chic-looking scarf, tied into a perfect knot around her neck, sways a little in the spring breeze.

Mel turns to look at her. "Hello there," he says. His mouth hangs open a little.

Vivian turns to face him without a trace of recognition. "Pardon me," she says, pulling her sunglasses lower on her nose. "Did you say something?" Her terrier yaps at her feet, just as a foggy film covers my eyes.

"No, no," he replies quickly. "Just saying good day."

"Well," Vivian says in a huff. "Good day to you, then."

"Hoity-toity," Mel whispers to me after she's out of earshot.

I rub my eyes, wondering how there could be love here. Mel, yes, he obviously has puppy dog eyes for her, but she doesn't appear to have any interest whatsoever in him.

"Well," he continues. I can tell he's injured by the way she regarded him. "I suppose you should be getting on to your date."

I smile at him. "Don't take that too personally," I say, hesitating for a moment. *Should I tell him?* "I think she . . . likes you."

Mel's eyes widen. "No, there's no way she likes me. I am a humble street vendor. And she probably grew up in a palace."

I shake my head. "None of that matters, and you know that. I still think she likes you."

"You're just being kind, Jane," he says. "It's OK. A man knows when he's out of his league."

"I don't think you are," I say. "She just doesn't know how she feels yet. You have to be patient."

He looks intrigued, and I hope I haven't given him false hope, but my eyes don't lie; at least, I don't think they do.

"OK," I say, squeezing his hand. "I'm off." I walk a few paces, then turn back to face him. "By the way, love the bow tie!"

He tugs at the edges, cinching the knot tighter, and casts an appreciative smile my way.

As I walk, I scroll through my Facebook mobile newsfeed and see that Mary's just announced her pregnancy. Beneath the sonogram photo are dozens of comments from elated family members and friends, peppered with Mary's gleeful responses. But between the lines, beyond the smiley faces and emoticons, I can sense my friend's deepest sadness.

I call her immediately. "I just saw the Facebook post," I say. "Let's pray to God this child looks like you."

"Thanks," Mary says. I can tell she's been crying.

"You hanging in there?"

"Trying," she says.

I hear a loud banging sound in the background. "What's that?"

"Oh, it's just Luca," she says.

"Luca?"

"He's my contractor. I'm remodeling my kitchen, remember?"

"Oh, that's right," I say.

"Yeah, I'm living in a construction zone. Dust everywhere. Doing the dishes in the bathtub. And Luca's English isn't good. But it's weird, Jane; I really like having him around. I actually don't know what I'd do if he weren't here right now when I'm missing Eli so acutely."

"Good," I say. "I'm glad he's giving you some comfort."

I hear her crying now. "Jane," she says in a weak voice, "how long do you think it takes for a heart to heal?"

"Oh, honey. You will heal. In time."

"But how long do you think it will take? Because, Jane, I'm not sure I'm strong enough to walk around with this gash in my heart forever. God, I feel like I'm leaving a trail of blood all over Seattle."

"It won't be forever," I assure her. "I promise you that." I pause for a moment and remember the way Mom grieved after my father left. "My mom used to say that for every year you loved someone, it takes a month to recover."

Mary sighs. "Nine years. Which means by the time I have this baby, I might be myself again."

"Not might, Mary, *will*. You *will* be yourself

again. You can't see this now, but *I* can. Every runner who ever starts a race cannot see the finish line. But it's there; it's out there. Just trust."

"Thanks, Jane," she says. "Come over sometime, OK? I'll show you the kitchen, and we can eat takeout on paper plates."

I arrive at Il Bistro five minutes early. The quiet Italian restaurant tucked beneath the street has been in the market almost as long as my flower shop. There is wisdom in the walls of long-standing establishments. I walk in and hang my coat on a rack near the door, and I think of all the proposals and breakups and declarations of love that have happened in this space. I see Cam at the bar, and I wave to him.

"Hi," he says, closing his laptop, then sliding a glass of whiskey my way. I take a sip.

"Working at the bar, huh?"

"Yeah," he says. "Big deadline tomorrow. Just finishing it up. How was your day?"

"Interesting," I reply.

The bartender walks over. "Can I get you anything, miss?"

"A Manhattan, please."

"And why was your day so interesting?" Cam asks.

"Well, for starters, I drank champagne in a bridal shop."

He looks intrigued. "I take it this isn't an everyday occurrence?"

I grin. "No, not exactly."

"I've been thinking about you a lot," he says, eyes fixed on me.

"And I've been thinking about you."

His eyes widen. "What about?"

"Well, lots of things," I reply. My eyes scan the bar as I collect my thoughts. "I have this feeling that I hardly know you. You definitely know more about me than I do about you."

He folds his arms across his chest. "Then what can I tell you?"

"Your career," I say. "You hardly talk about it. And yet, I've looked up your stuff online, and you're a pretty big deal in the world of science reporting. Why didn't you tell me that you won a Pulitzer?"

"Shy, I guess," Cam says, grinning.

"You are the last person I'd call shy."

"Well, would you have preferred that I bragged about it on our first date?"

"Good point," I say. "And what about you and past relationships? Have you ever dated someone long-term? Ever been in love?"

"Ah," he says. "The elusive topic of love."

"That's right. You don't believe in love; let's not let this fact slip our minds."

"That's not true," he says. "I told you I believe that love is a choice. It's about choosing and doing rather than just feeling."

"Ah, so you acknowledge that there *is* a feeling associated with love?"

"I guess there is truth in that, yes," Cam says with a brief conciliatory smile.

"And when have you felt that . . ."

"Feeling," we both say in unison, and I feel my cheeks burn and my heart rate quicken.

I think of what Flynn told me about the death of the woman Cam once loved, and I instantly feel guilty about prying.

"Her name was Joanna," he says, clearing his throat in a way that tells me the very sound of her name still moves him, deeply.

I place my hand on his wrist. "It's OK," I say. "You don't have to talk about it if you don't want to. I didn't mean to—"

"I want to go on," he says softly. "I want you to know this side of me."

I nod and listen as he tells me about the circumstances of her injury and her eventual death.

"I guess I feel, in some ways," he continues, "that by writing about the topics I do, I'm doing her justice."

"You are," I say tenderly. And, at once, it all makes sense: his secrecy, his caution about love.

"Hey," Cam says, breaking the silence. "I have to fly back to New York for meetings next week, and then I'll be on assignment in Chicago the week after, but my parents are flying up for a visit shortly after. And, well, I'd like to introduce them to you. I mean, if that's OK."

"I'd love to meet them," I say, beaming.

"I know it's a little early to 'meet the parents,'" he says with a grin. "I just don't have a lot of friends in the city yet, and believe me, you'll be doing me a favor. If I don't bring you, I'll have to endure a one-hour lecture from my mother about why I should be dating a nice girl."

I grin. "A nice girl, huh?"

He returns my smile. "Be my 'nice girl' for the night? Please?"

"I'd be delighted to."

He reaches for my hand and when he pulls me toward him, I feel a flutter in my stomach. "Want to get out of here?"

"Sure," I say. "Where to?"

"My apartment's just up the block, and I have a balcony," he says. "Want to order takeout and watch the ferries come and go?"

"Yes," I say, smiling. "That sounds nice."

On the walk to Cam's apartment, Flynn calls. "It's my brother," I say apologetically. "I'll just be a sec."

"No problem," Cam says, stepping back a bit on the sidewalk.

"Hi, Flynn," I say into the phone.

"How's my favorite sister?"

"Good," I say. "I'm with Cam."

"Put him on the line. I want to get his word that he's doing right by you."

I glance at Cam, whose eyes are fixed on his phone. I watch as the muscles in his forearms flex as he rapidly types a text or an e-mail. I can't help but wonder who the recipient might be.

"He's not available to talk just now, but I want to know when you get that promise out of him," I say. "How's everything with you? Who's the latest lady in your life?"

He pauses for a moment. "I'm not dating anyone."

"My brother, with no love interests? This can't be true." I laugh. "Wait, are you still obsessing over the girl in the apartment across the street?"

His silence tells me my hunch is correct.

"You are! Have you met her yet? Tell me you have at least taken this flirtation to real life."

"I haven't met her yet," he says. "And this is going to make zero sense, Jane, but I'm afraid to meet her. What we have is so intense from afar. I'm worried that if we were to meet, neither of us would live up to each other's expectations."

"So you'll just continue to flirt with her from your window until the end of time?"

"No," he says. "I mean, I don't know. I'm worried about her. She always seems so sad. I would give anything to take away some of that sadness from her."

"Then knock on her door."

180

• • •

Cam lives on the corner of Cedar and Elliott, in a new apartment building with dark hardwood floors and big windows that open onto a balcony overlooking Elliott Bay. "You're so neat," I say as I walk into his living room, which consists of a black leather sofa, a side chair, and a coffee table with three remote controls arranged in parallel formation. Even the decorative pillow on the chair seems to stand in submission.

"Not really," he says. "I don't own a lot of stuff, have a great cleaning lady, and am not home a lot. The neat-apartment trifecta."

I walk to the window. "The views are amazing from up here."

"Yeah," he says. "They are pretty great. I didn't expect to like Seattle as much as I do."

"The city gets under your skin, doesn't it?"

Cam uncorks a bottle of wine, pours two glasses, and walks to the balcony, where he stands beside me and offers me a glass. Our eyes meet. "You've gotten under my skin too," he says, reaching for my hand. I let him take it. "In the best of ways."

I take a sip of wine and smile. "Thank you."

His cell phone buzzes on the kitchen counter.

"It's OK if you want to take that," I say.

He makes an annoyed face in the direction of his phone. "I don't want to, but I probably should. I've been trying to track down a very important source all week, and this could be him."

I smile. "Go ahead."

He picks up the phone. "This is Cameron Collins," he says in a confident, businesslike tone. I love his voice, so confident and, well, sexy. "Yes, hi. Thank you so much for calling." He casts an apologetic glance at me and then holds up two fingers as if to say, "Just two minutes."

I nod as he walks to his bedroom down the hall. His voice is muffled from behind the partially closed door, but the intensity in his tone comes through.

He returns five minutes later, looking harried and distracted. "Sorry," he says.

"I'm enjoying the view," I say, reaching for his hand in an attempt to regain the closeness the call interrupted. "Thank you for telling me about . . . Joanna earlier."

"I wanted to tell you," he continues, sitting beside me. "It's important that you know the circumstances that have molded me." He's thoughtful for a moment. "You know, she was going to have surgery. A potentially life-saving surgery, one that could have cured her, but she passed away three days before the scheduled operation."

"I'm so sorry," I say in a hushed voice.

He rubs his forehead. "Yeah, you mentioned that your neurologist was in favor of your having surgery. I have to be honest and say that, well,

I'm worried about you. What if surgery really could prevent the type of cognitive decline your doctors are worried about?"

I sigh. "For now, I'm not ready to have the operation. Of course, Dr. Heller thinks I'm foolish, and you probably do too."

"I don't," he says. "But you know that I side with science. Still, it's your decision, Jane, and no one else's."

I nod. "I know it sounds crazy, but I believe that what I see is real."

"You mean, your gift, your ability to see love?"

"Yes," I say. "It's a gut feeling. And even in the face of Dr. Heller's warnings about the damage these episodes may be doing to my brain, I know I must complete my process."

Cam looks inquisitive. "You mean, identify the six types of love?"

"Yes."

He leans closer to me. "Do you ever wish that you could see love in your own life?"

"Yes," I reply. "It would make things a whole lot easier, wouldn't it?"

"Maybe, maybe not." He looks away suddenly and rubs his hand through his dark hair.

"Why do you say that?"

He shakes his head. "It's nothing."

"No," I say, a little more firmly than I intended. "Tell me what's bothering you."

He looks at me, hesitant at first. His eyes soften.

"She didn't know me in the end," he says. "After all those years of loving her, of caring for her, she didn't even know me."

"But it was her illness," I say. "Not her heart."

"That's what I tell myself," he says. "But I looked into her eyes in the end, and there was no love there."

"Surely she loved you, deep down," I reassure him. "She just couldn't access it anymore. She was ill."

He nods. "And yet it's nagged at me all these years, how love is like a switch that can be turned on and off with the flick of a finger. If it can be illuminated and then darkened so quickly, effortlessly, how can you trust it?"

"Oh, Cam," I say, reaching for his hand again. He takes it in his.

I inch closer to him. "I want to kiss you."

He smiles and leans toward me. His skin smells of soap, fabric softener, and man. "Thank you for telling me your story," I say. "I think I understand you now."

"I still don't believe in all the voodoo," he says, grinning. "And I may side with your doctor about there being a medical explanation—"

I place my finger on his lips. "Let's agree to disagree. For now, I just want to kiss you."

He smiles bigger, then pulls my hand to his mouth and kisses it softly, before cupping my cheeks in his hands and pulling my mouth toward his. He kisses me softly at first, then with a surge of intensity, and for a moment, I forget the season, the month, the day of the week. I am entwined with Cam, and he with me.

Chapter 13

342 Pine Street #4

Mel stares at his reflection in the bathroom mirror. It is the first of June, and he misses his late wife, as he always does this time of the year, when birds are chirping and couples walk hand in hand through the market. He can see her there, the way she used to be, standing behind him in the mirror, arms lovingly wrapped around his shoulders. The mirage feels so real, he swears he can smell her perfume.

As he walks to the elevator, through the lobby of his apartment building, and out to the street, he thinks of Adele. The two were married the first weekend of June fifty years ago, and he is sorely aware of this fact when he sees a wedding party in the distance, posing in front of the iconic Pike Place Market sign. He smiles and waves at the bride in a fluffy white dress, walking in heels along the Market's cobblestones, with her new husband beside her. A photographer follows behind, documenting their love in all its perfection.

Adele always loved weddings. She'd place her hand on her heart, and the other in Mel's hand, and say, "Look at them, dear. Aren't they beautiful?"

She was special, Adele. She could read him like a book, and even when she came across an unsavory passage, she never once set the book back on the shelf. She adored the story of their love, even the rocky chapters.

High school sweethearts don't often last, but Mel and Adele stood the test of time. And when her cancer came, Mel faced it fiercely. He could not fathom the idea of letting a disease take the love of his life. But it did. First it took her body, whittling her away to a mere ninety pounds. Then it took her mind, ravaging her brain, until she no longer recognized him.

Adele had died on June 2, eight years before. She took her last breath at a quarter past nine. Mel held her hand and watched her eyelids flutter for the last time, then crawled into her hospital bed and held her for hours, until her body grew cold beside his and the hospital staff told him he must go.

The night of her death, Mel went home to the apartment they had shared above the market, and for the first time, he felt like a stranger in his own home. Without Adele, home felt like a hollow place. Where there was once love and laughter, there was only sadness, grief. He couldn't bear to sleep in their queen-size bed with the quilt Adele had lovingly made. Instead, he retreated to the couch, where he has slept for the past eight years.

Sometimes, even now, and especially on warm

June days, he expects her to round the corner and appear in the distance, smiling. She'd hand him a sandwich, kiss him, and ask when he'd be home for dinner, though he was home for dinner at five o'clock sharp each day. She never got tired of asking him, and he never got tired of telling her. "When will you be home for dinner, dear?" "Five o'clock, darling."

There was a cadence, a rhythm to their life together that ebbed and flowed naturally, like the relationship between the moon and the tide—pulling, giving, balancing each other out. And so when Adele passed, Mel lost his moon. He lost his rhythm. Everything seemed out of step—sleep, meals, the hours of the day. He was like a tide that no longer knew when to come in or go out. He simply floated, the way a piece of driftwood in Elliott Bay might, caught in the current, pushed this way and that, until one day, it finds its way to shore on a sunny June day. And for the first time in a long time—years, maybe—it dries out in the warm sand.

Mel stands at his newsstand and feels the sunshine on his face. He is seventy-three, too old to be working day in and day out the way he does, but what else is there for him now? Take up golf? Sit in his apartment and watch sports? He bristles at the thought of retirement. Besides, he likes to be in the thick of life. The market is like a beautiful river, filled with people who stream in and out with their flowers and their bags of spring asparagus and bright red radishes and honeycomb in plastic cups. He likes to sit on the riverbank and wave and watch and take it all in. And occasionally someone passes who strikes him. A mother and a child. A young man and his prom date with a corsage pinned to her dress with shaking hands, no doubt. Or . . . a woman.

Vivian first appeared at the market on Christmas Eve. With her fur-lined coat, sharp temper, and British accent, she was a pay grade or two above him.

It was a schoolboy crush, he told himself, not unlike the time, before Adele moved to Seattle and enrolled at West Seattle High, he pined for Betty Lou Mansfield, the most popular girl in school. One Friday after school, he asked her to have a Coke with him at the diner, and she turned him down with such cruelty, he vowed never again to forget his place.

But now, with Vivian, he's steered back into Betty Lou territory. And though he has no real way of knowing whether Vivian is even remotely interested in him, his fascination with her is growing. He wonders, for instance, how she takes her eggs; if she likes the opera as much as he does; and whether she seeks the moon each night, if only a glimpse of it glowing behind the clouds, the way he has a habit of doing.

It's foolish, he tells himself, to think that she

might want to know him the way he wants to know her. And yet, when she walks by his newsstand, he cannot look away.

On this particular June morning, Mel finds himself in a starched shirt, with freshly combed hair (well, what he has left of it), at Vladimir's Egg Nest, in the market. Founded by a Russian immigrant in the 1970s, the restaurant serves the best omelets and eggs Benedict in Seattle, and every Friday, Mel sits at a corner table by the window. He likes to read the newspaper and watch the seagulls peck at clamshells on the ledge beneath the windowsill.

Vladimir's grandson, Johnny, approaches Mel's table. "The usual?"

"Yes, sir," he says with a nod. If he needed to state his order, which he doesn't, he'd say: "Two eggs, over easy. Dry wheat toast. And please bring out the Tabasco when you have a moment."

Johnny disappears into the kitchen just as the restaurant door squeaks open. Mel turns to see Vivian standing in the entryway. She looks beautiful in a black dress and gray cashmere cardigan. A strand of pearls clings to her neckline. She notices him and, just briefly, the edges of her mouth turn upward. Even the tiniest notion of a smile from her makes Mel beam.

"Table for one?" Johnny says, reappearing from the kitchen.

"Yes," Vivian says coolly. His question has

mildly irritated her. Don't people know that one does not draw attention to solitary dining?

He seats her at the table beside Mel. "Best view in town from right here," Johnny says, pulling her chair out for her.

"I can see that," she says, looking out to the bay.

Johnny hands her a menu, and Mel watches as her delicate, manicured hands hold it, closed.

"Two eggs, over easy. Whole wheat toast, no butter," she says, clearly speaking from experience.

Johnny exchanges a glance with Mel. "Excellent choice," he says. "I'll have that right up for you."

Vivian stares out the window. Mel folds and refolds the napkin in his lap a dozen times, and each time he opens his mouth to speak, he closes it quickly. For some reason, nothing he can think of to say seems worthy of her air space. And so he sits silently, relishing being near her.

When Johnny returns with their identical meals, he also sets a bottle of Tabasco at Mel's table. "Bon appétit," he says, turning to seat a group of people who have just entered the restaurant.

Mel douses his eggs with a generous dose of Tabasco. Before taking a bite, he looks up and his eyes catch Vivian's.

"Excuse me," she says. "May I borrow the Tabasco? There doesn't seem to be any at my table."

Mel's eyes light up, and he fumbles to set his

fork down. "My pleasure," he says, speaking two words that sum up everything he feels for this mysterious woman. It is his pleasure to sit beside her, to pass the Tabasco, to exchange sideways glances across breakfast tables.

It will be his pleasure.

After she has finished her meal, Vivian pays her bill and stands to leave, but before she walks out the door, she turns to Mel and offers two words of her own: "Good day."

And as the door closes and she disappears into the market, Mel thinks to himself, *Yes, it is a very good day.*

Chapter 14

June 9

I hear my phone ringing in the kitchen, where it's plugged into the wall outlet beside the counter, and I groan as I sit up in bed. Sam lifts his head up from the corner of the mattress, then sets it down, echoing my irritation at being roused before eight a.m. I was at the shop, up late into the night finishing the arrangements for Katie's wedding—sixty vases of white hydrangeas studded with irises, not to mention the elaborate ceremony decor for the church—and I was counting on at least another hour of sleep to provide the energy I need to be both the wedding florist and a bridesmaid today. Alas, I forgot to turn the ringer off last night, and now I am . . . awake.

I stumble to the kitchen and see Dr. Heller's name on the screen. "Hello?" I say groggily.

"Jane, sorry to call this early," she says. "But you've been on my mind. It's been a few months since your last office visit. And you know my position on surgery. It's a novel procedure, Jane, with minimal risk. I think it's the only option, and you must take it. I'm worried about you."

I sigh. "Dr. Heller, I'd like to live through this year without surgical intervention."

"You still believe what that woman told you, don't you? That your health condition is actually a gift?"

"Yes," I say. My heart beats faster as I think of Colette and her instructions to me about not failing in my search to identify the six types of love. "And as much as I trust you and understand your concern, I feel that I must see this through."

I can sense Dr. Heller's disappointment. "Even if that means destruction to your brain? We have measurable results about what your episodes are doing to your brain, Jane. With each episode, damage happens, eating away at your brain tissue. And it's getting cumulatively worse."

I sink into the couch. "You may be right," I say. "And I may regret the decision. But my sense is to keep moving forward. I can't explain why or how, but I know I must."

"I have made my best medical recommendation," Dr. Heller says. "I only hope you'll continue to consider it."

"I have, and I will," I say.

"And, Jane," Dr. Heller continues. "There's something else. And I hesitate to tell you, but . . . actually, no. I'm sorry. I . . . I . . . never mind."

"What do you mean, Dr. Heller?"

"I'm sorry," she says. "I shouldn't have said anything. It's not my place to meddle."

"I don't understand."

"Just be careful," she says.

"I don't have any idea what you mean."

"I've already said too much."

"What are you thinking about?" Lo asks, as I pause on the lower steps of the church and look up at the sky. The clouds appear rippled and wispy, like a fine layer of lace draped over the blue sky.

"My mom," I say, half-smiling. "She used to love weddings."

"I know she did," Lo says softly.

"She used to let me try on her veil," I continue. "The one she wore when she married my father. I used to pull up a stool and climb to the top drawer of her dresser and carefully unfold it. She'd clip it in place, and I'd feel like a princess."

Lo turns her gaze from the clouds back to me. "You're worried that you're not going to have your day, aren't you?"

I shrug. "A wedding, you mean? No, it's bigger than that. It's not the wedding I'm concerned about."

"But love," she says matter-of-factly.

I nod.

"Me, too," she continues, squeezing my hand.

Together we walk ahead up the steps. The ceremony is at three, and we have time to give the church flowers a final once-over—freesia and white roses, with a mix of hydrangeas in shades ranging from stark white to spring green.

Katie and her mother emerge from the bride's

room and gasp at the sight of the blooms. "They're perfect," Katie says through tears of joy. I bend over to retie a bow on one of the back pews that holds a nosegay in place. "Come on, you two, let's get you dressed. Mary just got here and she wants to give you updos."

"Updos," I say with a grin as Lo and I follow Katie down the hall.

"I love weddings," Mary says, taking a lock of my hair and threading it through the curling iron a moment later. "The sense of possibility. The way two people declare their love together so publicly."

I smile. "Me, too. Airports, weddings, and hospitals all give me that fluttery feeling in my stomach."

"It's beginnings and ends that are so poignant," Mary says nostalgically, pinning a curl to my head. "What did F. Scott Fitzgerald write? Something like, 'I love her and that's the beginning and end of everything.'" She nods. "I want to be loved like that. Decisively. Intentionally."

I know these words sting Lo, because when she sits down in the chair for her hair to be styled, she changes the subject immediately. "We need to get a girls' trip on the calendar. For the winter. Somewhere sunny."

Mary points to her bulging belly. "But I'll have to bring along a little guest."

"That's OK," Lo says. "We're baby friendly."

Mary smiles. "She'll fit right in, I think."

My eyes widen. *"She'll?"*

"Yes," Mary says. "I just found out. I'm having a girl."

"That calls for champagne," Katie says, walking toward us with a freshly uncorked bottle. She looks stunning in her gown, and I help her attach her veil to her intricate updo as Lo leans into the mirror and reapplies a bit of red lipstick.

"Maybe you'll catch the bouquet," Katie says, eyeing Lo and me.

I smile, but Lo looks taken aback by the comment. "I don't favor that tradition," she says, shaking her head vehemently.

I see that her eyes look troubled, and I make a mental note to ask her about Grant later. Something happened, or didn't happen.

Suddenly, Katie turns to me. "How much time do we have before the ceremony?"

I glance at my cell phone on the dressing table. "Five minutes."

She grimaces. "I think I have to pee."

"I'll take you," I say, smiling. "You're going to need help with all your . . . layers."

She grins. "I'm already second-guessing the shapewear."

We walk down the back hallway of the church and round a corner, which is when I notice Josh in the distance, in a well-tailored tux. His good looks equally match Katie's, but I know that their love is bigger than skin-deep. I've seen it. I've *felt* it.

"Stop!" Katie shouts down the hallway as soon as she sees Josh walking our way. "Close your eyes. Don't look at me! It's bad luck!" I close my eyes too. Their love is too powerful to look at.

But he doesn't obey. I watch him saunter toward us through squinted eyes. He's unable to take his eyes off his bride. And without uttering a word, or with any regard to my presence, he tucks his strong hands around the bodice of Katie's dress and pulls her toward him. My heart palpitates a little in the presence of their electric connection. I look away as he kisses her. Their love is intense, and I can't risk having an episode like the one I had the first time I saw them together, right before the ceremony.

"You," he says to Katie, "look divine. I have never in my life seen a woman more beautiful. Never."

She grins. "Thank you, handsome," she says. "But you're going to ruin my makeup and I haven't even walked down the aisle. And where is the bathroom?"

I point ahead. "Just around the corner, I think."

Josh gives her a final peck. "See you at the altar."

"This better not have been bad luck," she says.

Her husband-to-be shakes his head. "Nah, we don't believe in bad luck, remember?"

• • •

I intended that Lo and I be each other's date to the wedding, as we shared the work of the floral design and bridesmaid duties. She couldn't invite Grant, obviously. Despite her hope that they'd be able to bring their relationship out in the open by spring, he hasn't yet left his wife, and as a result, they have not yet stepped out of the shadows. When Katie insisted on meeting Cam, and Lo promised she didn't mind being dateless, I invited him.

"It's a good thing he's coming," Lo says with a sly smile as we check over the delivery of Katie's white roses. "We need to see how he looks in a suit. Baggy suits won't cut it."

In a Tom Ford suit, gray with detailing around the edges of the lapels, Cam makes his entrance at the reception. When he walks up to me and kisses my cheek lightly, Lo flashes me a triumphant, approving grin.

The lights are dim in the Four Seasons Hotel ballroom, but the table arrangements are perfectly accentuated by the glow of candlelight.

Cam leans in and whispers to me, "As far as bridesmaids' dresses go, you're rocking that one pretty well."

I smile and take a sip of my wine. In social situations, especially at weddings, I keep my head down as much as possible. If I look out into the ballroom, if I focus on the couples in my midst, my vision may completely shut down.

Lo looks sad, staring emptily at her phone beside me. "Have you heard from him?" I ask.

She shakes her head and sets her phone down on the table with a sigh. "No," she says. "And I won't. He has an event tonight. With his wife."

I lean back in my chair and sigh. "That can't feel good."

She nods. "It doesn't. But I'm trying to trust him through his process. He says he loves me. And, God, do I love him. I . . ."

Her voice trails off as her eyes wander across the room. And a moment later, I see what she sees: Grant . . . and his beautiful wife. His arm is tucked around the petite blond woman's waist. They're both smiling and chatting with Katie's parents.

Lo shakes her head. "I don't believe this," she says. "He's *here?*"

"Don't panic," I say. "So you have a shared connection. He probably couldn't get out of it."

"But look at them," she fumes. "They look so . . . *happy*. That is *not* the picture he painted."

I glance across the room. "Just because they *look* happy doesn't mean they are."

Katie, making her rounds, walks up to our table next. "Can someone spare a glass of white wine?" she whispers to me. "This meet-and-greet stuff is brutal."

I smile and pour her a glass, which is when she

notices the distressed look on Lo's face. "What is it, sweetie?" she asks.

Lo points to the corner of the room where Grant and his wife are laughing with another couple. "How do you know them?"

Katie squints, then nods. "The woman in the gold dress?"

Lo nods.

"I could be wrong, but I think that's one of Josh's father's colleagues and his wife," she says. She frowns. "Honestly, it's all a blur. My newly minted mother-in-law insisted on inviting every person in Seattle, apparently. I—" She pauses and searches Lo's face. "Is something the matter?"

Lo turns to me. "Do you see it, Jane? Tell me. Are they . . . ? I have to know."

Katie looks at us both, perplexed, but I focus ahead. I let my eyes wash over Grant and his wife. I can see Lo's distress. They certainly look the part of the happy, loving couple—both beautiful, all smiles, well dressed, body language that speaks to love, respect for each other. I stare, and I wait, and I wait.

"What do you see?" Lo asks impatiently.

"Nothing," I say finally, after a few moments pass.

She leans back in her chair, a little relieved but still disturbed. The weight of this love she carries is heavy, and I know she is weary.

Lo's eyes are fixed on Grant, and when he

looks in our direction, he sees her. I notice the way his eyes lock on hers, the long pause on his face, the one that tells me she reaches him as much as he reaches her. His expression is pleading, apologetic, begging her to understand. He whispers something in his wife's ear and begins walking toward us.

A moment later, he is standing beside Lo's chair. She looks ahead, unable to make eye contact. "Lo, I—"

"It's OK," she says. "You don't need to explain yourself to me." Her voice is resolute, strong. But I know she's broken inside and deeply confused.

I glance across the room and see Grant's wife watching the scene unfold, watching her husband pander to another woman. If she didn't know, she knows now. Anyone in the room, even without my gift, could see Grant's love for Lo. And just before Lo stands up to excuse herself, she looks at Grant, just one tiny glance. And that's when it happens. My vision clouds, slowly at first, and then with the same intensity I experience when I let my eyes alternate between Josh and Katie, the way their expressions intertwine and ultimately fit, like two puzzle pieces.

"I'm sorry," Lo says to Katie. "I . . . I'm not feeling well. I need to excuse myself for the night."

"Oh, honey," Katie says, placing her hand on Lo's shoulder. "Don't worry at all."

I rub my eyes, after Lo has left and Grant has returned to his wife's side. Cam, returning to the table with two champagne flutes, immediately recognizes what has happened.

"Sit down, Jane," he says softly.

"Is she OK?" Katie asks, kneeling beside me.

Cam is squeezing my hand. "Yes, yes," I say quickly. "I'm fine. I think I'm just getting . . . a migraine."

"She'll be fine," Cam assures her.

Katie shrugs. "My wedding party is dropping like flies."

I nod as my vision starts to come into focus again. "That man," I whisper. "Lo is in love with him, and he is with her."

Katie looks across the room, astounded. "Oh," she says. "It must have hurt something awful to see him here with his—"

"Yes," I say. "It's why she had to leave." I rub my eyes again. "She'll get through it."

"If you need to go home and rest," Katie says, "I will completely understand."

I shake my head. "Absolutely not. I'm staying." I turn to Cam. "I haven't danced with this fella yet."

He squeezes my hand under the table as Katie smiles and moves on to the next table. We both look on as Josh joins her a moment later, tucking his arm around her waist.

"They're an amazing couple," Cam says. "Obviously they are in love."

I nod. "Yes, and it's intense. I couldn't even look at them during the ceremony, or I'd have toppled over right there in the church."

Cam smiles as my cell phone buzzes on the table. I see that it's Elaine and decide to take it first making an apologetic face at Cam.

"Hi," I answer. "I've been trying to reach you for a few days."

"Do you have a second to talk?" Elaine asks. Her voice falters, and I can tell she's been crying.

"Yes," I reply. "I'm at a wedding reception, but I'll just step out of the ballroom so I can hear you better."

In the lobby of the hotel, I find an upholstered chair and sink into it. "OK," I say. "I'm all yours. What's going on?"

"Jane," Elaine says. "I'm a wreck."

"What's going on?"

"I'm falling in love with someone," she says. "Charles, from across the street. You met him at Christmas, remember?"

"I do." I don't tell her that I'm not surprised. I saw their love, as clear as day.

"Jane, I've been carrying this with me for so long now, I had to tell someone." She pauses, and I can hear her weeping. "I am so ashamed."

"Time out," I say. "Don't be ashamed. Yes, this is not easy for you; yes, it is unexpected; but don't think any of us should be ashamed about who we love." I think about Lo and Grant, and the power love has to be beautiful, or destructive, leaving a path of rubble in its wake. But even then, peel back the layers, disregard the circumstances, and love is love. Some of us just have the good fortunate of finding it under less taxing circumstances. I realize that now. "Elaine, I can't tell you why, but I've been doing some serious thinking on the subject. I've come to believe, deep in my veins, that we cannot help who we love. And the identity of our beloved can change over time."

I think about Matthew and Elaine. Did they ever really love each other? In all the years I've known them, I've never had an episode in their presence. But does that mean they don't love in their own way? Or maybe their love has simply changed. After all, love can ebb and flow. Or disappear completely, or hang on, in a quiet place in your heart for a half century, invisible to anyone, maybe even me.

"Yes," she says, gaining composure. "But, Jane, what am I supposed to do? I'm *married*. I have two kids. And I'm in love with the man across the street."

"You love him, yes," I say. "And I'm not telling you that you should do anything about it. I'm not saying anything. I just think you should own that love and not be apologetic about it."

"Yes," she says. "I was hardly going out looking for it. He just walked in my kitchen on

Christmas morning, and bam. It was that clear."

"I know," I say. "I saw it."

"You did?"

"I did."

"But you didn't say anything."

"It wasn't my place."

"Oh, Jane," she says. "What am I supposed to do?"

"Well," I reply, "what do you do when you're unhappy? What cheers you up?"

Elaine thinks for a moment. "Pies. I make pies."

"Then make a pie," I say. "Make two pies, and three. Lose yourself in the pies. And then sleep and when you wake up, you'll see more clearly."

"Yes," she says. "You're right."

"How is Matthew? Does he know?"

"No," she says.

"Give it time. Don't do anything rash. Not yet."

As we end the call, I see a familiar figure rounding a corner into a hallway of the hotel. I would recognize that distinctive steel-gray bun anywhere. Could it be Colette? Is she monitoring my progress?

"Sorry," I say to Cam as I slide back into my chair at the table. "A friend was having a crisis."

"Love life?" he asks.

"Yeah."

He smiles. "You could make a business of this. Jane Williams, Love Doctor."

"Ha," I say. "Not quite. I'd be about as successful at that as the fortune-teller in the bottom of the market."

He shrugs. "Well, if you really believe in what you see, you could do some good for people; help steer them in the right direction."

I shake my head. "I wish I had some other gift. Like a photographic memory, or the ability to predict the weather with an achy elbow or something."

Cam laughs. "I can assure you that your gift is much cooler than an elbow with meteorologist abilities."

I smile, then refold my napkin in my lap. "I wish my mom was here. She loved weddings."

"I'm sorry," he says. "I'm sure you miss her so much."

"I do," I say. "You're lucky that your parents are still living."

He nods. "They've been married for forty-five years, but I'm not sure how happy they are. I mean, they're happy, I guess, but there isn't any romance left in the equation." He nods toward Katie and Josh, who have just taken the dance floor. "I know you can see the love that those two have. It would be an interesting experiment to have you look at my parents. I'll bet your vision would be clear."

I try to laugh off the idea that Cam is proposing. "Your mom and dad and the state of their union aren't one of your science projects."

I think about my parents, and how little I knew of the love they shared, only that it had been love, and it had been true—I'd seen it once, for a brief moment—despite my father's departure from our lives. "My mom died when I was in high school," I say a little breathlessly. I so rarely tell people about her death, and it feels intimate to share this information with Cam now.

"I'm so sorry," he says quickly. "And your father? Are you close to him?"

I shake my head. "No, he's been MIA since I was tiny. I don't think I'd recognize him if I passed him on the street, and yet I think about him a lot. I wonder about how and where he's living his life. Perhaps he has a whole new family and I have half-siblings I've never met. I wonder a lot of things, like why he left my mom, and my brother and me. I know he loved my mother, but somehow his love for her wasn't enough for him to stay."

Cam nods, but he looks distracted, and I see that he's digging into his pocket for his phone. "Sorry," he says, looking pained. "It's work."

I nod. "It's OK, really. Take it."

"Thanks," he says, stepping away from the table. He's back in a few minutes, just as the song from the speakers changes. He smiles. "Do you know this song?"

I nod. " 'The Look of Love,' yes. A classic."

He reaches for my hand. "Dance with me?"

The music is mesmerizing, and so is Cam's gaze, and I raise myself to my feet and then step onto the dance floor with his arms around my waist.

"I want you to think of me, and this moment, whenever you hear this song," he whispers into my ear. "I want you to feel me."

"I will," I reply, resting my head on his chest.

The look of love. I may not be able to see it in my own life, but tonight, yes, I can feel it.

Chapter 15

2201 Hamlin Street
August

Elaine rolls out a sheet of pie dough on the marble countertop in her kitchen. Matthew will be home tomorrow, and the kids picked a bowlful of tart cherries from the backyard tree and painstakingly pitted them at the bar until their fingers were stained red. "Daddy will love our cherry pie," Ella says, grinning beside her brother.

Yes, Matthew loves cherry pies. Elaine remembers his delight upon discovering the old cherry tree in the backyard. It was the very first tree she'd climbed as a girl. The same tree that produced cherries for dozens of summer pies, lovingly baked by her grandmother.

Elaine combines sugar with the cherries in the bowl, then mixes in a pinch of cinnamon, just as her grandmother did. As she stirs the mixture, she remembers the way she sat on the counter as a girl, watching her grandmother make pies. Her grandfather would come into the kitchen and steal a taste of whatever was in process, only to receive a swift slap on the wrist from her grandmother. Their relationship was playful and loving, and Elaine considered it, as she still does, true love. She thinks of her husband. Matthew. Yes, he loves her. Of course he does. But he doesn't look at her the way her grandfather looked at her grandmother.

Ella pops a sugarcoated cherry in her mouth, then follows her brother to the backyard, as Elaine rolls the lattice pie crust cutter over the dough and tucks the long strips over the top of the pie. She looks up when she sees Charles's car pull into his driveway. He looks across the street and sees her through the window, and when their eyes meet, last night comes into focus like a film, replaying in a reel in her mind. Her heart swells.

They took the kids to a circus near Green Lake and spent the day shepherding them, with cotton-candy-coated faces, between the Ferris wheel, roller coaster, and arcade.

At the end of the day, they stopped at a flea market near the parking lot. Everyone was tired, but Ella, being an old soul, tugged at her mother's hand. "Can we go look, please, Mama?"

Charles smiled. "I love antiques and curiosities," he said. "Let's explore."

So they found themselves weaving from stall to stall, past tables of hand-knitted sweaters and kiln-fired pottery. Then, Ella ran ahead to a booth filled with antique jewelry, mostly gaudy costume baubles fit for girls' dress-up chests and little else. "Look," Ella said suddenly, lifting a charm bracelet from a rack at the far end of the table. "Didn't you have a bracelet like this once, Mama?"

Elaine rushed to her daughter's side. Her eyes filled with tears when they took in the sight of the charm bracelet—her bracelet, the one she'd lost as a girl of twelve, at a carnival just like the one they'd been at today.

"I can't believe this," Elaine said through tears, holding the bracelet in her hand. The charms were all still there: the cake, the spade, the half of the heart. "This is it. It's my bracelet. The one I lost as a child. I'm certain of it."

Before she even knew it was happening, Charles had opened his wallet and produced two bills. "Here," he said, handing them to the middle-aged woman behind the table, with a tattoo of a unicorn on her shoulder.

"It still fits," Elaine said, clasping it around her wrist.

Still under the spell of the afternoon's events, Elaine found herself alone that evening. Ella and Jack were at a sleepover with their cousins, and Matthew was out of town on business, so when Charles showed up on her doorstep with a bottle of wine, she didn't hesitate to invite him in.

It was against her better judgment, of course. But he was a neighbor, a friend, and yet so much more. They'd stood on the sidewalk watching their kids play together, exchanged hellos from opposite sides of the street, and slowly, their mutual attraction had reached a fever pitch, and there he stood, leaning into her doorway, a shadow of stubble across his chin, a look of longing in his eyes.

"Please, can I come in?" he said in a hushed voice.

"Yes," she responded. Just one word, but it said everything, the way a musician can draw emotion with a single note.

And so she invited him in. They drank. They talked.

"You lost something dear to you. That's why I bought you the bracelet, because I understand the feeling of searching in vain for what you know in your heart you will never see again."

"You must miss your wife so much," she said, with an open gaze.

"I do," he replied. "Every day. Everything reminds me of her. Music. Things our daughter says. Roses in the garden." He paused for a long moment, then looked up at Elaine with wide eyes. "You remind me of her."

"Would she like me?" Elaine asked then.

"Cara would have adored you," Charles said. His words made her heart swell. "I didn't think I could believe in romantic love again. And then I walked into your kitchen."

Their hands found each other first, then their lips, and their bodies. Elaine knew it was bigger than simple attraction, deeper than lust. She had known it when she'd looked into Charles's eyes that first day, that first moment in her kitchen months ago. Beyond the edges of his retinas, she'd seen life. A big, bold, beautiful life. A house and a garden. The sounds of children's voices. Christmases and Easters, birthdays and anniversaries. In those eyes, she saw love.

The flames flickered in the fireplace, casting dancing shadows on their naked bodies on the floor. Elaine hadn't drawn the curtains. Any neighbor could have strolled by—Mrs. Wilkinson with her poodle, or Jonathon and Lisa West walking their colicky baby before bed—and seen them lying together, bodies entwined, eyes locked on each other. It was reckless, Elaine knew. She wasn't behaving like herself, but like a sixteen-year-old version of herself. And yet, she had to have him, and he had to have her. To each, the other was the treasure they'd been in search of for a lifetime. The flea market find worth a million dollars, sitting in a dusty bargain bin, ripe for the taking.

And they took it, each of them. They lost themselves in it, this found treasure.

Elaine blinks hard and clutches around her wrist the bracelet that Charles purchased for her. He stands in his driveway across the street. She wonders if he's remembering the way he touched her, not more than twenty-four hours ago. The way she touched *him*. Does he hear her voice in his ear? Because she can hear him. She can still *feel* him.

"Mama, Mama!" Ella shouts from the back door, jarring Elaine out of her stunned state. "Daddy's home early!"

Elaine turns around and sees Matthew standing in the doorway to the kitchen. She didn't hear his car. How long has he been standing there?

He walks toward her. "I caught the early flight out of Chicago," he says, pausing to kiss her forehead.

Elaine reties her apron and wills herself to smile like nothing has changed. She is the woman he married after all. Loving, practical, incapable of betrayal. She turns back to the counter, to her lattice-topped cherry pie. Matthew presses his stomach to her back and wraps his arms around her waist, kissing her cheek from behind. Elaine looks up then. Charles stands at his mailbox. She knows he can see the two of them standing in the kitchen together.

"Think he'll ever have that house repainted?" Matthew asks, cocking his head to the right.

Their eyes meet again, and Elaine fights back the tears that so desperately want to spill from her eyelids. She wills them to stay inside. "Yeah," she says. "That blue is an awful color, isn't it?"

Matthew kisses the top of her head. "Cherry

pie, huh? How did I get so lucky?" He pops a cherry into his mouth before walking out of the kitchen.

Elaine stares out the window and clutches the kitchen counter. She feels as if her heart may burst.

❀

Chapter 16

September

L o sits behind the counter at the flower shop. She's wearing a blue dress with a black belt that makes her waist appear narrower than ever. She looks beautiful with her hair pulled up into a bun, but her eyes are sad, and when she glances up at me as I walk in the door, I can tell she's been crying. "He hasn't called or texted in a week," she says, staring at her phone. She lets out a long sigh.

Lo confronted Grant after Katie's wedding. Seeing him there with his wife had hurt her deeply, especially after everything he'd told her about his unhappiness at home and his vision for their future.

"It's OK," she continues, composing herself. "I've just got to stop obsessing over this, over him. He's obviously made his choice, to stay with his wife. Fine. But you know what I can't get over, Jane? You know what I just can't wrap my brain around?"

I walk toward her and set my bag down behind the counter. "What?"

"I've never loved this deeply," she says. "And I know he feels the same. This love is bigger than anything either of us has experienced. So I'm trying to figure out how he could walk away from that." She shakes her head in a sort of disbelief. "And then how do *I* walk away from that? How do I wake up every day, go on dates, knowing that I may never love this way again?"

I wish I could tell her that she will, that love is around every corner, that true love can be replicated, repeated, found again. And for some, I suppose it can. But when you've had big, bold love the way Lo has felt with Grant, can you find *that* again? I only know what I see, and I saw love between Grant and Lo. I saw intense love. And, like my friend, I wonder how the heart goes on when its match goes unmet.

"It's such a big risk, this love business," I say. "You love and you hope, but there are never any guarantees. You build your castle together, in your hearts, and it may all come crashing down at a moment's notice." I nod to myself. "I'm afraid of that too."

Lo looks up. "With Cam, you mean?"

"Yes," I say. "He invited me to meet his parents. They were going to come out a few months ago, but there was an issue with his dad's health, and, well"—I pause to let out a big sigh—"Lo, meeting the parents . . . isn't that kind of a big deal?"

"It *is*."

"But I can't tell if he's introducing me as a romantic prospect, or if he wants me along as some kind of research assistant. He's unusually fascinated by my brain. And maybe I'm being paranoid, but I don't want any part of his investigative reporting."

Lo shifts uncomfortably. "Jane, I wasn't going to say anything; in fact, I promised myself I wouldn't meddle." She sighs. "But what you just said, about being cautious, well . . . listen, I saw some messages on Cam's phone the night of Katie's wedding. He left it on the table. Even though I was in a state that day, I couldn't help but notice the text notifications popping up on the screen. There was some sort of all-caps text war in progress."

I think back to our romantic turn on the dance floor. Did I imagine that he only had eyes for me? "Did you read them?"

"I could only get bits and pieces," she says with a sigh. "But, Jane, he seems to be in some kind of trouble at work."

I'm too shaken to answer, so I change the subject. "I have an appointment to get these roots done in a few. Mind looking after the shop for the rest of today? I may go see my brother afterward."

Lo nods. "Totally fine. Tell Flynn I said hi."

"I will," I say. "And please, try not to worry too much about the Grant situation." I think of the old book Colette gave me, with the names of lovers from centuries past, examples of true love, fleeting love, all kinds of love. Lo and Grant will find their names in this book; I've known that from the day I first saw them together, even if I don't know the type of love they share or how their story will end—or not. And as hard as she wants their love to stand the test of time, to push past barriers, to be the seed that grows—flourishes, even—in a crack in the concrete, it isn't in her control, or Grant's.

"Look at you!" I exclaim, marveling at Mary's pregnant belly when I walk into the salon.

She smiles and rubs her stomach. "I know, I'm huge," she says. "If I had a dollar for every time someone asked me if I'm having twins, well . . ." Mary tucks a long strand of auburn hair behind her ear and sighs.

I squeeze her arm. "I know it's been so very hard, with Eli gone and all."

She nods. "I won't lie—it's been absolute hell. To be pregnant, and alone." She sighs. "Thank God for Luca."

"Luca?"

"You remember, my contractor," she says, as I sit down in the chair. "I never expected it, but he's become a great friend." She sighs again. "I'm going to miss him, actually."

"Miss him?"

She nods, dividing my hair into sections. "The remodel is almost done. Afterward, he plans to return to Italy. He's been hired by an American millionaire to lead the renovation on some mansion on Lake Como." She shrugs. "Maybe it's Clooney."

I sense hesitation, regret, in Mary's voice. "Does that make you sad?"

She quickly shakes her head. "No, no, it's nothing like that." She runs a comb through an under section of my hair. "It's just, well, I'll miss having him around; that's all."

As she sets the first few foils in my hair, I think about how love can either hit you like a ton of bricks or simply brush your face like a feather.

"Looking good, sis," Flynn says when I meet him at Beecher's in the market for a late lunch.

I run my hand through my newly foiled hair and grin. "Oh, thanks."

We both order crab melt sandwiches and walk to a bench overlooking Elliott Bay. Seagulls peck around our feet while we sink our teeth into lunch: sweet Dungeness crabmeat, roasted red peppers, and dill aioli sandwiched between two perfectly grilled pieces of bread. In other words, heaven.

"Remember how Mom used to like to sit here in the mornings with her coffee?" Flynn says, wiping the corners of his mouth with a napkin.

"Yeah," I say, pointing to the bench ahead, which is occupied by a young family. A toddler in Hawaiian print shorts is squealing as he tosses bits of bread at a group of eager seagulls. "She'd just sit there and look out at the bay." I crumple the sandwich wrapper and set it beside me. "You know, I don't think she ever got over our dad."

Flynn nods. "I don't think she did either."

"Even when she was happy," I say, "there was a sad quality to her eyes, as if she was always carrying the memory of him."

Flynn looks out at the bay, then turns back to me. "I know the feeling."

"What do you mean?"

"The woman, in the apartment across the street," he says, rubbing his forehead. "Jane, I don't know how to describe it. And it makes no sense. I still haven't even met her. I don't even know her name, and yet she's the reason I wake up in the morning." He smiles. "We have this unspoken language. We wave, we smile, we point and gesture. The other day I wrote on some butcher paper, 'What's your favorite flower?' She wrote on the back of a cardboard box, 'Orange roses.' And so I got a big vase of them and set them by the window, for her."

I smile. "That's right—Lo said you stopped in and asked for orange roses."

"She loved them," Flynn says. "It made her smile, and that's all I wanted. She doesn't smile enough. She carries some sort of incredible burden with her. And this man who continues to come see her. I think he's an ex-boyfriend. His visits leave her in tears. I see her crying, and I so desperately want to go to her. I want to take her pain away. I want to comfort her like I've wanted to comfort no other woman." He turns to me with wide eyes. "Jane, it makes no sense, but I think this is love."

"Or some form of it," I say with a grin. "Flynn, how can you know you love her if you've never spoken to her? If you've never even touched her?"

"I just know," he says simply.

And I know that Flynn and this mysterious woman will also end up in the ancient book. Theirs is a rapturous, rare, and intense sort of love.

"Ask her what her name is," I say. "I mean, make a sign asking her."

"I will."

Cam picks me up at four, and we board a ferry to Bainbridge Island to meet his parents for dinner at Hitchcock, a restaurant in the sleepy town of Winslow, where they are visiting a local relative.

"You look beautiful," he says with a grin as we step out of the car and walk hand in hand. It's a perfect late-summer evening—warm breeze, hazy cerulean sky overhead, couples strolling along the sidewalk, children licking ice-cream cones. "My parents are eager to meet you," he continues.

I catch a glimpse of my reflection in the windows of a storefront and eye my pale blue sundress and sandals. *Should I have dressed up a little more?*

"My mom grew up on Bainbridge Island," I tell him.

"What was she like?" Cam asks.

"She was the loveliest person you'd ever meet," I say. "Gracious, kind, a bit impractical." I smile to myself. "She once helped one of the fish-mongers in the market with a proposal to his girlfriend. Her favorite flower was this rare, and out-of-season, variety of lily. Of course, Mom shipped them in from Peru, at least two hundred stems, and didn't charge him a dime." I nod. "She did that kind of thing for people. She loved love."

"And you loved her," he says.

"I did, so very much," I reply.

We approach the restaurant, and I follow him into the dimly lit dining room. A gray-haired couple waves at us from across the room, and Cam smiles. "Mom, Dad," he says as we near the table. "This is Jane."

"So nice to meet you, Mrs. Collins," I say, setting my bag down by my chair.

She hugs me warmly. "Call me Claudia, please," she says. "And this is Gerald."

"Very nice to meet you, Jane," Cam's father says.

A waiter approaches and hands us all menus. Claudia opens hers and turns to Gerald. "Honey, they have gnocchi here; you love gnocchi."

"I do not love gnocchi," he says, grimacing.

"You do; you've just forgotten." She gives me a knowing smile. "He'd forget his head if it weren't attached."

Gerald frowns and sets his menu down. "Since you know so well what I like, why don't you order for me, then?"

Claudia nods confidently. "I will."

Cam fidgets in his chair. I can tell he's embarrassed by his parents' awkward exchange, and I realize he was right. His parents obviously aren't in love. I look back at Claudia and Gerald. And then it happens. My vision begins to cloud. I blink hard and grip the edge of the table to steady myself.

"You OK?" Cam whispers to me. "This can't mean that—"

I nod. "Yes."

"Dear, I hope you're not feeling ill," Claudia says, reaching across the table to pat my arm.

"I'll be fine," I say. "I'm just—"

"Jane gets migraines," Cam interjects.

I keep my eyes closed for a bit until the fog lifts. I'll be left with a dull headache through dinner, and I'll feel pressure behind my eyes, but

I know that I won't have another episode in their presence for the rest of the night. They never strike twice in the same interaction.

"You poor thing," Claudia says. "Gerald gets them too. He won't give up cheese. They bring the headaches on. He's also lactose intolerant." She shakes her head. "You'd think he'd give up dairy, but he absolutely will not see reason."

Gerald frowns. "Cheese," he says, shaking his head. "She wants me to give up cheese."

I look at Cam and smile. They love each other deeply, his parents. Through the years. Through the fights. Through the grumblings about life, and cheese. This is love.

Cam invites me back to his apartment, and as we settle in on the couch with two glasses of wine, he runs his hand through my hair. "You know, I can't believe it. I can't believe what you saw at dinner between my parents."

"Why not?"

He swirls the wine in his glass. "I was sure that any love they shared had evaporated over the years. They're always bickering."

I nod. "I heard that every love affair ends in pots and pans."

Cam grins. "Pots and pans."

"Yeah," I say. "But your parents show that there is still love in the pots and pans. Deep love."

He smiles as if he's somewhat astonished.

"Even in a forty-five-year marriage where all that's left to talk about is my father's lactose intolerance?"

I return his smile. "Love supersedes lactose intolerance, yes."

He leans in closer to me. "Do you think we could find love?" he whispers. "Do you think someone with your gift could see it in us?"

He's so close, I can smell his skin, his breath, sweet and intoxicating. My heart beats faster as I weave my fingers through his. I think of Colette and wonder if she'd see love between us. I both want to know and don't want to know. Mostly, I just want to lose myself in this moment. And as I press my lips against his, I do. Completely.

Chapter 17

4572 Sunnyside Avenue

Mary pulls her car into the driveway. She's happy to see Luca's truck parked on the street in front of her house; in fact, the sight makes her heart beat a little faster. It's late September. Because she decided to preserve the fireplace, the kitchen remodel and breakfast nook expansion are taking longer than expected, but she's secretly grateful for the delay. It means Luca will linger longer. And now that it's nearing the end, she's worried. She so despises being alone, though her child is soon to join her.

Mary hears the hum of a saw in the backyard and smiles to herself. Luca. His friendship has come to mean more to her than she could have ever expected. He helped her assemble the baby's crib and paint the nursery. In turn, she cooked for him, once the new stove was installed, or sometimes ordered takeout, and they'd linger over a meal, exchanging stories with tangled words and elaborate hand gestures. Mary sighs contentedly, remembering their dinner last night.

Luca had to turn the water off, temporarily, while the plumber installed the new faucet, so

Mary suggested they walk to Julia's, a little restaurant down the street. It was a warm night, and birds chirped from the maple trees along the sidewalk as they rounded the block. "Careful," Luca said, taking Mary's hand when she nearly stepped into an open manhole cover. Her belly was bigger than ever now, and on warm days like this, she often wondered how she would make it to her due date in December. As it was, most people stopped her on the street with the familiar question: "Are you having *twins?*"

It was the second time Luca had touched her. The first was an accident. They'd been hovering over the stove, inspecting the newly installed tile mosaic under the range hood. Their arms had brushed, and Mary's skin had erupted in a thousand goose bumps. Luca had stepped back and rubbed his forehead nervously.

Mary sets her keys on the side table, still thinking about last night. At the restaurant, the hostess led them to a little table in the back, where a fish tank housed two plump goldfish.

"I always wanted a goldfish as a child," she said to Luca. "But my mother never let me have one, though they're the easiest pets on earth."

Luca smiled and pointed to the smaller of the two goldfish. "That one is you," he said. "And the larger one is me."

"Look at them," Mary said. "They look so happy, even in that tiny tank."

Luca nodded. "You can be happy anyplace when there is love."

It was the most perfect English sentence he'd ever uttered to her, and she loved the way his eyes sparkled when he said it. He was right, of course. Since Eli had left, the beautiful home she used to take so much pride in didn't mean much to her at all now. Love was gone. But with love, she could live in a shack, a trailer . . . an aquarium made for two.

She peers into the kitchen, where Luca is hunched over a lower cabinet installing the knobs she purchased at Restoration Hardware. She went back and forth between the pewter and the brushed nickel, but opted for the latter, and they look perfect on the distressed white cabinetry.

The old fireplace, the one that Eli loathed, stayed. And Mary is grateful for it now, like an old friend.

"Funny," she says, looking around. "At the start, a remodel and a pregnancy each seems like a never-ending project, and yet, it's all gone so . . . fast." She feels a pang of regret then, both because Luca will soon be leaving and because Eli will never see the kitchen she intended to share with him, this gourmet kitchen they planned together. She had imagined all the Sunday mornings they'd spend, the two of them sipping coffee at the island, trading sections of the *New*

York Times, with bacon sizzling in a pan on the stove and blueberry muffins baking in the oven. Newsprint, bacon, and muffins. The smell of happiness.

But there's another tinge of emotion swirling in Mary's gut as she runs her hand along the butcher block island, sanded by Luca to smooth perfection. As soon as he finishes the trim on the doorway, he'll be gone, off to his next project, and that thought frightens her, deeply.

Over these months, and through her pregnancy, he's been a constant figure in her life, perhaps the only sure thing. She'd come home from a long day at the salon, and there he'd be—hammering, sawing, painting, nailing. Like the old chandelier in the entryway, he became a fixture in her home, and in her life, and she isn't quite ready to say good-bye.

Luca stands to face her and smiles. Mary loves his smile, so boyish, so joyful, so completely present. Eli never smiled that way. He never looked at her so expectantly, the way Luca does.

"There you are, my red fish," he says, taking a step toward her.

Mary can't help but laugh. "You mean, *gold-fish*?"

Luca smiles as he runs his hand through his dark hair. "Oh," he says with a laugh. "Yes, I meant goldfish. My English."

"No, no," she says, through laughter. "Red fish is better. So much better."

Their eyes meet and lock for a long moment. "Then you will always be my red fish," he says slowly.

A week later, Mary stands in her beautiful kitchen, in her perfect home. Luca is gone now. Her KitchenAid mixer, a wedding gift from one of Eli's aunts, whose name now escapes her, sits on the countertop where Luca's circular saw was before. And instead of the metal toolbox with its rusty hinges, the island is now home to a white bowl of shiny Granny Smith apples. Luca did a beautiful job, and Mary's architect, Stuart, even talked about sending in photos to *Architectural Digest* for their annual kitchen remodel feature. But as beautiful as the space is, she feels lost and lonely in it. Love does not live in her kitchen, or in her house.

Red fish. She smiles to herself, thinking of Luca. She misses him. Before he left, he wrote his phone number on a piece of paper. "If anything goes wrong, if something breaks," he said, "call me, and I'll fix it."

She looks at that piece of paper on the counter every morning. Sometimes she wishes the dishwasher would fail or that a cabinet hinge would appear misaligned or the faucet would leak. She longs for a reason to call him, to hear his voice again, to see him. He has been her friend all these months, and his absence now feels . . . achingly lonely.

Why not just call him? Mary thinks. *Why not just call him to say hi?* Like two old friends.

She picks up her phone and takes a deep breath. But she doesn't dial Luca; she calls her husband. They're estranged, yes, but Eli is still her husband. He's still the man she married. Her heart pounds in her chest, two beats for each ring. She can feel the baby kick too, and she rubs her belly on the spot where a little foot or knee or elbow just poked out. Their baby.

After four rings, there is a voice. A woman's voice. "Hello?" The voice sounds young, sexy . . . annoyed. Mary presses the end-call button quickly, then collapses into a chair at the table, in her perfect, lonely kitchen.

Chapter 18

October

"Morning," I say to Bernard as I step off the elevator with Sam.

"Morning," he replies with a smile, patting Sam's head as I exit onto the sidewalk. The Seattle air has turned crisp, and pumpkins are displayed on every available surface of the market. I stop at a vegetable stand to admire a row of sugar pie varieties. I buy three: one for Mel's news-stand, one for Elaine, and a third for the flower shop.

"Hello, beautiful," Mel says as I approach.

"For you," I say, setting a pumpkin near his cash register. "Happy October."

"A very happy October, indeed," he says, stepping closer to me as if he is about to reveal a secret. "Yesterday we talked about Parliament."

I give him a confused look. "Parliament?"

"Yes," he says victoriously. "We have breakfast together every Friday—well, at separate tables, but just the same. We eat our eggs together."

"Wait, Mel, who?" And then I see the sparkle in his eyes and it hits me. "Oh, yes, the Queen of England. Of course."

He beams. "Yes."

"Good for you, Mel. Why don't you ask her out on a date?"

"I'd like to," he replies. "I'm working up the courage."

"Well, don't wait too long," I say. "She might think you don't like her. We women can get impatient."

I wink at him as I continue along the sidewalk, stopping in front of Meriwether to tie Sam to a lamppost. Inside, Elaine is busily stocking the pastry case with fresh croissants. She smiles when she looks up and sees me.

"For you," I say, depositing a pumpkin on the counter.

"Aw, thanks," she replies, setting down an empty sheet pan. "I'm glad you're here. Do you have a moment to talk?"

"Of course," I say. She brushes a dusting of flour from her cheek and walks around the counter. Together we sit at a table by the window.

"It's Charles," she says. "It's the real thing, Jane. I'm in this. Truly, madly, deeply." The words fall out of her mouth like an avalanche.

I remember the way my vision fogged over in their presence. Of course Elaine is in love. I've seen it with my own eyes.

"People talk about soul mates," she says, "and all my life I never bought it. The idea that two people are meant for each other." She shakes her head. "But then I met Charles. And . . . well, I get it."

"What is it that you see in him, Elaine?"

"Hot air balloons," she says nostalgically. I notice the charm bracelet on her wrist.

I shake my head, not quite understanding.

Elaine smiles. "He loves hot air balloons. So do I. Matthew wouldn't go up in one to save his life, even for me. But Charles?" She sighs, and smiles to herself. "He's spontaneous, open, in a way that Matthew could never be. If I asked him to travel to Santorini with me tomorrow, by hot air balloon, he'd do it.

"But at the same time, it's terrible," she says. "I don't know what to do. Last night, Charles asked me to make a decision. Leave Matthew and start a life with him. I know it's agonizing for him to watch me draw the shades in our bedroom window every night. He sees me in the yard with Matthew and the kids, and all the while, he loves me, and I love him." She sighs again. "To go on like this anymore, Jane, it's going to destroy me. And it will certainly destroy him. He lost his wife recently. He's had more than enough emotional upheaval in his life."

"I worry about that," I say. "Do you think he's ready to love again? Could he be jumping in too soon?"

"I wondered that too. But I can see in his eyes that he is ready. He's all in."

"And his daughter? How does she fit into this scenario?"

She smiles. "We've talked about that. He's always wanted to live on the water, just like I have, and we imagined the idea of us moving to a houseboat on Lake Union, maybe somewhere near Lo." She pauses, as if to consider a beautiful daydream. "Bunk beds, barbecues on the rooftop deck, kids paddling around in kayaks." Her expression gets serious again. "He wants a *life* with me, Jane. A beautiful life. And I want it too."

"Wow," I say. "What are you going to do, then?"

"I just don't know." She pauses. "I could leave Matthew, and I could follow my heart, and embark on this new, bold life with Charles." She closes her eyes tightly. "I can see it, in all of its beauty. And it makes me feel absolutely *alive*. But there would be such regret—for my children, for my family. And I do love Matthew. I care for him, obviously. Hurting him was never my plan. I'm incapable of it, and yet, I . . . I would have to blow up my family to have Charles. And if I can't do that, I stay. And I have to live with the realization that I let love go, that I stood in the face of true and beautiful love, love that completed me in a way I never thought possible, and let it go."

"Oh, Elaine," I say. "It seems like an impossible dilemma. But I think your heart already knows the choice you must make. Our hearts speak to us all the time, but it takes practice to learn to listen."

In her eyes, I can see just how deeply entrenched

she is. "No major decision is made without carefu
consideration," I continue. "Tell Charles you neec
until January. That's ninety days. Big decision
take time."

And as I consider the enormous choice ir
Elaine's life, I can't help but also think of my
own: Colette, the gift, love, Dr. Heller. In January
I will have succeeded, or I will have failed
perhaps miserably.

Lo has decorated the window of the shop with a
display of pumpkins, some big and as bright as
orange sherbet, others white and ghostly. "You
beat me to the punch," I say, setting my little
pumpkin by the register.

"Grant asked me to go to Paris with him," she
says suddenly.

"When?"

"In December."

"So he left his wife?"

"Not yet," she replies. I can see that she's deeply
conflicted. "But he will. I know he will. He's
working through his process."

"Process," I say. "Sounds like a phrase from a
business plan."

She sighs. "I know."

It seems almost incomprehensible that Lo could
be in such a deflated state. She's a force. And somehow a man has knocked the wind out of her sails.

"Don't you worry about a thing today," she

says. "I know this is a big occasion for you. I've got everything covered here."

Lo remembers, as she always does, the anniversary of my mother's death. "Are you going to visit her grave?"

I nod. Mom wanted to be buried on Bainbridge Island, where she grew up. As a child she came to love a little cemetery tucked away along the coastline, near Hidden Cove Road. When I was a girl, she'd take me there and let me wander the rows of headstones. When Grandma died, I remember sprinkling freesia petals, her favorite, onto her casket before the men lowered it into the ground. And now Mom rests there, in this quaint little cemetery overlooking the sea. Oddly, it doesn't feel like a place filled with bones and sadness. It's a garden in its own right, bursting with flowers, bright pink azaleas and rosebushes dotted with vibrant orange and yellow buds. Perhaps that's why Mom loved it. And I do too.

"Here," Lo says, reaching behind the counter. "Take these." She hands me two bunches of red and orange dahlias, with sprigs of mint and greenery interspersed between the blooms.

"Thanks," I say, feeling fresh tears sting my eyes when I remember the way Mom and Grandma loved fall dahlias.

I let Sam leap into the back of my ailing Volvo station wagon, Mom's old car, which I've never gotten around to replacing, and set out for the ferry terminal on Alaskan Way. It's midday, and there isn't a line of cars waiting, so I drive right on and secure a primo spot at the front of the vessel. What did Mom used to say about ferries? I smile to myself. Yes, that they're the cheapest, most beautiful cruises in the world. She'd ride them back and forth when she wanted to clear her head.

I breathe in the smell of seawater and engine fumes, and at once, I am eleven again, sitting in the backseat with Flynn, who has his headphones on because he's annoyed that Mom's listening to her Billy Joel tape again, rewinding the song "And So It Goes" and listening to it over and over again.

I see tears in Mom's eyes. "You still miss him, don't you, Mama?" By "him," I meant my dad, the man I could barely recall.

She nods. "Yes, sweetie. I will always love him."

"How can you love him when he left us?" I ask.

"Yes, he left us," she says. "But when someone does a bad thing, a hurtful thing, it doesn't mean you stop loving them. You just change your course. You make adjustments. But love lives on." She presses her hand to her heart. "It lives here. You'll see, someday."

Love lives on. And I suppose I know that now, because I've witnessed it. The concept lingers in the eyes of Mel, when he speaks of his late wife, and in the interactions between Cam's parents, still connected after forty-five years of marriage. And I suspect it will for Elaine—no matter what her choice, she'll keep Charles, or Matthew, in a quiet corner of her heart forever. I think about all of it as the ferry glides across the calm October water. The sky is blue and clear, one of those stubborn fall days that's holding on, desperately, to summer.

My phone buzzes, and I look at the screen and find a text from Cam. "Thinking of you." I smile and write back, "You remembered. Thanks." He knows it's the anniversary of Mom's death. I told him on the phone last night, even though my first instinct was to keep it to myself. Mom was, and is, sacred.

I leave Sam in the car and walk up the stairs to the upper deck, where I buy a coffee, settle into a booth, and look out the big windows toward the water and the distant dot that is the island. A few moments later, I hear applause all around, and cheers from fellow passengers. At the center of attention is a couple in their thirties. They look like they stepped out of a Pinterest page. She's tall and stunningly beautiful, wearing a striped knit dress and a stylish denim jacket. I admire her wedge heels. He's handsome in a David Beckham way, with his dark fitted jeans, plaid shirt, and sport coat. Together they look like perfection, and I can see that the assembled crowd thinks so too, especially since he is down on one knee and has just presented her with a ring. A photographer in a navy sweater and a pair of blue Converse high tops snaps a photo.

All around, mouths are agape and eyes are wide as she lets him slide the diamond onto her hand. She hesitates for a moment, looks at the ring, then back at him, and smiles, then covers her mouth. "Yes," she says, finally. "Yes!"

Cheers and applause break out again as he takes her into his arms. I don't bother looking away; I've already seen too much. I brace myself for the foggy vision, the pressure, which is inevitably coming. I expect it to be intense. I mean, look at them. But I wait, and I wait. And it doesn't come. I blink hard. I take a deep breath and I refocus on the beautiful couple ahead. A couple that is seemingly wholeheartedly in love.

Except . . . they aren't.

The island is in sight now, so I get up, toss my coffee cup into the trash can, and head to the restroom, thinking about how someone can say yes to a marriage proposal when she is not in love. As I'm washing my hands, the newly engaged woman walks in and sets her purse down on the countertop in a defeated heap. I see the enormous diamond on her hand. It sparkles under the fluorescent bathroom lights as she looks at herself in the mirror. Her eyes are searching, unsure—frightened, even.

"Congratulations," I say to her when her eyes meet mine in the mirror. "I saw the proposal."

She forces a smile. "Oh, thank you. I . . ." She catches her own eyes in the mirror again and looks away quickly, as if she can't even bear the sight of herself.

"Something's weighing on you, isn't it?" I ask.

She rubs her forehead, then looks around the restroom, which is now empty. "God, what is wrong with me? I should be happy," she says, and points to the doorway. "The most amazing man I've ever met just asked me to marry him. I should be doing cartwheels right now. But I . . ."

"But you don't love him."

She nods. "I don't love him. I could learn to love him. I mean, look at him. He's—"

"He's not your love," I say, as my heart begins to beat faster. It isn't my place to interfere, but she already knows.

She nods. "You can see it, can't you? Is it that obvious?"

"No," I say. "It's not obvious at all. I just have a . . . well, a knack for these things."

"My mom's going to hate me," she says. "She wanted a summer wedding. She's already booked the ballroom at the Fairmont."

"But it's your life, not hers," I say. "And besides, your love is out there. Just be patient, and keep your eyes open."

She sighs. "I wish it were easier. I wish I could know my heart better."

"You already do," I assure her. "In fact, you're one of the brave ones who listen to it." I place my hand on her forearm. "You're listening to it right now."

The ferry horn sounds, and the captain announces over the loudspeaker, "Now arriving Bainbridge Island. Passengers, please return to your vehicles."

"Thank you," she says to me as we walk out together.

"You've got this," I reply, noticing the handsome, short-lived fiancé who waits a few feet away.

Sam wags his tail excitedly as I return to the car, and together we drive off the ferry onto the island, passing Winslow and continuing on for several miles, until I see the sign marking Hidden Cove Road beside a bank of big, fluffy fir trees. The cemetery isn't far. A moment later, I pull into the driveway, park, and let Sam out for a break before taking the flowers and walking along the moss-covered stone path to my grandmother's grave. I place one of the bouquets beside her headstone and smile. "Hi, Nana," I whisper. "It's me, Jane. I miss you."

Beside her is my mother's grave. "Oh, Mom," I whisper, as tears stream down my face. "How

I've missed you." I set her flowers on a mossy patch, then kneel beside the grave. I hear the crunch of gravel behind me, but when I turn around, no one is there. "I'm so lost, Mom," I continue. "You see, I have this gift, this ability. The eye problems I've had all my life are not a neurological disorder, though Dr. Heller would beg to differ. Mom, I have the ability to *see love*. The first person to show me true love was you. And now I have to figure out what to do about it. How to go on. What it means for me and the people I care about. And, Mom, I don't know. I just don't know. I wish you were here." I place my hand on her headstone, just as the wind picks up and blows a stream of chilly air through the cemetery. I shiver. A single red-tinged leaf drifts from a maple tree overhead and falls beside my leg.

I turn around when I hear footsteps behind me. A man is standing uncomfortably close, as though he might have been there for a while, listening to me talking. It takes a moment to connect the dots, but I recognize him, the photographer from the ferry. I notice his Converse sneakers, because in high school I had a weathered pair in the same shade of blue. "Excuse me," he says. "Do you think you can give me directions back to the ferry? I'm a little turned around, and the navigation function in my rental car doesn't seem to be working."

"Sure," I say. "Just turn right out of the cemetery. Then take a left at your first stop sign. Follow the road as it winds up to 305, then take a left. That will get you back to the terminal." I pause for a moment. "I think I saw you on the ferry earlier. You were taking a photo of that couple who got engaged."

He grins. "Yeah, they were cute, weren't they? I couldn't help but get a shot."

"What brings you here?"

"Oh," he says, pausing, "I'm a freelance photographer. Just taking some photos for an assignment."

I nod. "Well, good luck."

"Wait," he says. "Do you mind if I take your photo? I just noticed your green eyes. They're rare, you know. Green eyes. I'm doing a photo collection of green-eyed people. Just a little pet project, not sure if I'll do anything with it. I'd love to get your photo, right here, if you don't mind. The light is so gorgeous, the way it's filtering in through the fir trees."

I shrug. "Why not?"

"Thanks," he says with a smile. "Now, step back a few feet, and maybe lean against that tree."

I nod and follow his instructions.

"Now, lift your chin up a tad. . . . There, perfect." His camera clicks once, twice, three times. "Now turn to the right, as if you're looking out at the cemetery. . . . Perfect, just like that.

246

Just a couple more." His camera clicks several more times, before he pauses to look down at the screen. "Oh, these are amazing."

My eyes wander up to the sky, where dark, angry-looking storm clouds are hovering, ready to pounce. I wonder what Bernard would make of their form today. I don't see any image in particular, but their churning presence leaves me feeling uneasy.

"Yes, this is a strong series," the photographer says.

"Good," I reply. "Will you send me one?"

"Sure," he says.

I give him my e-mail address, and together we walk back to the parking lot.

"Your golden retriever?" he asks, placing his hand on the back window, when Sam jumps up and starts barking loudly.

"Sam, stop that," I say. "Sorry, he never does that. I think he's annoyed that I'm not taking him on a walk."

The photographer smiles. "Well, I'll let you go. Thanks again for the photos and directions."

A single orange-tinged leaf has fallen on the windshield, and when I lean over to retrieve it before getting into the car, a bolt of lightning flashes nearby, followed by a thunderclap.

"Let's go, Sam," I say, setting the leaf on the dash.

Chapter 19

1301 4th Avenue
November

F lynn inserts his key into the lock, steps into his apartment, and sets his bag down by the door. He drops his keys on the countertop, and the sound echoes into the air of his lonely home.

Cam was supposed to stop by the gallery tonight, but he didn't show. His friend has seemed preoccupied lately, but Flynn isn't going to let him avoid a heart-to-heart on the subject of Jane. He has to look out for his sister.

There were women at the gallery. Gorgeous women. A blonde in stilettos made a beeline across the room to talk to him. He could have had her; he knows that. He could smell her desire like a shark smells blood in the water. He could have taken her hand and pulled her into the back room of the gallery, pressed her up against the wall, pulled her panties down, and lifted those long legs up around his body. Then they could have come back to his apartment, where he'd light the candles in his bedroom and rip every shred of clothing off her body and tune her like a fine instrument until she released the kind of beautiful music he's so hungry to hear.

But Flynn came home alone, as he has done for months on end, because there is a woman in his life. She is both near and far. He can see her, but he cannot have her. He cannot touch her beautiful skin or let his hands wander the curves of her body. Not yet. She is delicious and enticing and intoxicating, and he would rather be in her presence, even separated by glass and concrete, than have anyone else standing beside him in the flesh.

The lights are on in her apartment, and her windows shine like a beacon in the night. Flynn can see a bottle of wine sitting beside two empty glasses on the kitchen island. Does she have a visitor? He scours the apartment, and at first he sees only her cat, who leaps from the coffee table to the couch. But then she appears, walking from the bedroom like a goddess. She wears a black dress that clings tightly to her figure. Just the sight of her sends electric pulses through Flynn's body, and he extends his hand to the window, fingering the glass lightly as if he expects to touch her soft skin.

She sees him then. She knows he's watching her. And she likes it. She likes his eyes on her. She likes how she can captivate him. And he captivates her. She watched him making coffee this morning. She let her eyes pore over his nude body as he stood in the kitchen, the curve of his shoulders, the strength of his back, and what lies below. Oh, it made her temperature rise, just the sight of him.

Flynn watches as she turns, suddenly, to the front door. Moments later, she invites a man inside. He is tall and good-looking, in a dark suit. Who is he? Other than the man who occasionally comes over, the one whose visits seem to disturb her, Flynn hasn't seen any other men in her presence. Could this be a new boyfriend? A date?

Flynn can't take his eyes off the two of them. He watches them together like an episode of a TV show in which there's about to be a major plot twist. And there is. The man suddenly pulls her toward him and kisses her. Their mouths are locked together for a long moment before he begins to undress her, tugging at the zipper on her dress until it relents. He carries her to the plush white rug beside the couch and lays her on her back as he unbuckles his belt and lets his pants fall to the floor.

Flynn's heart beats faster. He wants to shout, "No!" But it is not his place. He has no claim on this woman. He has no right to her body or her heart, and yet, his body pulses, and his heart aches as he watches this strange man press himself against her. It's horrible and wonderful at the same time, and he cannot look away. His eyes are fixed on that window, on the rise and fall of her body. He can imagine what she sounds like, her screams, the sound of her breath. He can feel her skin, so soft and taut. He can taste her.

She turns to look at him again, almost boldly.

She sees him watching her, and she reaches toward the window, just as Flynn raises a hand to his window.

Minutes later, the man gets up, dresses, and leaves her apartment. Flynn watches as she walks to the kitchen, bare breasted, wearing only black underwear, and returns with a large sheet of paper with two words written in all capital letters: I'M SORRY.

Flynn wipes away a tear from his cheek. He sees the sadness in her eyes. He feels her pain. Can she feel his? He remembers the large board of presentation paper he purchased recently for a meeting at the gallery. He retrieves it and quickly writes the words: IT'S OK.

She reaches toward the window again as Flynn writes a question on another piece of paper: WHY?

Her response, on a large piece of paper she finds in her kitchen, comes quick, and it hits him like an arrow to the heart. BECAUSE I COULDN'T HAVE YOU.

Her words are both tragic and comforting. He knows no other response but to smile. And she does too.

He holds up another sheet of paper: WHAT'S YOUR NAME?

CELESTE

I'M FLYNN

HI FLYNN

HI CELESTE

Chapter 20

1112 Broadway Avenue E. #202

Katie opens her eyes when she feels the morning sun on her face, streaming through the window of the bedroom she shares with Josh. He's still asleep, and she's careful not to wake him. She loves watching the rise and fall of his bare chest, this man she adores. She loves seeing him so perfectly peaceful.

Minutes pass, and Josh finally stirs. He turns to face her and smiles. "I will never grow tired of this face," he says, pulling her toward him.

He hungers for her in the morning, and within seconds their bodies are passionately entwined, just as they were last night. When they pull apart, Katie lies beside Josh smiling, sweat glistening on her skin. She cannot imagine greater happiness.

Josh stands up, and she watches the sculpted muscles in his legs as he walks to the closet to dress. He throws on a pair of jeans and a long-sleeved T-shirt before jumping on the bed again beside Katie. "I'm going to go grab some coffee at Ladro. I'll get you a double Americano. Want anything else?"

"A scone," she says. "The one with the currants."

He runs his finger from the top of her neck

down to her shoulder, and her skin erupts in goose bumps. He could have her again, right now, and she'd be his. It could go on and on, uninterrupted, all day. Their love is, in a word, electric, and in his presence, Katie feels sparks. Real ones.

"All right, a scone it is," he says, standing up.

"Hurry back," she says coyly.

He nods, and then he is gone.

An hour passes, and Katie finally gets up to dress. A sweater and leggings, hair in a ponytail. After another hour, she calls Josh, but there's no answer on his cell phone. By noon, she peers out the window. The car is still in the driveway. He must have walked. So she grabs her keys and sets out to the sidewalk. Maybe he ran into a friend and decided to grab lunch on Broadway.

She continues on, stopping at Caffe Ladro. She sees a plate of fresh currant scones in the case. Her stomach growls. "Excuse me," she says to the twentysomething clerk behind the counter. He has a nose ring and a sleeve of tattoos on his left arm. "Did you see a man in here earlier? Tall, navy blue long-sleeved shirt. Baseball hat. Good-looking."

"Yeah," he says. "A few hours ago. He was over at that table with a blonde."

She shakes her head. "A blonde?"

"Yeah, I think so. He ordered a currant scone, and"—he pauses and squints as if trying to recall something—"I think a breve."

She nods. "Yeah, that's him." In all of Seattle, Josh is the only person she's ever met who orders breves regularly. She teased him about it when they first met. "Do you know that a tall breve has a hundred and forty-six grams of fat in it?" Katie knew. She used to work at Starbucks in college.

"Thanks," she says, pulling out her phone again, annoyed. She dials Josh's number, but there's no answer. If he had a meeting with a colleague, or even a friend, why didn't he tell her?

She orders an Americano and walks home. Her mind is abuzz. Maybe he has a surprise for her. She inserts her key into the lock. After all, he surprised her with this very home. She smiles, remembering the way he carried her over the threshold, before they made love on the floor of what would be their master bedroom. Yes, it has to be some sort of surprise. He'll show up in a few minutes with her cold coffee in his hand, and it will all make sense.

But the hours pass, and it doesn't. The sun sets, and Josh doesn't come home. She calls his cell phone eleven more times, and then eleven more, but he doesn't pick up. She replays the morning over and over again in her mind. Did she say something to offend him? No. Was he mad when he left? No.

Finally, she calls his best friend, Joey. "Hey, it's Katie. Have you heard from Josh today?"

"No, why?"

"Well, he left this morning to get coffee and never came back."

"That's odd," Joey says. "Do you think something . . . happened?"

"God, I hope not," she says. "I just can't make any sense of it. He left around nine and said he'd be right back, but that was almost twelve hours ago. He's not answering his phone. Can you try him?"

"Sure, of course."

"Call me if you hear anything, OK?"

"I will."

Katie paces the floor, calls Josh's cell phone another fourteen times, eyes the window repeatedly, and finally decides to call the police.

"My husband didn't come home this morning," she says breathlessly into the phone. The words she just uttered are unfathomable. For a moment, she believes she might be dreaming, and when she answers the officer's questions on the phone, she barely recognizes her own voice.

Hours pass. She watches the second hand of the clock tick around and around, until her eyes are heavy and she closes them, alone, in their king-size bed.

The next morning, Katie opens her eyes, and for a blissful moment, she's forgotten that Josh is gone. The terror returns when she reaches over to his side of the bed and feels the coldness of the bare sheets.

She sits up in bed, reaches for her cell phone on the bedside table, and calls Josh again. When his voice mail picks up again, she sobs into the phone. "Josh, where are you? I'm so scared. Did something happen? I called the police. I'm so worried."

She stares at the phone for a long time. A minute. Five. Twenty. She has no sense of time as it passes, just that it's passing without Josh beside her. What if he was mugged? What if he was kidnapped? Or worse.

She turns to her phone, just as the screen lights up with a call. It's Joey.

"Hi," she says hurriedly. "Any news?"

"Ah, well, yes," he says cautiously.

"What?" Katie's heart pounds in her chest. "Is he OK? What happened?"

"Yes, he's OK," Joey says in a voice that is far from convincing. "Katie, I don't know how to say this, and I don't even quite know what Josh is going through, but I spoke to him."

"You did?" Her heart begins to race. "Where is he? What did he say? Why hasn't he called me?"

"He asked me to call you," he continues. His voice is hesitant, cautious. "He said he needs some time to work some things out. He needs some space. That's, well, that's why he didn't come home yesterday. And he feels like a coward, but he couldn't bear to tell you himself."

Katie shakes her head. "I don't understand. What the hell is that supposed to mean?"

"I don't really understand either," Joey replies. "It's like something snapped. I asked if I could see him. I thought I could talk some sense into him if I could just see him face-to-face, but he won't even tell me where he is."

"Joey, I don't understand this at all. It's like he's having a midlife crisis or something."

"I don't know," he continues. "He just wants you to know that he's OK, and that he needs some time to think before he comes home."

"Joey, do you know how messed up that is?"

"I'm so sorry, Katie. It is, and it doesn't sound at all like Josh."

She feels overcome with panic. "Maybe he's under duress. Do you think he's being held hostage?"

"No," Joey says. "It didn't seem like that at all."

"Oh." She pauses for a moment. "When I went to find him at Caffe Ladro, they said they thought they saw him there earlier with a blonde."

"A blonde?"

"Yep."

"Listen," Joey urges her, "don't jump to conclusions. Maybe he's going through some stuff and just needs some downtime. Guys do now and then."

"But he could have at least called me directly, Joey," Katie says. "I'm his *wife*."

"Just be patient," he says. "I'm sure he'll come around."

She sets her phone down on the bedside table. She buries her head in her hands and weeps. So much for perfect love. Because you can blink your eyes and it can vanish, without explanation, leaving you with only your memories and your tears.

Chapter 21

J ane, thanks for returning my call," Dr. Heller says. "The surgeon from Johns Hopkins can fit you in next month," she says. "I've had to move mountains to make this happen, and you'd have to fly to Baltimore for the operation, but I pray that you'll consent. Jane, if you don't have this surgery, I fear you will regret it for the rest of your life." She sighs. "That is, if you have the brain function left to even feel regret, or any other conscious thought. Jane, this is real. This is serious. If we don't operate, you will fall into irreversible cognitive decline."

I set a bucket of rosehips down and motion to Lo to help the customer who's just walked into the shop as I step into the back room. "I've trusted you my whole life, Dr. Heller," I begin. "And I have no reason not to trust you now. And, believe me, there are days I wake up and I just want to end all of this. I want to believe in science and let you fix me. But I can't. I can't, Dr. Heller. I have to see this through, even if it means a great health risk."

"I see," she says. "I feared you wouldn't change your mind."

"I'm sorry."

"Me, too," she replies.

I set my phone down and walk out to the shop, where I sit on the stool behind the counter and feign calmness.

Lo knows me too well. "What just happened?" she asks.

I shake my head. "Basically, my doctor says my brain is going to spontaneously combust if I don't have surgery."

She frowns. "And I'm assuming that this surgery would obliterate your . . . gift?"

"Yes," I say.

"What are you going to do?"

"I don't know."

"You need to talk to Colette. You need to check in with her. Because, Jane, you don't have much time left. Didn't she say you had to complete all of this stuff with the book before your thirtieth birthday?"

I nod.

"Honey, that's in a month."

"I know."

"Go see Colette. She'll give you some perspective."

I knock on Colette's door. When I hear footsteps, I'm grateful that she's home. I didn't call in advance; I simply left Pike Place and walked, deep in thought, to her building, where I stand on her doorstep.

"Jane," Colette says, smiling. "What a surprise."

"May I come in?" I ask. "I . . . I'm so lost, Colette. I could use some advice."

"Come with me, dear," she says. I follow her into the apartment, which looks more disordered than I remember. There are two boxes beside the dining room table and stacks of books all around. "I apologize for the mess. I'm . . . in the midst of . . . cleaning."

I sink into the threadbare velvet couch and sigh.

"How can I help you?" Colette asks, sitting beside me.

"I believe in this gift," I say. "I believe everything you told me. And yet, there's a logical side to my brain too. And a fearful one. My doctor says I need surgery, and forgoing it could mean grave health consequences. I have to be honest, that's weighing on me."

"Yes," she says. "But, Jane, you already know what you must do."

"Do I?"

She nods. "What would you tell yourself, if you were me?"

I sigh. "That the mind has an excellent way of causing us to second-guess our choices, but it's the heart that knows. The heart is always right. We just have to learn how to listen to it."

"Yes," she says, smiling at me like a proud teacher with her pupil.

I nod. "Then I think my heart is telling me to continue on my journey. I'm so close. I know I am. I'm nearly ready to record the names in the book." I take a deep breath, thinking about my contribution to its storied pages, passed down through the years. I've studied it carefully in the past months. Beneath each name, each woman with my gift wrote an account of the love she'd observed. Sometimes recorded in French, sometimes English, the vivid descriptions moved me, and in each case, I could hear their voices, feel the love they so intricately and intimately described. I'll have to do the same. Soon. "Colette, you said that if I fail, if I don't complete this journey, I will spend the rest of my life regretting it. I can't stop thinking about that."

She nods. "If you fail, you will end up like me."

"Like you?"

"Yes," she says. "I did not complete my journey."

I did notice that Collette's section of the book had been left blank, and yet I hadn't made the connection until now.

"I didn't believe in the gift until it was too late," she continues. "My time ran short."

"And what were the consequences, for you?" I gulp.

"A life without love," she says.

I shake my head. "You mean, you've never been in love?"

"Oh, I have," she says nostalgically. "There was a man, a long time ago, Pierre. I was twenty-nine, living in Paris. He walked into my life one day and, I suppose, my heart, and never left."

"And did he return your love?"

"No," she says. "It's the curse I live with. No one I ever love will return my love. It is my consequence, my destiny, now. It's why I came to America after my thirtieth birthday. I couldn't bear to live in a place where he was, if he could never love me." She closes her eyes tightly, then opens them again. "Jane, I don't tell you this to elicit sympathy. I only want you to succeed, and I hope you will learn from my mistakes. Because . . ."

I search her eyes. "Because what?"

"Because I saw you . . . with your date, at your friend's wedding."

"You did?"

She nods. "I was collecting some discarded flower arrangements from a previous reception, donated by the hotel, and I glanced into the ballroom, and there you were, dancing with him."

I swallow hard.

"Jane," she says. "I saw love."

"You did? You really did?"

Colette nods. "And I don't want you to lose it the way I did. I have never forgiven myself for that."

I shake my head. "But that's not how love works," I say. "Love is forgiving. Love is unconditional. It perseveres, and gives second chances. Colette, couldn't you be granted a second chance?"

She nods. "There is one way," she says. "Flip to the back of the book, and read the inscription on the last page."

"What does it say?"

"It says that those recipients of the gift who fail at following its mandates will be given one final chance. On the night of a full moon, when snow is falling, love can be restored."

"Do you believe that for you and . . . Pierre?"

"I don't know," she says. "But I will admit that I am hopeful. I have thought about the possibility often over the years. But I try not to dwell on it. After all, time has passed. I don't even know if he's still living. And if he were? It's foolish to think I could return to him and that he'd love me the way I have loved him all these years."

"But it's worth a try," I say.

She nods. "Love is always worth a try, yes. Even after my great failure. And it's worth a try for you, too."

I nod. "Colette, why did you choose me? Of all the babies at the hospital that day, why me?"

The edges of her mouth form a soft smile. "It was your mother," she says. "She exuded love in a way that I so admired and longed for. And I thought that anyone who was born from a woman with such a spirit had a legendary capacity to love and be loved."

"She had love in her eyes, yes," I say, wiping a tear from my cheek. "She always said that when you love someone once, it changes your heart forever. That it lives on in you. I never told her, but the idea of that frightened me. I knew what her love for my father did to her. I heard her weeping in her room late at night, or in the mornings when she thought I was still asleep. Her love persisted like a wound that wouldn't heal. It tormented her."

Colette gives me a knowing look. "And it's why you've closed yourself off to love."

"Yes," I say. "But something is changing in me. It's scary, and also wonderful."

"I know," she says in almost a whisper. I see tears in her eyes. "Enjoy every second of it, for to give love and feel it returned is life's greatest gift." Her nostalgic expression melts away as she straightens her shoulders. "Now go, and live out the final days before your thirtieth birthday, acting in accordance with the responsibility you have been given. And don't be afraid. I believe in you in a way that I never did in myself."

"Thank you," I say, giving her a hug.

Beside the door, I linger near the old flower cart. Its emerald green paint is buffed to a glossy shine, but I can see layers of rust where the top-coat has bubbled and chipped away.

"It was hers," Colette says.

"Whose?"

"The first woman who had our gift. Elodie, the flower cart girl. I found it at a flea market in

Paris. Her name is etched on the underside. I knew it wasn't happenstance that I found it, and I've kept it with me, always, as a reminder of the beauty and love she shared with the people of her city. All around her, she saw the same love that we see."

I run my hand along the edge of the cart, which is when I notice the French words engraved at the front: "Amour vit en avant."

"What do those words mean?" I ask.

Colette smiles. "Love lives on."

It's cold but clear, too nice a day to hail a cab, so I walk back to the market along First Avenue. When I pass Mary's salon, I peer into the window and see her sweeping the floor, alone, so I stop in.

"Jane!" she says, setting the broom aside.

"Look at you," I say, rubbing her belly.

"I'm huge, aren't I?" she says.

"And why are you here and not in bed with your feet up?"

She frowns. "Honestly, I hate being home. It's lonely."

"I'm sorry," I say. "It must hurt so much that he's not even going to be here for the birth of your baby."

She nods.

"My mom mourned the man who left her, my father, until the day she died. The sadness lived in her heart. She could never rid herself of it. I don't want that for you."

"Me, either," Mary says, sighing.

"Then don't be so focused on the past that you forget to see what's in front of you. My mother could never love anyone else because she was too busy looking backward. You must look forward to the life you are building, to the joy you have ahead."

"Yes," she says. "You're so right, Jane. And when I look forward, you know what I see?"

"What?"

"I see Luca."

I smile. "Did you tell him that?"

She shakes her head. "No, I didn't. It's too late, anyway. He already went home to Italy."

"It's never too late," I say. "Remember that."

I walk home along First Avenue with an undeniable feeling of heaviness. As I step into a crosswalk, the loud crash of metal on metal jars me from the depths of my mind. I stop, heart racing, and look up to see two crushed cars only a few feet in front of me. Smoke billows from a blue SUV, which is crumpled, accordion-style, into the side of a white Volvo station wagon. The woman beside me lets out an ear-piercing scream. "Oh my God!" she says. "I'm calling 911."

A middle-aged bald man in the Volvo springs from his car unscathed, though he's clearly horrified by what we all see: the spray of bright red blood on the windshield of the SUV.

I run to the side door, where a woman lies unconscious in her seat. The man beside her, presumably her husband, is awake, moaning something unintelligible. I open the passenger-side door, and his eyes flutter. He sees me. "Please, help us."

"Help is on the way," I say. "Just hold on."

"Is she hurt?" he cries. "My wife. Is she hurt?"

Blood drips from her nose, and I can't tell if she's breathing, but I don't say that. "Yes," I say. "But she's going to be fine. Just be still. Try not to move."

"We were fighting," he says. "Before the crash. She told me she was through with me. I . . . I . . . I did a terrible thing. I broke her trust."

"No, no," I say. "Don't think about that now. Please."

"This is my punishment."

"No, it's not," I say, looking over my shoulder, praying an ambulance is coming.

"She said she didn't love me anymore," he cries. "And it makes sense. After what I did, I don't deserve her love."

His wife sits lifeless in the seat beside him. Will the medics be able to resuscitate her? The faint sound of sirens is now in the distance, and I take a deep breath. "Help is coming. Just a few minutes more." I think of Cam and Joanna. I think of the desperation he must have felt after her accident. Did they also have an unresolved fight? Do these memories still jar his heart? Is it her face he sees when he closes his eyes each night?

The ambulance pulls up beside us. I step aside as paramedics rush to the scene. I watch as they extricate the woman's bloodied body from the vehicle and set her on a stretcher. The man, now in a neck brace, walks around and kneels beside his wife. "Please, honey, come back to me!" he screams. "I'm so sorry. So, so sorry."

And in that moment, through tears, my vision clouds. I steady myself and approach the tragic scene before me.

"I'm sorry, sir," a paramedic says. "We lost her."

"No, no, no!" the man cries. "No, it can't be. Try harder. Try again."

"I'm sorry, sir," the paramedic says, standing up and stepping back. "I'll leave you with her for a few minutes if you'd like. To say your good-byes."

"Dana," the man cries. "Dana, I'm so sorry. Honey, I love you. I love you. You are the only woman I have ever loved, the only woman I could ever love." He looks up at me then, tearfully. "I didn't tell her that enough. I did so many things wrong. And now it's too late. She didn't know how much I loved her. And how could she have loved me, after my betrayal?" He lays his head on her chest and weeps.

"She knew you loved her," I say in a faltering voice.

The man lifts his head. "What do you mean? How do you know?"

I kneel beside him. "Just take heart in knowing that she loved you, up until the end. And she felt your love, just as you feel hers. Keep that with you always; let it overshadow the pain. Love is bigger. And the two of you had it."

He lays his head back on his wife's chest, and I turn to the sidewalk, providing space for the moment he needs. For his good-bye.

I think of Mary's observations about beginnings and endings as I walk back to the market. Cam's ending with Joanna might have broken his heart, but I pray that there's still room for a new beginning. With me.

"Well, don't you look fancy tonight," Bernard says as I step off the elevator. I've had a few hours to rest, shower, and decompress after the dramatic scene downtown.

"Cam's taking me to Canlis for dinner," I reply, eyeing my black dress in the large wall mirror.

"Lucky you," he says. "I took my wife there on our twenty-fifth wedding anniversary. It's a special place."

I've learned to be cautious, when going to

restaurants, especially nice, special-occasion restaurants where love is prone to lurk, sometimes in every square inch.

I see Cam's BMW pull up outside, and he waves as he jumps out, dressed in his tailored suit and skinny tie. Time feels frozen as I watch him fiddling with his windshield wiper. A simple, everyday gesture. A moment that stands in stark contrast to the accident I witnessed earlier. And it gives me peace, somehow. *Cam* gives me peace.

Bernard grins at me. "You look stunned, like you've seen a ghost."

"That's Cam," I say, collecting myself.

"Have you ever heard that old quotation?" Bernard continues, "True love is like ghosts, which everyone talks about and few have seen."

"True love, huh?" I force a grin as I walk to the door.

We're seated side by side at Canlis, on an upholstered bench seat, which provides a complete view of Lake Union. I watch as a sailboat glides across the water and wonder about its passengers. A couple? A family? Two old friends shooting the breeze?

Our waiter pours the wine, then leaves us alone. I turn to Cam. "I've always wished I had some way to disguise my gift."

He grins. "Cloak-and-dagger?"

"Yeah, some way to throw a trench coat and

271

glasses on and not have to face what I see, or just have the freedom to see what I want without the constant worry of an episode happening."

"I'll talk to my neuroscientist friends," he says playfully, "and see if we can design a pair of specially patented sunglasses."

I laugh, then drift back to a thoughtful state. I tell him about the accident earlier today.

He looks out to the lake beyond the window. "I know what it feels like to watch someone you love slip away."

"I know." I reach for his hand under the table. "And I thought of you today in that moment. I thought of your loss and, well, how moved I am that after all of that, you're willing to begin again."

He turns to me, and his eyes search mine for a long moment. I feel a flutter deep inside. "I am, Jane." He smiles. "And I have this vision for a new beginning, for a new life. I lie awake at night thinking about it. About us."

"Us," I say, grinning. "We're an 'us.'"

"We're an 'us,'" he repeats, grinning back. "Tell me what you want, Jane. Tell me your vision for the future."

"What do you mean, exactly?"

"I mean, do you want a house, kids, a flower garden in the backyard? Do you want travel and adventure? Do you want security, to have and to hold, till death do us part, and all of that?"

"That's a huge question."

"It's an important one," he replies. "I want to know everything I can about you."

I let my eyes search his for a long moment. "Tell me first."

He nods and takes my other hand in his. "I want to play and laugh and fight. And have great make-up sex. I want to dream and grow and travel, but always come back to the same walls, the same person. I want to hear my children's laughter. I want to play catch on a freshly mowed lawn, with the smell of dinner on the barbecue in the backyard. I want to go to bed happy and wake up happier." He smiles. "And I'd like to have all that with you."

I feel an emotion I can't describe cropping up in my chest. It washes over me like a rush of adrenaline. It grows stronger when I look into Cam's eyes, when I squeeze his hands tighter. It's love; I know it's love.

"Now your turn," he says, smiling.

I blink back tears as I think of all the days of my life that have brought me to this place. Doubt. My mother's tears. Every flower I have ever placed into an arrangement. Every look of love I have ever seen on the faces of friends and strangers. And now I'm seeing my own love. He sits beside me, and he loves me in return. I know it, and I feel it. For so long, I have been on a journey, a race, that has been long and grueling, lonely at times, and uncertain. And I have made it to the finish line, tired and weak, but whole and grateful. "Exactly what you said," I reply, searching Cam's face and seeing our shared future in his eyes. "Every single word."

After dinner, we decide to go back to Cam's apartment, where I kick off my heels and curl up on his leather sofa, draping a soft throw blanket around me.

"Glass of wine?" he asks, heading to the kitchen.

"Sure."

He returns with two glasses, then sets the bottle on the coffee table beside us. "My editor gave me this bottle. It's supposed to be a pretty rare Bordeaux."

I glance at the year: 1984. "I was barely alive when this was bottled."

"I can't remember exactly," Cam says, eyeing the bottle, "but there's some story about why this was a really good year for wine in that region. Some sort of full moon harvest, during a freak fall snowstorm. I don't know." He eyes his laptop on the coffee table. "We could look it up."

I nod. "A full moon snowstorm? That's a coincidence. I was just talking to Colette—you know, the French woman who told me about my . . . gift." I pause for a moment. Even now, after months of getting to know each other, I feel self-conscious talking to Cam about my vision, as if he's evaluating the logic of it at every turn.

He looks interested. "What did she say?"

"Something about the fact that if we—I mean, I, or she—failed at love, there is always the possibility of a second chance, but only on the night of a full moon, when it is snowing, or about to snow, or something along those lines."

He grins. "Do you believe that?"

I smirk. "Well, you certainly don't."

"You know I'm a science guy," he says. "Your story, and how your gift came to be a part of you, is one that defies reason. When I want to understand a situation, I report it until I can articulate every nuance." He smiles, as if he's in the midst of an interview.

"Why would you put it that way? I'm hardly one of your subjects."

Cam reaches for my hand. "Listen, Jane, maybe I need to switch gears. I . . . I want to nurture what we have. I want to grow it. I guess what I'm trying to say is that . . . I love you."

I swallow hard.

"And it's not some sort of mystical thing. There are no stars or hearts floating over my head. Cupid hasn't shot me through the heart with his arrow." He smiles again. "I just know how I feel when I am with you and when I'm apart from you. It's love. Jane, I love you."

"You do?"

"I do."

I want to tell him that I love him too, that, just as he said, I've felt it in his presence and in his absence, that I've imagined our life together—how we'd wake up in each other's arms, walk to Meriwether for coffee and croissants in the morning, stopping at Mel's on the way to pick up a newspaper or the latest edition of *Time*, where I'd point to Cam's byline and brag to everyone within earshot that my husband is a famous writer. My husband. The vision is beautiful and vivid.

I open my mouth to speak, but Cam's cell phone is buzzing in the kitchen. "I'm so sorry," he says. "That may be my editor, and she's been pressuring me for answers. It's important, about a story. Sorry. I'll just be a second."

"Totally," I say with a smile. "Take it. I'll sit here with my rare wine." I swirl the burgundy liquid in my glass.

He walks to the kitchen to his phone and nods. "Yep, it's her." He steps into his bedroom and closes the door. I hear the muffled sound of his voice, but I can't make out any words.

I think of the story of the wine. The full moon, the snowstorm, the rare vintage. I set my glass down and reach for Cam's laptop. It powers up immediately, and as I'm searching for a Web browser icon, something on his desktop catches my eye. A folder, titled "The Look of Love/Jane."

My heart rate quickens as I click to open it. I feel a pang of guilt, but I can't help it. My curiosity overpowers me. Inside is an assortment of Word documents titled "Interview Notes—Dr. Heller," "Interview Notes—Jane's Father," and "Neurological Research Study."

Suddenly, I feel hot, like I've just sprinted a lap around a track and have begun to sweat. I peel the throw blanket off my legs and click on a document titled "Jane-Look-of-Love-First-Draft." When the Word document opens, I almost don't believe my eyes:

The Look of Love
By Cameron Collins

Jane Williams is not a clairvoyant or a fortune-teller or a mind reader. But if you ask her, she may tell you about her gift, one that is highly improbable, one that defies science, and one she fiercely believes in. Jane Williams can see love.

I shake my head. I can't read another word. Tears well up in my eyes as I click on a PDF titled "Proposed Cover." And there I am, on the cover of *Time*. I recognize the photo immediately. It was taken at the cemetery on Bainbridge Island. The photographer was working with *Time*.

I close the laptop and set it back on the coffee

table. I feel like a fool. I trusted him, believed him. And he betrayed me.

Cam walks out of his bedroom and sets his phone on the coffee table. "Sorry about that. I swear, sometimes I think my editor is the most unreasonable woman in the world."

"Oh?" I say, trying hard to disguise the anger I feel. "And why is that?"

He places his hand on my leg. "Let's not waste our time talking about boring work stuff."

"As in, the article you're writing about me?"

His face looks ashen.

"I know," I say. "I saw it on your laptop."

"Jane, I—"

"This whole time, it's only been about your story, hasn't it? You saw a cover story in me, and you jumped at the opportunity."

"No, no," he says. "I mean, yes, it may have started off that way. The magazine told me in no uncertain terms that I needed a revenue-generating cover story. But I assure you, though my initial interest in you might seem mercenary, it grew into something genuine and pure. And when I realized, when I knew—"

"That you loved me? Yeah, you really expect me to believe that?" I point to the laptop. "Is that something you do to the person you love?"

He closes his eyes tightly and sighs. "Jane, I promise, the story wasn't going to run. It's what I was talking to my editor about on the phone just now. I told her I refuse to publish it. I'm forcing her to kill it. It will never run, Jane. Please, believe me."

I slip my feet into my heels and stand up. "I don't think I'll ever be able to believe you from now on."

Cam follows me to the door. "Jane, please. Please, let's talk about this. Don't go yet."

"Good-bye, Cam," I say as I reach for my purse and walk out the door.

So much for love. It was only an illusion.

Chapter 22

220 Boat Street #2
December

L o spritzes perfume on her neck, the kind tha drives Grant wild. He's told her so on many occasions. She loves the way he compliments her. The way he praises her beauty, the way he notices when she wears something new or does her hair in a special way. Grant notices her in ways she has never been noticed before. And there is no doubt in her mind that she's becoming addicted to this brand of being noticed. She craves it, needs it, like a drug.

Tonight will be special. Grant is coming over for dinner, and even though he has only a few hours, Lo will squeeze every ounce from them. An hour or a minute—she'll take any amount of time he can give, and these days, it's less and less.

She sets her lipstick on the bathroom counter when she hears a knock at the door.

"Hi," she says to Grant.

"Hi," he says back.

She loves the way they can just say hi, and it can mean everything and immediately bridge the gap between them. Hi. It's their way back to each other, time and time again.

Inside, he kisses her passionately. He is hungry for her love, just as she is hungry for his. Never mind that the risotto is warm and ready to serve, that the salad is dressed and tossed. They don't care about dinner, or the bottle of wine he has set on the kitchen counter. Lo takes his hand and leads him up the ship's ladder to her loft bedroom. She wants to feel his skin on hers. She wants to taste his mouth, to hear his breath in her ear. And she does. They devour each other, over and over again, until they are lying still in each other's arms.

Grant brushes a strand of hair out of Lo's eyes. "For the rest of my life, I only want this."

"Me, too," she says, her eyes locked on his.

In this perfect moment, she wishes she could forget that he has a wife, children, a family across town. But these facts linger like a dark cloud; they hover with them in bed, nudge at them when they kiss, follow them with their every step. And Lo knows that the time is coming: She must receive Grant's full, complete love, or she must find a way to live without him—forever, maybe.

"What are you thinking about?" he asks, running his hand along her arm.

"Our future," she replies. "And the steps we need to take to get there."

He nods soberly, the way he always does when she brings up reality. "Yes," he says with a sigh.

"I've been thinking a lot about that. You know I have been. It's all I think about. Because you are my love. You are all I want. And yet, it's so hard. Every day I go home, and my wife is there, cooking dinner. The girls are seated at the island helping, chopping vegetables, smiling. They're all unaware that at any moment, I might drop a bomb on their world and destroy it. I feel like I'm premeditating a crime, wandering around my house as if it's the site of a future crime scene. The victims are all in place; they just don't know what's coming." He kisses Lo's hand. "Listen, I know what I want. And it's you, but there are times that I don't know that I have the guts to do what I need to do to get to you."

She sits up, her mind coursing with a thousand emotions: shame, for interfering with a family; fear, that Grant won't be able to pull the trigger; love, for a man who may never fully be able to commit himself to her.

"Baby, don't cry," he says, wrapping his arms around her. She loves the way he embraces her, with his full self. She is his, and he is hers. Except that he is not entirely hers. She will say good-bye to him tonight, and he will go home to another woman, whom he will lie beside. They will talk about their children, laugh about something funny one of them did today. He'll watch an episode of *True Blood*. She'll pull up a TED Talk on her iPad. Their arms will brush as he pulls the covers up over himself, and they'll fall asleep together. And Lo will be alone.

"I can't do this much longer," she says. "I can't share you like this. It isn't right. It isn't fair to your wife, and it isn't fair to me."

"I know, I know," he says with a long sigh. "It's on me. It's all on me. I need to do what I need to do."

"Then do it," Lo says. "We can't go on like this forever. It will kill me; I know that for sure."

"Believe in me," he says.

She nods.

"But do you?" he asks, tilting her chin up so that her eyes meet his.

"I do."

"Good. Because you know what we are?"

She shakes her head. "What?"

"We are unbreakable."

She nods. "Unbreakable."

"And we will be unbreakable in Paris."

Paris, with Grant. It's everything Lo has wanted, and yet, somewhere in a far corner of her heart, she worries that the trip is simply a consolation prize.

"I can't believe we're leaving on Christmas Day," Lo says.

"Yes," he replies. "It was tough on the home front, but I'll open presents with the kids when I get home tonight. And believe it or not, it was easier to get two first-class tickets out of Seattle

283

on the holiday than before or after." He smiles. "Maybe we can drink eggnog on the plane."

She laughs. "Eggnog?"

"Good, then," he says. "I'll swing by and pick you up in the morning." He grins devilishly. "Bring that red dress I love."

"Paris," Lo says wistfully. But she knows it's not Paris they need; it's for Grant to make his decision—to be all in, or all out. But Paris is a beautiful, shiny distraction. It'll numb the anxiety, the fear, for a little longer. And it will mean more time with Grant. She'd do anything for more time with him.

He stands up and puts his pants on, then buttons up his shirt, before glancing at his watch. "I'm sorry, I have to go. I said I'd be back a half hour ago."

Lo frowns. "But you haven't even had dinner. I made your favorite, risotto."

"Next time," he says, leaning in to kiss her once more.

She always hates when their time together comes to an end. She hates to watch him slip away from her world and return to his. And as he climbs down the ladder, she listens as he grabs his keys from the counter and closes the door to the houseboat behind him. His footsteps clack on the dock, until they disappear into the winter night, and he into his life, his real life. Back to his wife, back to his children.

Lo wipes a tear from her cheek. She dresses and descends the ladder to the kitchen, where she grabs a spoon and eats her risotto alone, right from the pot. She pours herself a glass of wine and takes a sip. Her keys sit on the countertop, and without a second thought, she reaches for them, and then her coat.

She knows where Grant lives, in a beautiful home on Queen Anne Hill. He recited the address to her once. It's easy to remember because as a high school student she babysat for a wealthy family on that very street, and the Flower Lady has many long-standing clients in the neighborhood, one of Seattle's finest.

She gets into her car. Tonight she wants to see his world. She wants to drive by his house, to see where he comes home to every day after work, where he rests his head at night. And there it is, the big, beautiful Tudor on Highland Drive, with its gabled roofs and leaded glass windows.

Lo's heart races as she stops on the street in front of Grant's house. She turns off the engine and the headlights and looks into the big living room windows. And there he is: Grant, wearing the same shirt she just tore from his body, standing beside his two daughters. They're talking, smiling, in front of their enormous Christmas tree, which is beautifully decorated, not an ornament askew. A moment later, his wife walks over and completes the picture-perfect scene. Lo feels a wave of nausea as his wife hands him a glass of wine and tucks her arm around his waist, nestling her head against his chest.

Lo begins to cry, and as she turns on the engine and drives down Highland Drive, away from Grant, back to her world, she realizes what heartbreak truly feels like.

Chapter 23

The air outside is icy, and it stings my cheeks as I step out of my apartment building to the sidewalk. White frost covers the roof of the market, where vendors are clothed in heavy coats and hats. I cinch my scarf tighter around my neck and smile as a station wagon with a Christmas tree strapped to the top drives by. I think of Mom then, the way she used to let Flynn and me pick out the biggest Douglas fir in the lot, and somehow she'd wrangle it onto the car and drag it up to our apartment. It must have taken so much effort to pull it off every year, but she managed to make it look easy. And with our faces sticky from candy canes, we'd watch her fit the trunk into the tree base.

I miss her, as I always do so acutely at this time of year.

I unlock the shop and turn on the lights. For the first time in more years than I can count, Lo called in sick. She was crying on the phone, so I know her malaise is more emotional than physical, but it worries me just the same, or perhaps even more.

"Take all the time you need," I said. And yet, with the rush of orders coming in for Christmas Day, it's the worst time to be running the shop solo, especially after the drama with Cam. So when Flynn calls and offers to lend a hand, I'm beyond relieved.

"How's it going, sis?" he asks, setting his messenger bag beneath the counter.

"Honestly, not great," I say, scrolling through the newest orders that have come in from the website. "I'm still dealing with Cam's betrayal."

I told Flynn about Colette, my gift, all of it, months ago, but the existence of his sister's mystical gift was less shocking than a best friend who could betray her. I sigh. "They were going to put me on the cover, Flynn."

He shakes his head. "I still don't believe it."

"Believe it," I say. "And he interviewed Dr. Heller, and apparently even our father."

"What?"

"Yeah," I say. "I saw the interview notes. It seems he tracked him down in Oregon."

"So our deadbeat dad surfaces in Oregon. That's unexpected news."

"I know."

"I'm so sorry, Jane," Flynn continues. "At least you found out, before . . ."

"Before my photo was plastered all over every newsstand in America?" I sigh. "And the crazy thing, Flynn, is that I thought it was love. I thought I was actually in love, and that he loved me."

"Maybe he does love you," he offers. "But I'd still like to wring the guy's neck."

I shake my head. "No. But anyway, throwing

someone under the bus for your own interests, career or otherwise, is not love."

"But didn't you just say he was going to pull the plug on the article?"

"Yes, he said that, but how am I supposed to believe him?"

Flynn nods. "I thought he was a friend, or I never would have introduced the two of you. Now I understand why he's been avoiding me. He was too ashamed to face your big brother."

I direct him to a shipment of holly and greenery, which he begins moving to the back room.

"How about your girl?" I ask. "The one in the apartment across the street. Tell me you've finally met her."

He shakes his head. "Not yet."

"Flynn, what would it take, really, to just walk across the street, take an elevator up, and knock on her door?"

He smiles. "I know, I know. It makes no sense that I haven't done it yet. I guess I'm afraid."

"Of what? That she'll speak in a Miss Piggy voice?"

"No," he says, laughing. "I mean, maybe. I guess I'm afraid that in-person won't be as amazing and wondrous as adoring her from afar. Does that make sense?"

I nod. "Sure. You've fallen in love with a fantasy. And it's become sort of a game."

"Yeah," he says.

"But games end, remember."

"I was thinking I could bring her flowers tomorrow, for Christmas," he says.

"And my birthday," I say, mostly to myself, thinking of Colette and her warnings about what will happen if I turn thirty without fulfilling the obligations of the gift.

Flynn is still thinking of his lovely neighbor. "If she's alone," he continues, "which I'm sure she'll be, I can cheer her up."

I smile. "I think that sounds like a perfect plan. I'm proud of you."

"I'm proud of you too," he says.

The shop phone rings, and I run to answer it.

"Jane, it's Dr. Heller."

I'm silent.

"Jane, are you there?"

"Yes," I say stiffly.

"Cam called to tell me that you discovered the article. Jane, I'd love for us to talk. Could you come into my office today?"

"Dr. Heller, I don't know that there's anything left for us to discuss."

"There is," she says. "I'd like to apologize to you in person, and I won't feel right until I can explain myself. Can you be here in an hour?"

"All right," I say. "I'll do my best."

I walk into Dr. Heller's office that afternoon and feel a pang in my heart. Although I didn't read

Cam's interview notes with her, the mere fact that she'd even think to speak to a journalist about me gives me pause. It has rattled my trust in her, trust I've built since childhood, when she'd dangle stuffed animals above my head to get me to focus while she examined my eyes. Today, I want to look her in the eye and ask her how she not only betrayed my trust but violated medical ethics.

"I'm glad you came," Dr. Heller says when she walks into the room. "Please, let's go talk. Maybe in the cafeteria? I'll buy you a coffee."

I nod and follow her to the elevator. We ride to the third floor in silence, and when the doors open, the smell of boiled broccoli and burnt French fries hits my nose.

We stop at the coffee cart. Dr. Heller orders two coffees, and we head to an empty table.

"Let me start by saying that I didn't know he was recording me," she says. "I asked him to keep my comments off the record."

"Off the record, or on the record," I say. "Dr. Heller, I'm honestly shocked that you'd even think to speak about my condition to anyone without my consent."

"I know, Jane; I was wrong. And I violated some established medical ethics. I'm not proud of that. But, please, I hope you know that it came from a place of good intent. You know I have cared about your health since the first day you came into my office as a young child. And when you refused the surgery, I felt that maybe by talking to Cam, you'd come around. Maybe together, with his understanding of science and my medical knowl-edge, we could convince you to make the right choice for your health. For what it's worth, I believe he cares about you and ultimately wanted you to see that surgery was the only way."

"And betraying me was his way to do it?" I shake my head and sigh.

Dr. Heller refolds her hands in her lap. "I realize I handled this all wrong. I only hope that someday you can forgive me, and also Cam."

I take a deep breath. "I cannot forgive Cam. But, Dr. Heller, of course I forgive you. You have been like a mother to me. I know you only have my best interests in mind. I just wish that you would have understood that no matter how much science or medical data, I have to make the right choice for me, even if it seems illogical or foolish."

"You're right," she says. "And I am grateful for your forgiveness." She pauses for a moment. "And what about Cam? Can you ever forgive him?"

I shake my head. "Colette told me she saw love between us, but even that knowledge is not enough. He wanted to sensationalize my story, to capitalize on it. He saw me as a great byline—the moment he met me last New Year's Eve, in fact. I know that now."

"That may be true," Dr. Heller says, "but what you can't deny is how his feelings may have changed and grown over this year. I believe he loves you, Jane."

I shake my head and smile to myself. "No, it's not love. It was a figment of it. A hologram."

"But you believe in love, Jane," she says. "I know that about you."

"I believe in it for others, just not so much for myself."

Just then, Dr. Heller's nurse, Kelly, waves from across the room. She holds a tray from the cafeteria as she approaches our table.

"Please, join us," I say.

"No, no," she replies. "I don't want to interrupt. I'll just grab another table."

"Kelly, please, feel free to sit down," Dr. Heller says, smiling. And as Kelly takes her seat, I feel pressure behind my eyes. It's light at first, and I almost dismiss it entirely, but then it intensifies, and I blink hard when a film of fog envelops my vision. I can hardly believe it. I've gotten it all wrong. All this time, I thought Dr. Heller was in love with Dr. Wyatt. But no. Dr. Heller loves Kelly. And Kelly loves her in return.

"Jane," Dr. Heller says, jumping to her feet. She kneels beside me and holds my wrist to take my pulse. "You're having an episode, aren't you?"

I nod.

"Can I get you some water?" Kelly says nervously. "Can I do anything?"

"No," I say. "I'm OK." I sit still for a long moment, and when the fog lifts, I turn to Dr. Heller, who's still kneeling beside me. Her eyes are moist, as if tears might spill from her lids at any moment. And I realize, for the first time, that she believes.

"You understand now, don't you? You finally get it."

Dr. Heller looks at Kelly, then back at me. "I do," she says, wiping a tear from her eye.

"Now you see," I say, standing up. "That's what true love does to me."

Kelly smiles at Dr. Heller. I turn to the elevator, then look back at the two of them. "I'm so very happy for you."

As I drive out of the hospital parking garage, I reach for my phone to call Colette. Tomorrow is my thirtieth birthday, and I am ready, finally, to write my findings about love in the book. I want to tell her about it. About Cam. About the jumble of thoughts pulsing through my brain and heart.

I dial her number, but there's no answer, so I decide to drive straight over, parking on the street in front of her building. I take the elevator up to her floor and see from a distance that her door is ajar. "Hello," I say, peering inside. "Colette?" My voice echoes back to me.

As I push the door open wider, I'm shocked at the sight before me. The apartment is empty, the bookcases bare. The old velvet drapes hang limp and lonely from the bay window ahead. Colette is gone, and the only sign that she ever lived here is sitting at the center of the room. The old flower cart, which once brimmed with blossoms on a Parisian street, now sits empty in an abandoned apartment in Seattle. I reach for the envelope taped to its side.

Dear Jane,
I must leave you now, for my work here is complete. You must continue on as I have done before you. I wish you happiness, but most of all, I wish you love. Don't ever lose sight of it.

Yours,
Colette

I can't believe she's gone. I think of her flying into New York City. Or Rio de Janeiro. But I really hope she has gone to Paris. I hope she will take a second chance at love, and I hope she will succeed.

I wheel the old cart to my car, and I'm happy to see that it fits, with a little angling, in the back of the station wagon. As I climb into the driver's seat, my phone rings. It's Mary. "Jane, tomorrow's the big day. I want to make sure you can still be there to meet my baby girl."

"I wouldn't miss it for the world," I say. "What time is your induction?"

"It's been moved to later in the afternoon," she says. "With any luck, I'll be holding her in my arms by evening. You can be the first to hold her, after me."

I know it then. The final piece of my journey that I have been most concerned with now makes sense. I will give Mary's baby girl my gift. I think of Mary, wide-eyed and kind; hurt deeply but not hardened. Her heart, somehow, has remained tender and beautiful through her pain, like my mother's. Yes, I think to myself. Mary's daughter will have access to her heart, to love, in the very same way. And she will see the world through the foggy lens of love the way I have done. She will find her way, just as I have, even when it doesn't always end with the loose ends tied up neatly in a bow. That is life, and that is love.

After I hang up the phone, it buzzes, and I glance at the screen to see a text from Cam that reads, "I'm so very sorry."

I sigh and tuck my phone into my coat pocket. I am too.

Chapter 24

Jane, it's Katie." She sounds scared, frantic.

"What's going on?"

"I don't know how to say this. . . . Josh left me."

A customer walks into the shop, and I motion to Lo for assistance. "Wait, what?"

"Yes, he left me. He walked out of our house to get coffee and said he'd be back soon, but instead he had breakfast with a blonde and decided not to return."

"Katie," I say with a gasp. "This makes no sense. I have never seen two people more in love than the two of you. Surely you're mistaken."

"I'm not," she says. "He hasn't even come home to get his stuff. He's done. Done with everything. I just wish I'd known this was coming. There were no signs. Not even one."

"Honey, I don't even know what to say. This makes zero sense."

"I know," she says. "But I do know that if he's chosen to leave, I need to move on. I can't sit around in this house we used to share and wait for him to come home. I'll have to sell the house. Jane, I feel like I'm living a nightmare right now."

"It does sound like a nightmare," I reply. "I'm so sorry. Is there anything I can do?"

"No," Katie says. "Actually, yes. I think I need to get out of town. How do you feel about going somewhere sunny and beachy with me soon? Next month, maybe. Mexico? Hawaii? Somewhere away from here. With fruity cocktails. Let's get Lo to come too. We can sit around by the pool and drink ridiculous amounts of alcohol and not think or talk about men."

"That sounds like heaven," I say.

"Good," she says. "I just need to get my mind off all of this. Jane, I'm so heartbroken." She sighs. "I'll look at flights and let you know."

"OK," I say. "And, Katie, I don't know what is going on with Josh. And it doesn't sound good. But here's what I do know: I have seen you two together; I have witnessed your love, and it is real. Don't ever discount that, OK?" I know she's crying. I can hear the faint sounds of sniffles. "Promise me?"

"I promise," she finally says.

"It's Christmas Eve," I say to Lo. "Time to head home."

"Nah, I'll stay. There's more to do."

"No, there's not," I say. "And what am I? Scrooge? Go home, drink some mulled wine, listen to Bing Crosby."

She nods. "Alone."

"Me, too," I say. "Though, honestly, I'm so tired after this week, I really don't mind. I just want to

298

sleep, for a thousand years." Lo has been sad, introspective for the past few days. "You need rest. Aren't you leaving for Paris in the morning?"

"Yes," she says, forcing a smile.

"Then get out of here," I say. "I am going to shoo you out with a broom if you don't leave right this second."

She slips her apron off and hangs it on the hook behind the counter. "OK, boss," she says with a smile.

Just as she walks out the door, I hear the bells jingle again, and a wave of cold air breezes through the shop. Without looking up, I say, "Sorry, we're closed. I—"

And then my eyes meet a man's. The customer who comes in every year on Christmas Eve, the one with sad eyes who walks with a limp, and tips heavily, for a reason unbeknownst to me.

"Oh, hello," I say, recognizing him immediately.

"I'm sorry," he says with a shy smile. "My train was late." He's a little out of breath. "I was worried I wouldn't make it before you closed."

"Train?"

He nods. "I live in Portland."

My eyes narrow. "Portland? So why does someone from Oregon come to a Seattle flower shop every year on Christmas Eve?"

His expression is serious and his eyes, sad. "You have the best flowers," he says after a long moment.

"Well, then," I say. "Let me get started on an arrangement for you."

"No," he says quietly. "Don't put yourself through the trouble. I'll take something from the case." He points to a vase of red roses and greenery. "That is perfect."

I carry it to the front counter. As I reach forward to rearrange a rose that looks a little off kilter, I feel a prick on my index finger.

"Darn," I say, as a drop of blood pools on my skin. "The growers always get sloppier around this time of the year. If I had a dollar for every thorn I've seen on a stem this month, well."

The man nods. "And every time I've held a rose, it seems I only felt the thorns."

"Billy Joel," I say with a smile.

"Yes," he replies. " 'And So It Goes.' "

"It's a beautiful song."

I bandage my finger, as he hands me a check.

"Merry Christmas," he says, heading toward the door, before turning around once more. "That was your mother's favorite song."

I am too stunned to speak, frozen in place as the door closes and the man walks out to the street. I look down at the check and read the name printed on it: Eric Williams.

My father.

An hour later, I close up the shop, carrying an extra wreath and a holiday arrangement with me, and walk through the market. It's quiet, almost eerily so. I hear Christmas music coming from an idling car ahead. Inside the SUV is a man and his wife, and their three children, two boys and a girl, who are licking candy canes in the back-seat.

The air is crisp and cold, and I can see my foggy breath all around me, and Mel in the distance. His suit looks like it might have fit him well—in 1983.

"Jane!" he exclaims. "Just the lady I was hoping to run into."

"Merry Christmas, Mel," I say softly.

"Merry Christmas, beautiful," he replies with eyes that twinkle under the streetlights. "I need your finest bouquet of flowers. I'm going to give them to Vivian tonight."

I smile at his enthusiasm. Even in one's seventies, love can be young. "Here," I say, handing him the arrangement I made for my mantel: green chrysanthemums, interspersed with yet-to-bloom lime-green hyacinths, Mom's favorite Christmas bouquet. "Take her these. She'll love them."

"But I couldn't—"

"Please, I want you to." I feel the sting of a tear in my eye when I think of how much my mom would have loved giving flowers to Mel and shooing him off to woo his beloved.

"Thank you, sweetheart," he says.

"I hope they do the trick."

He straightens his tie with his left hand. "Me, too."

I walk past Meriwether next and admire the rings of fruitcake and braided bread in the window. Elaine is probably home putting the finishing touches on the kids' Christmas stockings, but I know her mind—and her heart—is full with weighty decisions.

Bernard is just packing up to leave as I enter the lobby of my apartment building. "I'm so glad I caught you," I say, reaching into my pocket and handing him an envelope with a little Christmas cash. "Merry Christmas," I say, smiling.

"Merry Christmas, and an early happy birthday," he replies. "Oh, that boyfriend of yours, what's-his-name . . ."

"Cam," I say. "And he's no longer my boyfriend."

"Oh," Bernard replies. "Well, he was here earlier today to see you. He said he stopped in at the flower shop but didn't find you. Anyway, he asked me if I'd give you this." He places an envelope in my hand. "I was about to slide it under your door before I left. I get the feeling that it's urgent, something you should read tonight instead of finding it in your mailbox in a few days."

"Thank you," I say curtly, tucking the envelope in my pocket.

"Can I give you some advice?" he asks.

"Sure," I say cautiously.

"Whatever you're punishing him for," he says, "don't do it for too long. Forgive him. Life is too short not to extend forgiveness, even for the worst offenses."

I nod and venture a smile. "I'll think about it," I say, stepping onto the elevator as I give Bernard a parting smile. "Merry Christmas."

After I greet Sam, I pour a glass of wine and turn on a Johnny Mathis Christmas CD. It reminds me of Mom, and I ache a little, for Mom, for my past, for the future that—if Dr. Heller's predictions are accurate, or if I fail to adhere to the rules Colette has laid before me—I might never know.

My coat is draped on the couch, and I reach for the envelope in the right pocket, tearing it open and pulling out the single page inside:

Dear Jane,

I won't be here to wish you a merry Christmas and happy birthday, and even if I were, I know that you wouldn't want to see me anyway. What I did was wrong, and you have every right to blame me, to hold a grudge against me for the rest of your life.

I'm going back to New York for a few weeks. After I refused to turn over my notes for the feature about you, my editor was forced to kill the story. They've laid me off as a result, so I'm pursuing other opportunities. I've just been offered the science editor position at *Newsweek*. It will mean moving back to New York. I don't want to go, and yet . . . is there anything for me here anymore?

I felt something big with you, Jane. Something I haven't felt since my fiancée died, and then I went and screwed it all up. For that, I will always have deep regrets.

I have never met a woman like you, and I know I never will again. You changed me. You made me see the power of love. You taught me to believe in it, to trust it.

I will always love you, Jane. Always.

Cam

A single tear falls from my eye and lands on the letter. I run my hand along Cam's signature, studying the curve of his *C*. And then I take a deep breath and tuck the letter back into the pocket of my coat.

Chapter 25

342 Pine Street #4

It's Christmas Eve. Tonight there's a candle-light service at the Presbyterian church on Fifth Avenue. At breakfast, Vivian said she was going, and even though Mel has never considered himself religious in any way, he has never felt more drawn to a church service in all his life.

He selects a tweed suit from his closet, the nicest one he owns, which isn't saying much. Adele patched the elbows years before. He dresses and then combs his hair, what he has left of it, at least. Should he get her a Christmas present? He scolds himself for not thinking of that ahead of time. He's never been good at presents. But Vivian deserves something. He can't afford anything fancy, certainly not the expensive jewelry she's accustomed to. But something. Surely, he can think of something. He glances at his watch. Most of the shops at the market will be open for another hour. Flowers. He'll stop at Jane's shop and get Vivian the most beautiful bouquet he can find. That's the ticket.

The air outside is cold. Cold enough to snow, maybe. But the sky is clear, and he's glad of that.

The walk to the church on Fifth would be complicated in the snow.

Mel is disappointed when he notices the lights are dim in the flower shop ahead, but he breathes a sigh of relief when he sees Jane approaching and she kindly offers him the vase of flowers in her arms.

Jane's voice sounds cheerful, but her eyes don't match. They look weighted down, heavy with some matter of the heart, and he worries about her the way a father might worry about his daughter.

"You're not going to be alone tonight, are you?"

She deflects his concern with a smile. "I have Sam, don't forget. And where are you off to on this wintry Christmas Eve?"

He smiles shyly. "A church service." He lowers his voice. "Where Vivian will be."

Jane smiles. "And you're going empty-handed?"

"Well," he says. "I was hoping to bring her some flowers, but I see that you're all closed up for the night."

Jane regards the arrangement in her arms. "Take these," she says suddenly. "They'll be perfect. Everyone thinks they want red roses to express their love. And it represents love, yes, but more of a fleeting love. A fire that burns hot but ultimately burns out. You want to show her the purity, the realness of your love. And this arrangement will make your point." He can see tears in her eyes then. "I promise you that."

Mel beams. "Thank you, sweet Janey."

Jane can tell he wants to linger. He wants to make sure she is OK, but she waves him on. "Go," she says. "Go find her."

He winks at his young friend and continues along the sidewalk. It must be thirty degrees, definitely below the freezing point, but Mel doesn't feel the cold, not really. He's warmed by his love.

The church is just ahead. A glow of orange bathes each street-facing window as he makes his way up the steps. Inside, the sanctuary is filled with the quiet hum of an organ and the sweet voices of the children's choir singing "O Holy Night." He takes a seat in one of the back pews and scours the church for Vivian. He doesn't see her at first, but then he notices a woman sitting tall in the pew, with an elegance that could belong only to Vivian. In the dim candlelight, she turns slightly, and he can see the curve of her beautiful cheeks, her exquisite mouth, her regal nose. It's her. And as the children's choir shifts octaves to begin "Silent Night," Mel notices the man sitting beside Vivian. He's impeccably dressed, tall, and broad shouldered. His suit, well pressed and expensive looking. Yes, this is the type of man she deserves, his Vivian. And as he sits in the back pew, holding the bouquet of flowers, listening to the choir, Mel is struck with the realization that he only wants the best for her. And as much as his love is true, he is not the best for her. He will never be good enough for her.

She turns her head then, and their eyes meet, only for a moment, and her regal face melts into a smile. Mel stands to leave, and on his way out to the reception area, he hands the vase of flowers to a man in the entryway. "I have to go," he says. "But would you mind giving these to someone?" He describes Vivian to the man and then walks out to the street alone.

Chapter 26

Christmas Day 2013

I open the old book and reach for a pen. It is my thirtieth birthday, and I contemplate my year. When I think of Cam, my heart twinges. I was wrong about him, so wrong. But I can finish my journey. I can finish it, and I will own it.

I nod to myself and stare at the brittle page before me, yellowed over the years. I think of the first type of love: Pragma, love driven by the head, not the heart. Elaine called me last night, in tears. She'd made her decision. I write "Pragma" on the page, followed by her name, and Charles's. And then I let loose my pen to describe their love.

2201 Hamlin Street

Elaine feels Matthew's eyes on her, even before she opens her own. It's Christmas morning, and she can't help but remember how her life changed when Charles walked into her kitchen last year.

"Morning, beautiful," Matthew says, stroking her cheek softly.

"Morning," she whispers. "Are the kids up?"

He nods. "They're waiting for us downstairs. We wanted to let you sleep a little longer."

Elaine looks at her husband, this man who loves her with such sincerity. She loves him too, of course. How could she not? He is her partner. He is her best friend.

"Mom, Dad?" She hears her son Jack's impatient voice coming from downstairs.

"You go ahead," Elaine says. "Tell them I'll be down in a minute."

Matthew kisses her forehead and heads downstairs. When she hears his footsteps on the stairs, Elaine walks to the window that looks out to the street and feels a pang in her chest as her eyes survey the house that once belonged to Charles. Her Charles. The for-sale sign still stands out front, even though it sold last week, to a nice family from Cleveland. The moving truck came three days ago, and just like that, Charles and his daughter were gone.

Elaine touches the cold glass of the window, tracing the outline of the house with her finger, remembering the way he looked at her before he left, feeling his love wash over her all over again. And in an instant, she is in his arms once more, steeped in the same joy and shame of loving a man who isn't her husband, loving a man whom she can never have a life with, because she already has one with someone else.

She brought over cinnamon rolls on the Thursday

night that Charles told her about the job offer in San Francisco. "Come with me," he pleaded. "Let's start a life together. Let's do this."

No one would ever know how much she wanted to set the cinnamon rolls down that day, just drop them on the ground, reach for Charles's hand, and catch the next flight out of town. They could be together and then sort out the rest later. For once in her life, she could follow her heart, instead of her head. She could choose love. But instead, Elaine trembled from a place deep inside. Because she knew she could never leave Matthew. Leaving wasn't a part of her DNA, even for great love, for true love, for the one and only love of her life.

And so she said good-bye to Charles. She kissed him once and walked home, where she collapsed in a heap in her kitchen and burned the cupcakes for Ellie's school bake sale.

"Mama, are you coming?" Elaine turns to see her daughter standing in the doorway.

"Yes, honey," she says, collecting herself.

Downstairs, the Christmas presents are opened with the same fury that they are every year, and then silence descends upon the house again. When Matthew gets up to make coffee, Ellie suddenly squeals. She runs to the tree and finds a tiny box, wrapped in gold paper, that got lost in the piles of crumpled wrapping paper and torn-open boxes. "Look," she says. "Another present!" She pauses to read the tag. "It's for you, Mama."

Ellie hands Elaine the box, and she stares at it curiously for a moment before untying the ribbon and unwrapping the gold paper. When she lifts the lid of the box, she's perplexed for a moment, and then her heart seizes. Inside is a charm for her bracelet: a tiny hot air balloon, attached to a delicate silver clasp. "I . . . ," she says in a faltering voice. "This is . . ." Her voice trails off as Matthew returns to the living room with two cups of coffee.

"Are you OK, Mama?" Ellie asks, wrapping her arm around her mother.

"Yes, honey," Elaine says through tears.

Ellie's eyes are big. "Is it a charm for your bracelet?"

Elaine nods.

"Did Santa bring it to you?"

Matthew smiles at his wife. "Santa's sorry for getting it wrong so many years before."

Jack and Ellie run upstairs to their rooms to play with their new toys, and Matthew nestles beside Elaine on the couch. "I thought you could fill the bracelet with memories we make together," he says, watching as she attaches the charm to the bracelet that clings to her wrist. "Starting with a hot air balloon ride. What do you say?"

"Yes," Elaine says through tears. "Yes."

I sigh and look to the next line in the book, where I write "Agape." Unconditional, altruistic love. And below it, I record the names Mary and Luca. I'd never mentioned it to my friend, but I'd seen the two of them together, unexpectedly, one night at Julia's, where I'd stopped for takeout after a meeting with a vendor in Wallingford. I remember how my vision had changed and the way my heart felt warm when it happened; then I begin writing.

4572 Sunnyside Avenue

Mary reaches for her bag when she hears the cab honking outside. She locks the door behind her and feels the baby kick on the way to the hospital. A baby girl. Her baby girl. She checks in at the reception desk, then sits down in an uncomfortable chair and fills out her paperwork on a clipboard. Eli should be sitting beside her, of course. But when she closes her eyes, it's Luca's face she sees. She blinks hard. *Funny how life turns out,* she thinks.

"Ms. Sherman?" She looks up to see a woman in her early twenties with a nose ring beside a wheelchair. She wears a pair of turquoise scrubs. "If you're ready, I'll wheel you up to your room now."

Mary nods and hands the woman the clipboard,

then sinks into the wheelchair. She tucks her bag on her lap and sits back as the woman wheels her to the elevator. It jerks upward, then stops on the third floor. When the doors open, Mary sees someone she recognizes in the distance. At first she hardly believes her eyes, but he sees her too. She opens her mouth to speak, but the elevator door closes.

"Did you see someone you know?" the woman behind the wheelchair asks.

"Yes," Mary says. "At least I think so."

In her hospital room on the fifth floor, she changes into her gown, which barely contains her swollen belly. She takes a long look at herself in the bathroom mirror of her hospital room and frowns at her hair, pulled back into a messy ponytail. A hairstylist ought to have better hair on the day she'll meet her baby girl. But there wasn't time for a highlight or cut. At her doctor's appointment yesterday, Christmas Eve, her OB was nervous about her rising blood pressure, so they scheduled an induction, for Christmas Day.

The nurse returns, and Mary watches in silence as the woman attaches various cords to her belly and arms. Eli won't be coming, of course. He's in New York or Paris with his new girlfriend. Good riddance, she thinks as she climbs into her hospital bed, but Mary is overcome with a feeling of loneliness as the fetal monitor beeps quietly beside her. The nurse asks for her right arm to start the IV, and Mary closes her eyes as the needle meets her skin. She barely feels the prick. She barely feels anything. She is numb.

"Will you be having any visitors?" the nurse asks. The question is benign enough, but Mary can sense the prying tone of the nurse's voice and the real question veiled beneath: "Is the baby's father going to be present for the birth?"

"No," Mary says quickly. "I mean, yes, well, my friend, Jane. She'll be here in a few hours."

The nurse nods and smiles before heading to the doorway. "Just buzz me if you need anything."

Mary's mind turns to Luca. She remembers the way he held her hand so tenderly on that walk so many months ago, the way he fixed the drip in her leaking faucet, painted the baby's nursery. And then she stares out over her enormous belly. She feels foolish, suddenly, to even let the thought cross her mind. Luca deserves so much more than this, a brokenhearted woman carrying another man's baby. She can't ask him to be the glue that puts all her broken pieces back together. It's too much to ask another human being. Besides, he's gone home to Italy.

She remembers their tearful good-bye. She turned away when he looked at her as if he wanted to kiss her. She would not let him spend his love on her. He'd spend it until he was broke, and she didn't deserve it. There's someone else for him, someone better than she.

She wipes a tear from her cheek as the nurse pokes her head in the doorway with a knowing smile. "You have a visitor," she says.

Mary glances at the clock. Jane isn't supposed to arrive until this afternoon. "Oh, she must be early," she says.

The nurse looks confused. "She?" Behind her, Luca appears in the doorway holding a vase of white roses and a pink balloon, shaped like a heart, that reads, "Our Baby Girl."

Mary sits up, beaming. "Luca!"

The nurse smiles. "I'll be at the desk if you need anything."

"I hope it is OK," he says, setting the flowers down on the table by the window.

"You didn't have to," Mary says through tears.

He sits on the bed beside her and weaves his fingers through hers. "I *wanted* to." He takes a deep breath and looks intently into her eyes. "I love you. Do you know?"

She smiles. "You do?"

He nods. "Yes. I love you, my little red fish." He reaches for the bag beside the balloon and pulls out a copy of Dr. Seuss's *One Fish Two Fish Red Fish Blue Fish*.

Still smiling through her tears, she says, "But I don't deserve your love; I'm . . ." She looks down at her belly.

"I have been thinking," Luca says. "If you let me, I be her father. I will love her, Mary. I will love her . . ." He pauses for a moment to find the words. "To the moon and back." He clears his throat. "Mary, please, let me be your husband, and this child's father. It would be my greatest honor."

She touches his face lightly. "Do you really mean that? Do you?"

"I do," he says. "I want to be there for my red fish today, and tomorrow, and for all the tomorrows after that."

"To infinity," Mary says.

He looks puzzled.

"It means forever and ever and ever," she says.

"Yes," he says, grinning. "And even this 'infinity' wouldn't be enough time with you."

A tear falls down Mary's cheek as the door to the room opens, and a man in a white lab coat approaches. "Hello, I'm Dr. Carter," he says. "I'll be seeing to your induction today. With any luck, you should have a baby in your arms by five o'clock. Now how does that sound?"

She nods through her tears. "It sounds wonderful."

"Now," the doctor continues, "I assume Dad will be cutting the cord?"

Luca nods. "Yes," he says with confidence.

Mary reaches for his hand and squeezes it. "Yes," she whispers to him. Then she smiles to herself. "I saw someone today, on the third floor."

"Oh?"

"Yes, a friend of someone I know," she says, reaching for her cell phone. "Before this baby comes, I have to make a call."

I set the book aside and get up to make a cup of coffee, then return to my kitchen table. In three hours I'll need to be at the hospital. I promised I'd hold Mary's hand through labor. But first, I'll finish this page. I look to the next line and write "Mania." I remember Colette describing this type of love—obsessive love, filled with highs and lows—and pause only for a moment before writing the names Flynn and Celeste on the line below. I swallow hard before I begin to write their story.

1301 4th Avenue

Flynn wakes before sunrise, which is unusual for him, and especially unusual given that he drank good whiskey with friends last night, perhaps too much of it. But he wakes fortified with energy. Because he's made a big decision. After months of admiration from afar, he's decided to knock on Celeste's door. He knows that when she opens the door and sees him, she will let him take her into his arms. And he knows she will feel as intensely about him as he does about her. It will be the beginning of a beautiful love story. Their love story.

As Flynn showers, he thinks about all the women he's had. The ones who have sauntered in and out of his door, his bed, his life. Their faces are fuzzy, their names a blur. None have retained so much as a centimeter in his heart. And now, all he sees, all he knows, is Celeste, this woman he hasn't uttered a single word to yet. As he shaves, he marvels at the absurdity of falling in love from afar. And he doesn't even flinch at his word choice. *Love.* He knows it. He feels it. And he can see the way she looks at him through the windows. She feels it too.

As he dresses, he thinks about the way he's watched her late at night chopping vegetables for salads in her bra. He recalls the way she looked up the other night, gazing into his apartment, knowing he was watching all the while, and smiling in his direction, that sad, beautiful smile, as she pranced by the window in her lacy black panties, tempting him, taunting him, making his feelings for her deepen with every step across her mahogany floors.

He walks into his living room and looks out across the street. The air is thick with fog. A low cloud hovers in the space between their apartment buildings, obscuring his view into her windows. But it doesn't matter. Rain, snow, sleet, fog—none of it will stand in their way. Today is their day. Today he will declare his love for her. Today is the first day of the rest of their lives.

From his wine rack, he selects an expensive bottle. He knows she likes French wine, Bordeaux. His binoculars are high-powered enough that he could read the label on the bottle on her counter yesterday. He tucks it under his arm, reaches for the vase of orange roses he bought for her yesterday, then places his hand on the door. Just twelve paces to the elevator, then sixteen to the sidewalk, and then another seven off the elevator to Celeste's apartment, or at least that's how he imagined when he'd counted it all out in his head. He can hear only the beat of his heart. He's so lost in his thoughts when he steps into the hallway, he doesn't immediately notice the little white envelope lying by his door.

He bends down to pick it up. His name is written on the front of the envelope, and he tears the flap open hastily.

Dear Flynn,

I am so sorry that I left without saying good-bye, or even hello. But the circumstances in my life gave me no other option. Some things aren't meant to be. And some love is ill-timed. And yet, I think I could have loved you. I think I did love you, even if it was only through two layers of glass.

I will always be yours,
through the window,
Celeste

P.S. Look after Cezanne for me, please?

The wine and vase of flowers drop from Flynn's grasp and fall to the floor, shattering in a mess of crimson-stained petals and jagged glass shards. Flynn doesn't notice or hear, though. He begins running, down the hall, to the elevator, out the lobby to the street, and into Celeste's building. He doesn't even hear the doorman's greeting. His lips simply move, and there is only the sound of his own beating heart. It pounds in his ears like a bass drum. *Boom. Boom. Boom.*

The elevator deposits him on the eleventh floor, and he runs down the hallway to Celeste's door, which is slightly ajar.

The space is completely empty. Flynn's shoes clack on the hardwood floors and release a lonely echo in the air. The furniture is gone. The walls are bare. And he can feel it, that palpably empty feeling. Celeste is gone.

He falls to his knees then. Couldn't she have waited? Just a few hours longer? He was coming, for her. He buries his face in his hands, just as he feels a soft nudge against the side of his knee.

A fluffy white cat purrs beside him.

"Cezanne," he says, lifting the cat into his arms.

Flynn wipes away a tear, then nods. "Let's go home."

In his apartment, he sets the cat down, and she saunters to the couch, where she nestles beside a pillow in a way that seems as if she might have done it a thousand times before, and will a thousand times after.

The low clouds still hover outside, but they're dissipating now, and Flynn walks to the window. With each moment, the view into Celeste's empty apartment becomes clearer. And yet, Flynn wonders. Was she an illusion? Was she a figment of his imagination all along?

He closes his eyes and sees her again. Her beautiful nude body walking through her living room. That sad face looking over her shoulder at him from her kitchen.

Cezanne has leapt from the couch and now rubs her head against his leg. Flynn opens his eyes and places his hand on the glass once more.

Celeste was the very best illusion.

I wonder how Flynn's doing today. He seemed on edge yesterday. I consider calling him but decide to finish the entries in the book. There isn't much time left now. I move to the next line and write

"Storge." As I do I think about the way Colette smiled to herself when she described this type of love. Love born from friendship. And I smile too, when I write the names Mel and Vivian on the next line and sit back to write their story.

342 Pine Street #4

The smoke alarm wakes Mel from his Christmas Day nap. He leaps to his feet and runs to the kitchen, where smoke billows out of the oven in a torrent. What was supposed to be a roast for his Christmas dinner is unrecognizable in its charred state. He turns on the kitchen fan and throws open the windows, immediately regretting his plan to cook when he might have been satisfied with sandwich fixings. Yes, Adele would have made dinner. It would have been perfect. Adele made everything perfect.

He extinguishes the smoldering roast in the sink with cold water, then retreats to the couch and stares down at his feet, and he thinks, as he does each Christmas: *How will I get through this day?*

A half hour passes, and he opens a beer and turns on the television. There's a can of chili somewhere in the cupboard. He'll find it later, after this episode of *Seinfeld*.

And when a knock sounds at the door, he hardly hears it at first. But then he turns the volume down, silencing Newman. Probably the landlord, here to complain about the smoke. He braces himself as he opens the door. And there, standing in the hallway, is Vivian.

"Oh," he says, stunned. "This is a surprise."

"Thank you for the flowers," she says. Her eyes look soft in a way he hasn't seen before.

"How did you know they were from—"

Vivian says, pushing past him, "I figured you'd be no use in the kitchen today," she says, waving her hand in front of her nose. "What did you burn? A duck?"

"I take it you could smell my disaster throughout the market?"

"Yes," she says, setting a paper bag down on Mel's dining room table, stacked high with books, newspapers, and boxes of this and that. "So I thought I'd share my Christmas dinner. It's nothing much, just some pâté and crudités. But it has to be better than what your contingent plan entails."

Mel smiles. "Canned chili," he says, eyeing the plastic containers of food Vivian is setting on the table. "So, yes."

He runs his hand through his sparse hair nervously. He wishes he'd put on a fresh shirt this morning and cleaned his living room. The dishes in the kitchen sink date back to three days before. "I'm afraid my apartment's in a bit of disarray."

"You do not live with a woman, nor have a housekeeper," Vivian says with a knowing smile. "It's a forgivable sin."

He watches as she confidently navigates his apartment, first dropping her coat on the over-stuffed chair by the fireplace. "Now," she says, rolling up her sleeves. "We'll just need two plates and a couple of wineglasses."

He sheepishly fiddles with his watch. "The plates are all in the sink, and I'm afraid I don't have any wineglasses. Or wine. Just beer, in the fridge."

"Fine, then," Vivian says without a moment's hesitation. "You sit. I'll just wash us a few plates." A few moments later, she sets out a veritable feast on the coffee table: a plate of cheese, pâté, crackers, and sliced vegetables. Two cold cans of beer round out the spread. She cracks open one of them and smiles.

"You should be drinking champagne out of a crystal flute," Mel says.

"I've done that all my life," she says, staring into his eyes. "Believe it or not, it gets a little dull."

He thinks of Adele. And he wonders if she can see him now. He wonders if she'd approve, but somewhere deep down, he already knows the answer. His heart feels full, and tears sting his eyes. "Why did you come, Vivian?"

She takes another sip of her beer, then sets it down daintily on the coffee table and folds her hands in her lap. "Because, for every reason I can think of not to like you, there are ten reasons why I do," she says, slowly extending her hand to meet his. He takes it.

"I like you too," he says.

"Besides, no one should be alone on Christmas. It's criminal."

"Indeed," Mel agrees, returning her smile.

"The flowers are the most extraordinary range of greens," she says. "I've never seen such an array."

"That's the work of Jane, the Flower Lady. I'll have to introduce you, but not today."

"What artistic vision she has. I look forward to meeting her."

"I . . . I wanted to give them to you myself, but I saw you seated beside a man. I didn't want to interfere."

"My driver, you mean?" She smiles, and he smiles back. "You know something?" she says, turning to the fireplace, where a log crackles and hisses behind the grate. "I didn't think I could feel this way again. After my husband died, I went through so much grief, some that I'm still sorting through. And I suppose that process may continue for the rest of my life. You see, when you know love once, you can feel as though you'll never know it again. But then came you."

"And then came you," Mel says, eyes locked on hers. "It feels right, doesn't it?"

"It does," Vivian says.

"Merry Christmas," he says, holding his beer up to hers.

"Merry Christmas," she says. "To new beginnings."

"To the most beautiful new beginnings."

Just a few more now, and my journey will be complete. On the next line, I write "Eros." I think about this form of passionate love. And I write Josh's and Katie's names in the book. I can almost feel their names pulse on the page. And yet, their story is raw and unfinished. I begin writing.

1112 Broadway E. #202

The real estate agent will be over tomorrow, and Katie knows she should tidy up. She feels a lump in her throat then, thinking about the first time she and Josh made love in this bedroom, on the bare hardwood floors.

Josh paid well above market price for the home, and she's nervous she may not even break even on the sale. But instead of blitzing the windows with Windex and restacking the books on the coffee table in a neat row, Katie pulls up her laptop and rereads the e-mail she received from Josh, sent from God knows where.

Katie,

It's better this way. Trust me. I had to leave. I'm sorry that we won't have the future we planned. Someday I hope you'll understand. But for now, the house must be sold. I want the very best for you. I can't see you now, but have all the documents faxed to my office and my assistant will make sure I sign what I need to.

Please take care of yourself,
Josh

When she reads his words, Katie bursts into tears all over again. How can he be so very cold? How can he treat her like a business transaction? They were in such deep love. They planned a life together. And for Josh to just get up one morning and leave, without so much as an explanation or even a good-bye?

Of course, he met a woman. Katie is sure of it. He was so good with her, sexually. He knew how her body worked, and he played it with precision, like an instrument he'd mastered with virtuoso skill. She imagines him touching someone else now and her stomach turns. Of course he's touching someone else. Josh needs that. Just as she does.

When the phone rings, she almost doesn't answer it, except it's her hairstylist friend Mary, who's about to have her baby. Maybe she needs help. Katie reaches for the phone. "Hi, Mary," she says, collecting herself.

"You OK?" Mary asks.

"You're the one I should be concerned about," Katie says. "Are you in labor?"

"Yes," Mary says. "At least, I will be soon. I'm at the hospital. They're inducing."

"Oh, wow. You must be so excited."

"I am," Mary says. "But that's not why I'm calling. Honey, I . . . I have some news for you."

Katie's heart beats faster. It's about Josh; she can feel it. In a moment, Mary will tell her that she saw him at a restaurant with another woman. Or maybe the other woman came into the salon, and Mary foiled her hair and listened as she talked about Josh, unaware of the connection between Mary and Katie.

She braces herself. "What is it?" she says cautiously.

Mary takes a deep breath. "I saw him, Katie. I saw Josh."

"You did?" Katie exclaims. "Where?"

"Here, at the hospital."

"What do you mean, at the hospital?"

"After I filled out paperwork at reception, they had an orderly pick me up in a wheelchair," Mary continues. "We got on an elevator, headed for the fifth floor, but we stopped on the third to let some other people on, and I saw Josh in the distance. I just caught a glimpse of his face down the hallway. He was sitting in a chair beside the nurses' station."

"Are you sure it was him?" Katie gasps. "Maybe it was just someone who looked like him."

"No," Mary says. "It was him. He recognized me too. Our eyes met, just before the elevator doors closed. I would've stopped to talk to him for you, but I had to get hooked up to this damn Pitocin drip."

"I—I—" Katie stammers. "I don't know what to say. Why would he be at the hospital?"

"Maybe he's visiting someone here."

"Maybe," Katie says. "But I'm coming down there. Right now. What floor did you say?"

"Third floor."

As she races out the door to her car, Katie doesn't think of anything. Not readying the house for the real estate agent tomorrow. Not locking her front door. Not even her cell phone, which she leaves on the coffee table. All she can think of is Josh, and now that she knows where he is, in this moment, despite the painful circumstances, all she knows is that she must go to him. She must see him.

She parks her car in a physician parking spot on the first floor of the parking garage, knowing that the price of a steep parking ticket will pale in comparison to missing Josh today. What if he already left? What if he's here to see someone? Another woman? Katie runs to the elevator and jams her finger on the Up button. *Third floor. Third floor. Third floor.* Her heart beats wildly as the elevator jerks upward.

"Can I help you?" a mousy-looking nurse at the desk asks.

"Yes," Katie says, out of breath. "There was someone here about a half hour ago. A man. His name is Josh Parker. You see, my friend called me from the hospital and she thought she saw him here, right down—"

"And are you a visitor?"

"I'm his wife. He was here?"

The nurse's eyes dart around her desk nervously. "Ma'am, I've been told that—"

"My God," Katie cries. "Josh is a patient?" She scours the whiteboard behind the nurse's desk with frantic eyes until they lock onto "Parker/ Room #319." She takes a step back. "What floor is this?"

"Third," the nurse says.

"No, no, I mean, what floor is this? Oncology? What?"

"This is the rehabilitation wing."

"Rehabilitation?"

"Yes, it's where patients who have undergone traumatic brain injury or paralysis are taken for recovery."

"Paralysis?" Katie looks right, then left, then runs down the hallway until she sees a sign that reads "319." She doesn't knock, nor does she turn around when she hears the nurse calling out behind her. "Miss, you can't go in there. It's against our policy."

Katie opens the door and pulls back the curtain. And there is Josh. Her Josh. There is stubble on his chin, and his face is much thinner now. But his green eyes, those eyes she loves, are just as she remembers. And when they meet hers, it touches her in a place deep inside. Her legs feel weak as she rushes to the bed where Josh is lying. She doesn't deny her urge to run to him, to wrap her arms around his shoulders and kiss him with the love she still feels, that she will always feel.

"Why didn't you tell me?" she says. She is both exhilarated and angry. "Why did you go dark? Why?"

"Sir, is everything all right?" Katie turns to the door. It's the mousy-looking nurse from the desk. "If you'd like, we can—"

"It's fine," Josh says.

The nurse stares at Katie for a long moment, then nods and closes the door.

When they are alone again, Josh looks out the window. Katie watches as the light hits his eyes, which are moist with fresh tears.

"Josh, please," she cries. "Talk to me. What happened? Please . . ."

He's silent for a long moment; then he turns to face her. "I was going out to get you coffee, but also to meet with a landscape architect. I wanted to surprise you with those raised vegetable beds you're always talking about."

She nods. "The blonde," she says to herself.

"I was leaving the café, walking past a construction site, where they're retrofitting an old building." He swallows hard. "I didn't see the scaffolding fall until it was too late." Tears spill from his lids. "Katie, it was too late. It pinned my legs. I was out for twenty-four hours, and when I woke up, they told me." He looks out the window again.

"Oh, Josh," Katie says through tears. "They told you what?"

He swallows hard. "I'm paralyzed, Katie. From the waist down. I can't walk. I can't . . ."

She buries her face in his chest. She feels his arms touch her back lightly, and her neck erupts in goose bumps. "Why didn't you call me?" she cries. "Why didn't you tell me? I thought you'd left me for another woman. I thought you hated me."

He frowns. "I wanted you to hate me. I wanted you to hate me enough to move on, to find someone who could love you the way I can't."

She shakes her head and wipes the tears from her cheeks. "Did the accident paralyze your heart? Did it take away your mind?"

Josh looks away, but Katie presses on. "Did it? Did it?"

"No," he says, "but, Katie, I can't . . . God, I'll never be able to make love to you again. I'll never be able to—"

"And you thought that I would walk away from you because of that?" She shakes her head.

"That's just it," he says. "I knew you wouldn't. But how could I enslave you to a life of platonic love? A life where I could not make you scream with pleasure the way you deserve? I just couldn't do it. I couldn't bear it."

Katie walks to the window and stands in silence as the tears stream down her cheeks. "No," she finally says, turning around. "No, you're wrong, Josh Parker. You're so damn wrong."

She climbs onto the bed and straddles his limp body. "Yes, we had it good in that department. Oh, honey, we had it so good. But here's what you're forgetting." She looks deep into his eyes. She wants to be sure he sees her, feels her, hears everything she has to say. "Our love is deeper than physical. Don't you see that? Don't you know that? You must know that."

A tear streams down his handsome face, and she flicks it away with her finger, then reaches for his hands. Weaving her fingers into his, she grins mischievously. "Your hands still work, don't they?"

He nods, looking up at her through his tears.

"You'd really want to be with me for the rest of my life? You really think you could be truly happy?"

"Baby," Katie says, leaning closer to him, "I wouldn't be happy with anyone *but* you." She kisses his lips and then nestles beside him in the bed. "Tell me you're not giving up on our love."

He turns to face her again. "Oh, Katie," he cries. "Forgive me. I was just so afraid."

"You don't have to be anymore," she says, pressing her nose against his. "I'm here. I'm never going. I'll always love you. Even if your face was maimed, or if you developed a case of late-in-life Tourette's and cursed at me every five minutes." She shakes her head and points to his chest. "It's what's in here that I love. It's you." She wipes a tear from her eye. "Always."

"Always," Josh says, pressing his cheek against her shoulder. "Always."

I yawn and drop my gaze to the next line. Just one more to go and then this strange journey is complete. Well, *complete* is hardly the word. My own story has no ending. I think of Cam, and my heart flutters. I collect myself quickly. He isn't the one. If he were, it would have worked out. If he were, he would be here.

I think of Lo instead and smile to myself, before

writing "Ludus" on the line above her name. Oh, the game of love. If anyone can play it and keep the upper hand, it is Lo. But will she ever be happy? I think about her and Grant now. Though I saw the look of hesitation in her eyes earlier at the flower shop, they are supposed to be on a plane bound for Paris now. Or are they? I turn to the page and begin writing.

220 Boat Street #2

Lo opens her eyes before sunrise and reaches for her phone, as she always does when she wakes up. She scrolls through the list of texts that have popped in overnight and in the wee hours of the morning from the various men in her life. Conor, the surgeon. Jake, the sommelier. Ryan, the Australian with green eyes and stubble on his chin. They know she's off the market, and yet they continue to reach out.

And then there's Grant. They're supposed to fly out this morning for Paris. First class and a pair of champagne flutes.

She sits up in bed and peers out the porthole window in her bedroom. The lake is gray and choppy, and she can feel her houseboat swaying ever so slightly in the wind. Didn't she hear something on TV last night about the possibility of a Christmas Day windstorm? She knows she should get up and shower and pack for Paris. Grant will be here to pick her up soon. But instead, she settles back in bed and lets her head sink deeper into her pillow. She thinks about her life, and men. And she realizes there has never not been a man in her life. She has always had someone. But why? What's wrong with being alone?

Lo puts on her robe and climbs down the ladder to her living room. She knows the answer, but she's afraid to admit it. So she makes a cup of coffee instead and sinks into her couch, where she scrolls through her texts. Conor wants to see her tomorrow night. Jake can't stop thinking about her, still, even after months since they dated. And Grant says he'll be over in two hours to pick her up. Her heart lurches in her chest.

She sets her coffee cup down and picks up her phone. There's momentum building inside her, and her heart beats faster as she dials Grant's number. He's broken her heart. He's broken her. For the first time ever, she was willing to give herself to a man completely—body, mind, soul. But, most telling, heart. And he waffled. He was dishonest about his intentions, about his situation at home. He carried on with Lo and kept playing house with someone else, with no real intention of making any changes. Even in the weeks following Katie's wedding, when his wife combed through phone records and exposed her husband's affair with Lo, Grant still did not leave, or formulate any plan or exit strategy. Instead he smoothed things over at home and begged Lo for more time.

But she doesn't want to give him any more time. He's taken so much already and made promises she knows he won't keep. And now Lo has an angry woman to deal with. She received a nasty e-mail just this morning from Grant's wife, Jennifer. The things she wrote hurt, yes, but they're true. And Lo might have written the same words had she been in Jennifer's shoes.

This has to end.

"Hi, baby," he says, picking up after one ring. "Ready for Paris?"

"Hi," she says vacantly. "I'm so sorry, Grant. I don't think I can go."

"What do you mean?" he says. "I don't understand."

Lo takes a deep breath. "I've been thinking about this so much," she says. "And, Grant, what we had was real, and true. I will always believe that. But in the end, it . . . just wasn't meant to be."

He's quiet on the other end of the phone. She knows she has stunned him. "And I realized something this morning," she continues. "Something I've been trying to ignore about myself for a long time."

"Baby," Grant says, pleading, "what are you talking about?"

She doesn't want him to call her baby. Not now, not when he probably calls his wife that too. While she used to love hearing the word cross his lips, now it sounds so cheap, so generic. "Grant," she continues, "all this time, with you, and with other men in my past, I've only wanted to have the emptiness in me filled. I thought men could do that for me. But here's the crazy thing: I could have filled that space myself a long time ago. I just didn't know it."

"I don't understand," he says. "Was it something I said? Did? Do you want me to leave my wife? Is that what this is all about? Because I told her this morning that we need to talk. I told her I am unhappy and that we need to figure some things out. It's my process. My process for coming to you."

"Your process?" Lo says with a laugh. "Grant, if you were coming to me, you would have been here months ago."

He's silent.

"Listen," she continues. "Go to Paris. Meet a French girl. Drink wine. Eat the most glorious food. Stay out late. Better yet, take your *wife*."

"But I want to do all that with you," he says, injured.

"I can't," she says. "Not anymore. I don't deserve to find love, real love, until I can learn to love myself a bit more." She lets out a nervous laugh. "I'm almost thirty years old, and I've never really been alone. There's something not quite right about that." She pauses for a long moment. Tears sting her eyes. "Good-bye, Grant." She doesn't wait for his response before ending the call.

The wind picks up that afternoon, and when the lights flicker that evening and eventually go out, Lo lights candles in her houseboat. She sits in the semidarkness and considers calling Ryan or Jake or maybe even Conor. She could call any of them, really, and they'd be on her doorstep within the hour, with a bottle of wine and arms to fall into. They would help her pass the time, help her not feel alone. Band-Aids for her emptiness. Well, mandaids. She smiles to herself, then shakes her head with resolve. Men can't fill the hole in her heart. Only she can do that.

She turns her phone off and tucks it in the kitchen drawer. She will pour a glass of wine, open her laptop, and start writing that memoir Jane always said she should write. Tonight she will not be alone. And she isn't. She has herself.

Nat King Cole's voice seeps through the speakers of her radio. *Have yourself a merry little Christmas.* She glances at the lonely Christmas tree in the corner of the room, the one she hasn't had time to decorate. A box of ornaments from her grandmother's estate sits beneath, and Lo kneels beside it. She reaches inside and unwraps a star-shaped ornament she remembers from childhood. She touches the words her grandmother painted on the edge: "Christmas 1984."

She stands up and hangs the little star on a branch in front of her.

Have yourself a merry little Christmas.

Yes. She will.

Three days have passed when Lo gets the call. She has just stepped out of the shower when she hears her phone ringing from the kitchen. Normally she'd wait, just let it go to voice mail. Whoever's calling can be called back. But in the back of her mind, she'll admit, she wonders if it could be Grant calling from Paris. He's been silent for three long days. And although she said her good-byes, love lingers. And perhaps it always will.

She wraps a towel around herself and runs to the kitchen, hair dripping along the wood floors.

"Hello?"

"Lo?"

"Yes, this is."

"Lo, this is John, Grant's best friend."

Her heart begins to beat faster. She met John once, just briefly. He's the only person from Grant's life she ever formally met. "John, yes, hi," she says, mind racing.

"I'm so very sorry to call you like this, with this

news." His voice falters a bit. "But I know he'd want you to know. I know he'd want me to call you."

She clutches the phone tightly. "What is it? What's going on?"

"Lo, Grant died."

"He . . . what?" She's breathless. Her mouth feels dry.

"We just found out. He went out for a meal in Paris and died at the restaurant. He was alone. It was an aneurysm. There wasn't anything that could have been done. It was his time."

"No," Lo cries, falling to her knees. "No."

"I'm so very sorry." He pauses for a long moment. "I wanted to be sure you knew about the funeral. The service will be tomorrow afternoon, at Saint Luke's." There's another long silence. "You know he loved you, don't you? He loved you so much. I've never seen a man more in love."

Lo walks into the church in a black dress and dark sunglasses and inconspicuously files into a back pew. She doesn't want to be seen. And a part of her knows she doesn't deserve to be seen. She was in the shadows of Grant's life when he was living, and in the shadows she remains in death. To Grant's friends and family, she is a blip on the timeline of his life. To his wife, a fly she'd probably like to swat away. But to Lo, Grant was the man who taught her to love wholly and completely. And even though their story was ill-timed, fraught with deception and pain, and despite the fact that she feels great sorrow for the pain she's caused his wife, Lo does not regret loving Grant. Not ever. Remorse and regret are two very different things.

A man takes to the piano at the front of the church and begins to play, just as the funeral procession begins. The minister walks up the aisle first, and then the casket, carried by John and Grant's three brothers. Tears spill from Lo's eyes then. She can no longer contain them, or her sadness. In that wooden box is the man she loved with all her heart. A man she might always love.

Jennifer walks behind her husband's casket. She looks beautiful in her long-sleeved black dress. The handkerchief slips from Lo's hand as she passes, and Jennifer stops to pick it up, then turns to face her. The two women's eyes meet.

In that moment, Lo feels panic wash over her. She feels shame. She feels sorely out of place and wonders if she should leave. Perhaps it was the wrong decision to come. She does not belong here. And her presence is only adding more pain. But just before she stands to depart, Jennifer places the handkerchief in the pocket of Lo's coat, then extends her hand.

Lo weeps as she stands and takes it.

"Walk with me," Jennifer says calmly, through tear-filled eyes.

Lo nods, astonished.

"Grant loved you," she whispers. "I saw it in his eyes that day at the wedding."

"I, I'm—" Lo tries to whisper her apologies. She tries to think of something to say in this moment, this profound moment.

"He'd want you to stand with me," Jennifer says, nodding. "He'd want me to forgive you, and him. And that's a gift I can give him today."

The two women walk together behind the casket, both with hearts aching, with love for a man they will never see again. And yet, Jennifer's love for her husband is bigger than the anger and hurt, the broken promises, the deception that rattled her world. Her love is not prideful or self-serving. In the end, it's love.

Just love.

Chapter 27

Christmas Day

I have to hurry. It's late in the afternoon, and it won't be long before sunset, before the end of my journey, my year. Just one more task lies ahead, the biggest one of all.

I tuck the flower arrangement for Mary in the passenger seat of my car—a square vase packed tightly with pale green blooms—and drive to the hospital.

The elevator deposits me on the fifth floor, Labor and Delivery.

"Hi," I say, out of breath, to the nurse at the desk. "I'm Jane Williams. I'm here for the birth of my friend Mary's baby. She's expecting me."

The nurse lowers her glasses on her nose and scrolls through a screen on her computer. "Yes, I have your name down," she finally says. "She's in room 523. She's not far from delivering now. You're just in time."

I hurry down the hallway and knock when I reach her door, then poke my head in. "Mary, it's Jane. I'm here!"

"Come in," Mary says, and I find her sitting up in bed, legs parted, about to endure another contraction. Luca clutches her hand, invested in

345

every cry, every push, every word from the doctor, who is at Mary's feet.

"Just one more push and you'll meet your little girl," he says. Mary obeys, and a moment later, the room is greeted with the high-pitched cry of new life.

I set the flowers down on a side table and watch as a nurse gives the baby a quick bath before swaddling her in a blanket, then handing her to Luca, who proudly tucks her in Mary's arms.

"Jane," Mary says, beaming. "Come meet her."

I walk toward the bed, with shaking hands and a heart that booms in my chest.

"She's beautiful," I say, swallowing hard.

"Look, she has green eyes like you." Mary wipes away a tear. "Grace. I'm going to call her Grace."

"A beautiful name," I say.

"Would you like to hold her, Jane?"

"Yes," I reply, unable to prevent a tear from spilling out onto my cheek as I take the baby into my arms. I touch her cheek lightly, and I feel it then, a warmth that flows through me. A transfer of energy from one soul to another. It has happened.

It is done.

Chapter 28

January tiptoed in quietly. On New Year's Eve, Jane sat in front of the TV, watching the ball drop in New York City with Sam, thinking about the year before, when she'd spent a life-changing evening shivering on a balcony with Cam.

Cam . . . Jane said her good-byes, and yet Colette's vision of the two of them lingers. She completed her journey, fulfilled the prophecies of the gift, and even Dr. Heller agrees that surgery is no longer needed and might not have ever been. Although her brain scans continue to be puzzling, Dr. Heller concedes that some things may defy medical explanation. Jane's work is done, her health intact. And yet, her heart feels . . . empty.

Hawaii was nice, Jane thinks as the plane begins its descent into Seattle. A proper girls' getaway, with plenty of sun, sand, and booze. Mary is brave to take an infant on a plane, but Grace has been the perfect travel companion. She's sleeping soundly in Mary's arms when Jane glances at the two of them across the aisle. Katie and Lo are asleep in the seats on either side of her. Lo's black silk eye mask looks lopsided with her face pressed up against the side of the seat. Katie i snoring. She got wind of Mary and Luca' situation and was able to help iron out hi immigration issues from Hawaii, pulling a fev strings with the right judge in Seattle, even, an to Mary's delight, it looked like he would soon b a permanent resident of Seattle, and employed Matthew put the word out in his architectura circles about Luca, who'd recently started his owr construction company, and he's apparently beer flooded with calls.

As the plane touches down, Jane considers the past year, all of its ups and downs. Her journey successfully completed; the handoff of her gift to little Grace; reuniting with her father, and having brunch with him and Flynn on New Year's Day; and yet, there's still a big gaping hole. Love.

She thinks of that as they walk to baggage claim and stand beside the carousel, waiting for their suitcases, which they retrieve and wheel outside. Katie's father-in-law is in town, and he pulls up with Josh in their new handicap-accessible van. The house she was intending to sell in his absence has been retrofitted with a ramp to the front door, and the lower-floor guest bedroom is now the master. She waves and runs to the van. Lo boards a shuttle to the airport parking lot to retrieve her car. Luca drives up next and jumps out of the car to handle Mary's luggage while she buckles the baby into her car seat.

And then Jane is . . . alone. She stands on the curb and hails a cab. The Seattle air is frigid, and she smiles to think that she can still feel sand between her toes.

"Where to, miss?" the driver asks.

"Pike Place," she says. "I live on Pike."

The driver nods and turns out onto the road. Jane thinks of Cam then, how they parted. Tears sting her eyes, and she fights them back before they can spill out onto her cheeks. She had every right to be angry. He deceived her, after all.

But she loved him. Oh, did she love him. And she still does. She knows it with every beat of her heart. It's the fact that clings to her now as the cab speeds down I-5. It's the whisper in her ear as twilight sets in. The city is in sight. Her Seattle. The skyline is like a hug, a reminder that she will be OK. But will she?

Cam's somewhere out there, she thinks. Yes, January 19. He was supposed to get home from his trip today. Maybe they even passed at the airport unknowingly. But what does it matter? Jane shakes her head. It's over.

The cab turns onto First Avenue, then proceeds down the hill. She feels the familiar bumps and grooves of the cobblestones beneath the tires of the cab. Home. Her beloved Pike Place Market, welcoming her back. A few moments later, her building is in sight.

"Thank you," she says to the cabdriver, handing him two twenties.

The driver thanks her, then fiddles with the radio. A second later, Dusty Springfield's smoky voice fills the cab: "The look of love is in your eyes. The look your heart can't disguise." She remembers the dance she and Cam shared at Katie and Josh's wedding. She remembers the way he held her. What did he say that night? "I want you to think of me, and this moment, whenever you hear this song. I want you to feel me."

And she feels him now, deeply. She wheels her bag onto the sidewalk and stands in front of her building. A young couple strolls past, hand in hand.

It's nearly seven, and Bernard walks out of the building. "Jane," he says when he sees her. "Just getting back from vacation?"

She nods.

"Just in time for the storm."

"Storm?"

He points to the sky. "Those are snow clouds up there."

"I know," she says, remembering her first lesson in clouds, given by Bernard more than a year ago. She feels a snowflake hit her cheek.

"But you never told me what you saw in the clouds that day." He smiles. "Do you remember?"

"I do," she says. "The image still jars me, in fact."

"What was it?"

"It was a heart," she says softly.

Bernard nods knowingly. "I expected as much," he says approvingly. He tips his hat. "Good night, Jane."

She turns to face the street, and in the far corner of the night sky, there's a moon. Snow clouds are moving in, but they haven't obscured it entirely yet, and when a wispy cloud passes, Jane can see its full round form. Her heart begins to race. She remembers what Colette told her about second chances, how love can be restored on a snowy night, with a full moon presiding overhead.

For a moment, the world is nearly frozen into stillness. A seagull flies above, but its wings barely move. The couple on the sidewalk pause in an infinite embrace. Even the snowflakes themselves seem suspended in midair, enraptured in this moment. Jane is too. And when the cab begins to pull away and she opens her mouth to hail it back, her lips don't seem to work. Her voice is muted. But the driver sees her somehow, and stops the car. She gets in and scrolls through the e-mails on her phone until she finds the one Cam sent her in Hawaii about how he had rented a house in Wallingford after his lease downtown expired. She didn't respond to it, of course, but now she wishes she had. "I have to see someone," she says, breathless. "Can you take me to Wallingford? 4634 Densmore. Please, hurry."

● ● ●

Across town, Cam is stepping out of a cab in front of the house he's just rented, one of those old Craftsmans, quintessentially Seattle. Jane would like it; he's sure of it. Of course that old Dusty Springfield song would play on the radio on his drive home from the airport. Jane haunts him still. And maybe she always will.

Cam sighs as he pays his fare and slides the strap of his bag over his shoulder. He thought about Jane every minute of his time in New York. He feels a snowflake on his cheek, and looks up at the streetlight. *Or is there?*

The wind is picking up now, swirling a pile of shriveled autumn leaves this way and that. It's weeks into winter, but a single leaf clings to a high branch on the old maple tree in the parking strip. It's seen sleet and snow and wind, but it stubbornly hangs on. Could their love survive this? Could it hold on, just a moment longer?

Cam feels the bitter air brush his cheek. A cold north wind. A dog barks in the distance, and he hears a child laughing from a nearby front porch. A college-aged guy pedals past on a bike, leaves crunching beneath his tires. And then Cam sees the moon, big and bright and full, carving a hole through the clouds, hovering over him.

He knows he has to see her. Those green eyes. One last moment.

"Wait," he calls out to the cab, which has

already started off down the street. "Stop," he says, dropping his bag, waving his arms. But the driver doesn't see him. He motors away, oblivious to the part he might have played in this developing love story in which each moment is precious.

Cam looks down at his feet. The snow is falling harder now. He picks up his bag and walks back to his house, where he slumps over on the front stoop, staring ahead for several minutes as the snow falls. And then, headlights strobe through the snowy night like two giant sunbeams.

Jane's cab pulls onto Densmore, and she wipes the foggy window with the sleeve of her coat. Her heart is in her throat now. Every year, every day, every second of her life has led her to this moment. The cab stops, and she reaches for the door handle. Her heart is so full she feels it may burst. It is January 19, and Jane knows it is the first day of the rest of her life. Cam is in the distance, sitting on his stoop. And for the first time, she can see clearly.

Epilogue

Pike Place Market
Christmas Eve 2042

Cam stands beside me in our bedroom. He looks sharp in his tux, even for a man of sixty-two. But I always knew he'd age well. He presses his nose in the place between my neck and my shoulder, which still sends a tingly feeling down my back, even after all these years. "You'd better get dressed," he says. "The ceremony starts in an hour. The kids are all there."

I tighten the right strap of my white silk slip and stare at my reflection in our bedroom mirror. I turned fifty-seven last year. There are wrinkles around my eyes now, and my hair has lost its luster. But I feel beautiful, because to Cam, I am.

"Shoo," I say to my husband. "It's bad luck for the groom to see the bride in her dress before the wedding."

He takes my hand lovingly in his. "To think that I was never going to get married, and not only did you get me to marry you; you're getting me to walk down the aisle again. You're either really good or I must really love you."

I grin. "Both."

He kisses the top of my head, then rests his chin on me and we stare into the mirror that we face together. "Honey, I'd renew my vows every day of the week if I could. But get dressed! Everyone's waiting."

I smile. "I will. You go on ahead to the church. I'll meet you there in a half hour, promise. There's something I need to do first."

"All right," he says. "Don't leave me at the altar, now."

"Promise," I add with a wink.

After he's closed the door behind him, I slip into my white silk floor-length dress and give myself a once-over in the mirror before letting my eyes rest on the framed photo of my family on the table beside the mirror. Cam and our two sons. Darby is a physical therapist; Landon, an attorney. I'm proud of them, exceedingly so.

I smile as I reach for the ancient book in the drawer to my right. I run my hand along the spine and study the lettering on the leather cover just as I did the day I first took it into my own hands. I think about the woman I was then—a little jaded, lost, unsure. But this book set me on the journey of discovery, a journey that taught me about love. I nod to myself as I reach for the birthday card I purchased last week. It nestles in its pale pink envelope. I reach for my pen and write:

Dear Grace,

Happy birthday. I am an old friend of your mother. I knew you as a child, before your parents moved to California. You see, twenty-nine years ago, I was there when you came into the world. I know that you are, like I was, lost when it comes to love. The year before my thirtieth birthday, a stranger wrote me a birthday card, and in the card, she told me something about myself that changed my life forever. And that is what I must do for you. Grace, you have a gift, a very special gift. And a beautiful one. I've enclosed my card. Please call me when you receive this. There are many things I must tell you, things that will alter your life forever, for the better, if you trust your heart as I did. You get to choose. But, if I may say, love is always the best choice. And I challenge you to be brave. I will be here when you're ready to talk. Oh, and do we have much to discuss.

Sincerely,
Jane Williams

I tuck the card in the envelope and address it to her at the university in Italy where she is studying abroad, in her adopted father's homeland. I find postage, enough for the letter to travel a good long way, then affix the stamps. It's half past one. The ceremony will begin in a half hour, just enough time to walk the three blocks to the church.

I reach for my sweater and step outside to the street. Pike Place looks just as glorious as it ever has, and as I navigate the old cobblestone streets, I think about my journey, and the people along the way. Pigeons congregate on the corner where the old newsstand once was, and I smile when I think of Mel and his beloved Vivian, rest their souls. Elaine's daughter, Ellie, runs Meriwether now, and I still stop in for chocolate croissants on occasion, but not often enough. Flynn and his cat, Cezanne III, share an apartment a block away. He'll be at the ceremony, as will Katie and Josh, who just welcomed their first grandchild.

I stop at the Flower Lady and poke my head in the door. My assistant, Alise, shakes her head in surprise. "What are you doing here? Don't you have a wedding to go to? As in *yours?*"

I grin. "It can't start without the bride. Besides, I forgot to pick up my bouquet." I poke my head into the refrigerator behind the counter and retrieve it. "Gorgeous job, by the way, Alise."

"Thanks," she says. "I've learned from the best." She sets down a vase of white daffodils and then turns to me with big eyes. "You'll never believe who just came into the shop."

"Who, Brad Pitt?"

"Eww, he's so old," she says with a grin. "No. Lo Hemsworth. The mega-best-selling author."

She shakes her head. "I still can't believe she used to work here with you."

I smile to myself. Lo, who'll be at the ceremony later, went on to write four critically acclaimed books on love and dating. The first received a generous (and life-changing) endorsement from Oprah Winfrey.

"She bought herself a bouquet of roses," Alise says.

"Ah," I say with a knowing smile. "Yes." Lo's life changed when she finally realized she didn't need a man to buy her flowers. She could do that for herself.

"All right, dear, I'm off to my wedding."

Annie grins. "I'll sneak into the back pew just as soon as I can close things down."

"Hurry," I say. "I want you to be there." I hold my bouquet in one hand and the pink envelope in the other. On the next block, I stop and take a deep breath as I let the birthday card fall from my hand into the dark abyss of the mailbox on First Avenue.

I smile to myself as a seagull squawks overhead. And so begins another woman's journey. Love is waiting for her, in all its forms, ready to be discovered, reveled in, felt, and seen from every angle: the raw and the beautiful, the joyful and the sad, the temporary and the eternal, and every shade in between. And love can be hers if she's brave enough to look for it, and ultimately, to see it.

SARAH JIO is the *New York Times* and *USA Today* bestselling author of *The Violets of March*, a *Library Journal* Best Book of 2011; *The Bungalow*; *Blackberry Winter*; *The Last Camellia*; *Morning Glory*; and *Goodnight June*. She is also a journalist who has written for Glamour; *O, The Oprah Magazine*; *Redbook*; *Real Simple*; and many other publications. Jio's books have become book club favorites and have been translated into more than twenty languages. She lives in Seattle with her three young boys and an elderly golden retriever. Learn more about her at
sarahjio.com or
facebook.com/sarahjioauthor.

Center Point Large Print
600 Brooks Road / PO Box 1
Thorndike, ME 04986-0001 USA

(207) 568-3717

US & Canada:
1 800 929-9108
www.centerpointlargeprint.com